Paul Burston was born i   d
now lives in London. A jo   s
appeared in *Time Out*, the
the *Independent* and the *In*
Four. He is the author of se   ...st novel
Shameless, and *Queens' Cou...y... iour Around the Gay Ghettos,*
Queer Spots and Camp Sights of Britain. His most recent novel,
Lovers and Losers, is also published by Sphere. Visit his website at
www.paulburston.com.

'A fun tale of celeb shenanigans'
Star

'*Star People* is a caustic but compassionate slice of Hollywood
life brimming with unforgettable characters and a plot that
races along like a rollercoaster. A perfect summer read'
Attitude

'A highly readable trek through the sleazy side of LA'
What's On In London

Also by Paul Burston

Shameless
What Are You Looking At?
Gutterheart
Queens' Country
Lovers and Losers

as co-editor
A Queer Romance

Star People

PAUL BURSTON

sphere

SPHERE

First published in Great Britain in 2006 by Time Warner Books
This paperback edition published in 2007 by Sphere

A CIP catalogue record for this book
is available from the British Library.

ISBN 978-0-7515-3849-6

Papers used by Sphere are natural, recyclable products made from
wood grown in sustainable forests and certified in accordance with
the rules of the Forest Stewardship Council.

Typeset in Berkeley by M Rules
Printed and bound in Great Britain by
Clays Ltd, St Ives plc
Paper supplied by Hellefoss AS, Norway

Sphere
An imprint of
Little, Brown Book Group
Brettenham House
Lancaster Place
London WC2E 7EN

A Member of the Hachette Livre Group of Companies

www.littlebrown.co.uk

For Stately, who was always there in spirit.
And for Paulo, who arrived just in time.

When they say you're a faggot, that's when you know you're a star.

JACK NICHOLSON

All actors are liars. I've never met one that wasn't.

TRUMAN CAPOTE

PART ONE

Billy

CHAPTER ONE

Billy came to Los Angeles looking for love but soon found other ways to pass the time. That was the thing about LA — you had to be willing to make some adjustments. Learning to live with the smog and the daily gridlocks was the easy part. The key to keeping heart and soul together was knowing when to lower your sights a little.

Of course not everyone was as flexible as Billy. Each week he watched the new arrivals come pouring into the bars and restaurants around West Hollywood and Melrose. The faces changed, but the expressions were always the same — fixed grins and eyes that could work a room in seconds, desperate for that first big break, hungry for fame, quietly convinced that, somehow, it would all fall neatly into place. Soon they would wind up waiting tables, or join the swarms of ageing wannabes who hovered around industry types at Morton's or The Ivy — skins thickened by years of rejection, hands brandishing personalised business cards proclaiming themselves models, or actors, or whatever it was they still dreamed of becoming one day, however remote their chances. It was a running joke in LA that anyone over the age of thirty with a business card but no health insurance could be dismissed as a 'model/actor/whatever'. 'Maws', the locals called them, and to Billy's mind there were few things more pitiful than a maw with the determination to succeed but neither the looks nor

3

the talent to back it up. Angelenos could forgive many things, but failure wasn't one of them.

So compared to some, Billy's dreams were pretty modest. While others came to LA seeking fame and fortune, all he'd ever really wanted was to fall madly in love, the way people did in the movies. He'd been waiting for that innocent, timeless rush of love all his life, but so far it seemed to have eluded him. He'd had devastating crushes. He'd fallen asleep in a stranger's arms, quietly wondering if this was The One, before waking up in the cold light of day to discover that no, actually, it wasn't. But he'd never been in love. Not really. Not on that grand scale where emotions run riot and movie clichés are made flesh. He'd never known love at first sight, or lost his heart across a crowded room. He'd never experienced that swooning sensation often indicated by a camera circling two lovers locked in an embrace and a sudden stirring of strings. He'd never kissed someone and felt the world fall away. He'd never been the star of his own love story. And for all his bravado, there was a part of him that still held out a glimmer of hope that such things were possible – even for someone in his position.

Naturally this wasn't something he shouted from the rooftops. In LA, it was customary for people to wear permanent expressions of perpetual boredom, and to speak in carefully measured tones of casual indifference hardly conducive to talk of love. And in the relentlessly hedonistic, reassuringly superficial West Hollywood world Billy inhabited, even the slightest suggestion of a romantic nature was generally frowned upon. Boys like him were expected to hide their true feelings behind a cocky grin, not mope around like lovesick puppies. But every so often his loneliness would get the better of him and his mask would slip, the way it had that first time he got wasted in Casey's small apartment off Santa Monica Boulevard.

4

Casey came from Memphis ('the same as Justin Timberlake') and sometimes gave the impression that he'd just stepped off the Greyhound, slipping into a deep Southern drawl whenever a little extra colour was called for, or he felt he wasn't getting enough attention. In reality, Casey had lived in LA for the best part of ten years – long enough to lose all but the faintest trace of his accent, and to develop a keen understanding of local mating rituals. Like many Angelenos, Casey operated a strict turnstile policy on relationships. He dated plenty of people, but he never hung around long enough to risk discovering anything remotely lovable about any of them.

'If it's love you're after, you've definitely come to the wrong place,' he said sagely, passing Billy the joint and shaking his head. 'People here don't have time for all that romance and shit. That stuff's just for the movies. Sorry to disappoint you, Billy boy, but you've about as much chance of finding love in this town as you have of running into ET.'

But Billy wasn't stupid. He knew life wasn't like in the movies. In fact, he was counting on it. In the movies, people who fell in love tended to be beautiful and thin and straight. Billy was aware that many people considered him beautiful. A born looker with hair as blond as the beaches at Santa Monica and eyes as blue as the desert skies, he had that rare, unblemished beauty that inspired the work of certain male fashion photographers, and drove some of the city's most gifted cosmetic surgeons to despair, weeping behind the windshields of their SUVs at the futility of their profession. And despite a high-carb, low-fibre diet no self-respecting movie star would consider unless they were bulking up for a role, Billy had never been in any real danger of getting fat. But straight? Well, that was a different story – and one that rarely made it on to the big screen, at least not in a way he recognised. In the

Gospel according to Hollywood, people like him didn't meet and fall in love. They were too busy camping it up on the sidelines, or being hunted down as serial killers, or dying of AIDS. Love was strictly for the straight folks.

Despite all this, Billy loved the movies with a passion even staff at *The Hollywood Reporter* sometimes found it hard to muster. It didn't really matter what kind of movie it was. High concept or low budget, big Hollywood blockbuster or small independent offering, dumb action thriller or classy romantic comedy, he greeted them all with the same level of enthusiasm, always ensuring that he arrived at the movie theatre in plenty of time for the previews and rarely leaving his seat until the final credits had rolled. Casey found Billy's behaviour extremely odd. Try as he might, he couldn't understand how someone could watch so many movies and not develop a fondness for one genre over all the rest. But since Casey's favourite movies tended to be those filmed in the San Fernando Valley and commonly referred to as gay porn, he was hardly in a position to comment. And as Billy tried to explain to him, it was a bit like James Dean responding to the question of whether he was bisexual by saying he wasn't willing to go through life with one hand tied behind his back. That was how Billy felt about the movies. When the lights went down, he didn't care what kind of movie it was. Nothing could dampen his enthusiasm – not even the names Tom Hanks or Meg Ryan in the opening credits.

Such slavish devotion took some explaining, and Casey for one wasn't convinced. 'I still don't get it,' he said, puffing away on the joint. 'I mean, I know I'm no movie buff. But Tom Hanks? You have got to be kidding me!'

So Billy finally opened up and revealed the true nature of his addiction, in terms he was certain his friend would understand. As he confessed to Casey that long night, going to the

6

movies was a habit he developed around the time he first began to masturbate. Relieved of sexual tension but riddled with guilt, he would sneak out of the house while his parents were asleep and lose himself for a few hours in some late-night double bill at the local fleapit. Sometimes the manager would let him slip in for free, and Billy would feign innocence as the old man ushered him up to the projection booth, each of them knowing what the invitation meant but neither one willing to risk acknowledging it and facing the consequences. He must have watched over a hundred movies from up in that booth, until one day the old man finally wised up to the fact that he wasn't getting anywhere and the invitations to free screenings dried up. Not that Billy really minded all that much. He may have saved himself a few dollars, but given the choice he would much sooner sit in the front row of the stalls, where everything looked far larger than life and his concentration wasn't broken by the whirr of the projector or the unwanted attentions of a man even older than his father.

'Not that there's anything wrong with older men,' Casey interjected. 'Older men have been a great source of comfort to me over the years. But I hear what you're saying.'

These days Billy went to the movies in much the same way that some people went to church – not quite religiously, and never really believing in everything he heard and saw, but always willing to suspend disbelief in the hope that, for the next few hours, all his problems would disappear. Once he even persuaded Casey to join him on a pilgrimage to the famous Mann's Chinese Theater. They arrived to find the hallowed forecourt littered with gum and coachloads of tourists kneeling at the foot- and handprints of Hollywood's great and good. One woman was busy fingering Marilyn's signature while her boyfriend encouraged her to wiggle her fat ass at the camera. Nearby, a man was treading the remains of his hamburger into the small patch of concrete immortalised by Dean Martin. 'Gross,' Casey said with a look of horror, and for once Billy was forced to agree.

Persuading Casey to join him at the movies had proved even more difficult after that particular episode, but in all honesty Billy was just as happy to go alone. Many an afternoon had been whiled away at the Sunset 5, which was walking distance from his apartment and handy for the gym, and where the latest independent offerings attracted a quieter, more sophisticated audience than the popcorn-munching masses who flocked to the larger multiplexes. But more often than not he would climb into his red Volvo convertible and drive over to Westwood village, where many of the original movie palaces still towered above the modern sprawl of Starbucks and Urban Clothing Stores.

Driving along Wilshire with the wind in his hair, Billy would try to imagine what Westwood was like in the old days, before the multiplexes arrived and the premieres moved downtown. Grander and more lavish than the theatres in Hollywood, the Westwood movie palaces were reminders of a time when stars were regularly referred to as gods and goddesses, and studios were still in the business of selling dreams. Hollywood must have been magical back then, before the familiar tales of infidelity and drug addiction brought the dream into disrepute.

Arriving at the theatre, he would hand over his ten dollars and feel the familiar flutter in his chest. Nothing compared to the giddy excitement he felt at the movies. Sitting there in the dark, with that long funnel of smoky light stretching out over his head, he would lose himself in the intimate workings of other people's lives, played out for him in revealing close-up. Sometimes he even pictured himself up there on the screen with Tom or Brad or Leo or Colin, only in Billy's version of events the boys invariably cruised off into the sunset together, leaving their female co-stars crying into their pillows or ready to try their hands at lesbianism. But then the movie would end and the credits would roll and Billy would emerge blinking into the light, wondering if life was ever as good as the movies or if this was the best he could hope for. Moving to LA had provided him with far more opportunities than he would ever have found back home. The city was home to some of the most beautiful men in the world, many of whom were gay and up for a good time seven nights a week. But for all the parties and potential sexual partners, love was no easier to find in West Hollywood than it had been in northern Wisconsin.

Still, Billy was a survivor. He knew how to adapt. Billy wasn't even his real name. His mother called him Jamie. His father had called him many things – pretty boy, sissy, faggot – until the booze and the bitterness finally got the better of him and he dropped dead of a heart attack at the ripe old age of forty-two. It wasn't like in the movies. There was no big scene, no final dramatic flourish. He simply slumped to the floor one evening after dinner and quietly died. Jamie was seventeen at the time, and to say that he was moved by his father's death would be putting it mildly. Emotions bubbled up inside him like molten lava and he ran upstairs to his room, terrified that he might explode. Seeing his mother numb with shock and visibly choking on her own grief only made matters worse. The truth was, he wasn't the least bit sorry his father was dead. Any love he might have felt for that man had been knocked out of him years ago. Maybe now the hate would slowly fade away too, until one day he'd wake up and there'd be nothing left but cold indifference.

He didn't attend the funeral. He pretended he was feeling sick that day. Then he waited until the house was empty, packed some clothes into a holdall and hitch-hiked his way to LA. The first car to pull over was a blue station wagon, driven by a man who looked a bit like Jack Nicholson and who assured Billy that he'd be glad of the company, 'it bein' such a long drive an' all'. It didn't take too long for old Jack to make his move, and for Billy to find himself dumped at the edge of the freeway, swearing that this was the last time he put his trust in someone simply because they happened to resemble a famous movie star. He waited a while before finally accepting a ride from a young college student who didn't look the least bit like anyone even remotely famous, and who was driving all the way to LA to audition for a part in a new reality TV show, the details of which he was happy to bore Billy with for the best part of the journey. As they approached the city, the desert gave way to a landscape of neon signs, fast-food stops and anonymous motels offering clean sheets and cable TV for $50 a night. Billy knew they'd arrived when he saw a giant billboard that read: *LA, where the people are fake. It's the earthquakes, fires and riots that are real*. At the time, he didn't know if this was intended as a joke or not. What was more, he didn't care. Whatever the city had to throw at him, it couldn't be any worse than the mess he'd left behind.

Six years on, he still hadn't been back home. There were too many bad memories tied up in that house, and very little to be gained from raking up the past now the old man was dead and buried. His mother had lived the best part of her life in blissful ignorance, and Billy didn't want to be the one who brought reality crashing down around her. So he sent the occasional letter to let her know he was doing okay, sometimes with a few hundred dollars enclosed but always without a return address or telephone number lest she was tempted to write back or call to ask him why he never visited. He was grateful that his mother wasn't the adventurous type. The chances of her tracking him down in a place like LA were pretty slim. Strange cities had always frightened her, almost as much as they had always excited him.

Of course much of the excitement he felt when he first arrived in LA had rubbed off by now, along with many of the vestiges of the person he used to be. People changed when they moved to a big city, though how much of this was caused by the city itself and how much was due to the baggage they brought with them he'd never really worked out. Certainly, most of the people he'd met during his time in LA seemed to be running away from something. Some tried to hide it by constantly moving forward, trying new things, seeking spiritual enlightenment through home furnishings or building a better future by investing in a bigger hot tub. Some insisted that this was simply a stopgap until something better came along. Some even claimed that they had just landed here by accident, and were too busy or too lazy to even think about moving on. But really it all amounted to the same thing. LA wasn't a city of angels at all. It was a city of exiles, which made it the perfect hiding place for people determined to change.

The first thing he'd changed was his name. After that, the rest hadn't seemed so difficult.

CHAPTER TWO

To: gary.koverman@foxstudios.com
From: lee.carson@leecarsonassociates.com
Subject: Matt Walsh

Gary, I know what game you're playing and I'm telling you now
the shit won't work. If you want this movie you're going to
have to pay for it. And if you don't, there are plenty of people
who will. So do us both a favour and either piss or get off the
pot. I'll expect to hear from you by the end of the day.
Lee

The email was short, sharp and to the point – rather like the
woman who'd written it. Lee Carson wasn't known for her
tact. But she was certainly known. Lee was one of a rare
breed – one of a handful of high-powered Hollywood man-
agers/agents/publicists who, though not nearly as famous as
the clients they represented, were seen by many as celebrities
in their own right.

Liz Rosenberg owed her share of the limelight to a certain
ambitious blonde named Madonna. Pat Kingsley spent years
basking in the glow of Tom Cruise's megawatt grin. As for
Lee, she represented the man *People* magazine had recently
named 'The Sexiest Man Alive', the same man who'd just
made the *Vanity Fair* Hollywood power list for the first time

in his career. Almost two decades after he first strutted in front of the cameras, Matt Walsh was at the top of his game. Every inch a star (and a good four inches taller than Tom Cruise), Matt could finally command twenty million dollars a movie, and Lee could take her place at all the top tables in town, confident that her reputation not only preceded her but was guaranteed a good brown-nosing from the maître d' at Morton's.

How a woman of Lee's limited abilities had managed to scale such dizzy heights was a matter of some dispute. Some put it down to good old-fashioned luck, a simple case of being in the right place at the right time. Others suggested that darker forces were at work. But what nobody could deny was that Lee Carson had made it on her own terms, with a single-mindedness second to none and a sense of her own importance that was awesome even by Hollywood standards. All the stars had their 'people' – armies of anonymous managers, agents, assistants and publicists who quietly kept things in order but whose influence was barely detectable and rarely acknowledged. Not Matt Walsh. For as long as anyone could remember, his affairs had all been handled by one person, an individual whose name was as familiar to the Hollywood rank and file as the star she represented, and whose influence was so palpable it was felt by everyone who crossed her path.

Sure, Lee had her underlings. Contrary to popular opinion, she was only human after all. There were only so many hours in the day, and with the best will in the world no amount of multi-tasking could meet the demands of such a demanding business. Tough as it was for her to admit, even she was forced to delegate every now and then. Still she made her presence felt. Every memo, every press release, every detail of every deal was personally approved by her on a daily basis.

Nothing escaped her attention, and woe betide the employee who tried to win her approval by showing some initiative. People had been fired for less. The sign above the door of her office on Wilshire may have read *Lee Carson Associates*, but nobody in Hollywood would ever make the mistake of thinking that any of Lee's associates had played even the smallest part in Matt's success. The recognition she'd craved for years was finally hers. There wasn't a single industry insider who didn't know the name Lee Carson and wasn't obliged to treat her with respect – at least to her face.

Lee knew only too well that people bitched behind her back. There was a saying in Hollywood – 'It isn't enough to succeed; in order to be truly happy you have to see someone else fail' – and it was a long time since Lee had given anyone the satisfaction of seeing her fail. So a certain amount of back-biting was inevitable. Besides, she hadn't got where she was today without making a few enemies along the way. When it came to bearing grudges, journalists were in a league of their own. Desperate to be seen as proper writers rather than the hired hacks they were, they resented Lee and everything she stood for – each precondition of every interview she granted a painful reminder that they were little more than an extension of the PR machine. They hit back at her the only way they knew how. Her name appeared in the gossip columns on a regular basis, and rarely was she portrayed as anything other than a hard-faced bitch.

Take today, for example. She'd only been at her desk for a little over an hour, and already she was making news. An item in this morning's edition of the *Star* referred to her as 'Matt Walsh's personal Rottweiler' and repeated the famous story of her once settling an argument by taking a bite out of a producer's ear. Never mind that the story was ten years old and the producer was about to have his ears pinned back anyway.

The way the *Star* reported it, anyone would think she made a habit out of this sort of thing.

Still, it was a reputation she was more than happy to live with. Although physically rather small, she was larger than life in every other respect. Five foot four in her spike heels, she was every inch her own woman. Nothing had been left to the vicissitudes of nature. Painfully underweight, with nails like talons and red hair so heavily lacquered it could withstand a minor earthquake, she was pushing fifty, looked ten years younger and wore the permanently incredulous expression of someone who was no stranger to Botox and was widely rumoured to be on her second, if not third, facelift. She was like a painting by Picasso – all sharp angles and improbable dimensions. It wasn't a look that suited everyone, but for her it worked very well. She could turn on the charm at a moment's notice, but preferred to remain prickly and impenetrable whenever possible. She may have possessed her fair share of feminine wiles, but softness and curves had never been part of the package.

When it came to her wardrobe, the look was very Jackie Collins, but without the obvious sex appeal. Like Jackie, she had a passion for animal prints, although in Lee's case they were worn purely as battle dress, with none of the sexual overtones commonly associated with the first lady of trash fiction. Today she'd opted for a leopard-print jacket with black pants and snakeskin ankle boots. On anyone else this might have signalled an air of availability. On her the overall effect wasn't so much seductive as savage. Indeed, there were people in Hollywood who swore blind that she skinned the animals herself, with her bare hands, each morning on her way to the office. Where she was supposed to track down such creatures amid the urban sprawl and busy freeways Lee had never been able to work out. LA had more than its fair share of exotic occupants, many of whom had crossed continents to get here, but they tended to be of the human variety. Tales of tigers and zebras roaming the streets of Beverly Hills did seem a little far-fetched – even for Hollywood.

Not that she was particularly bothered by people suggesting she was capable of such savagery. She had never cared much for being liked anyway, and in her line of work it was far better to be feared than have people think they could walk all over you. This wasn't a popularity contest, it was business. And Hollywood was a tough town. People were expendable here. Faces came and went. Friendships were forged over breakfast, consolidated over lunch and forgotten about by dinner. In such a fast-track, unforgiving world, the only survivors were those who had the foresight to put themselves and their careers first. Not that you'd think it to hear the way some of them talked. The industry was full of people willing to make out that their jobs weren't that important, especially in the current climate. 'We're only making movies,' they'd say. 'We're not curing cancer.' And there they were, hunched over their desks by 7.30 every morning, poring over the day's editions of *Variety* and *The Hollywood Reporter*, timing their calls, discussing projects, plotting their next move. Hypocrites, every last one of them.

Whatever else people said about her, nobody could accuse Lee of false modesty. She may have been described by one gossip columnist as having more faces than a town clock, but her dedication to the job was legendary. She worked every hour God sent, rarely took a holiday and had never taken a day's sick leave in her life. Her personal life was practically nonexistent. She lived alone. She had never married, rarely dated and harboured no regrets about never having had children. What little maternal instinct she did possess she reserved for her client, although it was clear to anyone that it was maternal instinct of the most primitive kind – more *Aliens* than *Stepmom*. Nurture wasn't part of her nature, and she made very little attempt to disguise the fact. Once, purely to antagonise some studio exec who was making that tired old comparison between making movies and curing cancer, she interrupted him to say that she had recently bought herself a dog. 'Really?' the exec asked, startled. 'What breed?' 'A chihuahua,' she replied. 'Odd little thing. Looks as if half his fur is missing. I call him Chemo.'

That little gem had made it into the gossip columns, of course. She laughed out loud when she read it. And when it was suggested by another columnist that the reason Lee Carson never got sick was that even viruses were afraid of her, she laughed that off too. Because it didn't really matter what people wrote about her. All that mattered was what they said about Matt Walsh. In a world where any piece of trailer trash could claw their way into the tabloids, or achieve cheap-grade semi-celebrity status on the back of a reality TV show or a bust-up on *Jerry Springer*, stars of Matt's calibre were few and far between. At a time when most Hollywood 'stars' possessed all the charisma of black holes, and studios squandered vast sums promoting the pumped-up heroics of Vin Diesel or the pretty-boy posturing of Brad Pitt, Matt was one of the few movie stars truly worth his salary. Matt Walsh didn't just pose for the camera. He teased it, flirted with it, seduced it, willed it to love him with a combination of plucky arrogance and heart-stopping vulnerability that great swatches of the movie-going masses found virtually impossible to resist. Whether their devotion was undying, or was destined to fade as he faced his forties, nobody in Hollywood could say for certain. But in a town where few people could see beyond the opening weekend grosses, there was one thing everyone was agreed on – Matt Walsh sold a lot of popcorn.

Of course he had his detractors. The kinder of his critics said he was cursed with a talent for making everything look too easy, as though he were always simply playing himself. Others suggested that this was the only role he was capable of playing, given his obvious limits as an actor. One recent review opened by saying: 'Beauty brings many privileges, but do they have to include Matt Walsh's bad acting in this movie? He smirks when he means to be suave and mugs at the camera when he means to be charming. Not since Richard Gere admired himself in *American Gigolo* have we seen a man so in love with his own image.'

Lee grimaced as she recalled it, then reminded herself that the author of that particular review was known neither for his looks nor for his talents as an actor. Besides, critics who compared Matt's shameless displays of male narcissism to the pumped-up posturings of a glorified male hustler were only showing their ignorance. It was like those critics who accused the Oscars of having turned into nothing but a crass commercial platform for promoting movies. Where was their sense of history? The Oscars had *always* been a crass commercial platform for promoting movies. Similarly, there had always been male movie icons who were accused of putting the 'Ho' into Hollywood, long before Matt Walsh came along. Some of the greatest male screen icons of all time had suffered similar taunts, from Valentino onwards, and their legends would live on long after these third-rate hacks had pissed away their pension plans in some Florida nursing home.

Nobody would ever claim that Matt was the greatest actor of his generation. But as Lee always told him, that was merely an epithet invented to console those bright young things who weren't blessed with matinée-idol looks. Plenty of people could pass themselves off as actors. Very few had what it took to be a star, least of all these days. Critics would do well to remember that, the next time they complained about Matt's decision to turn down an interview, or Lee's strong-arm tactics with the world's media. Stars like Matt Walsh were a dying breed, and as such they deserved the same level of protection as any other endangered species. People could bitch and complain all they liked, but without the likes of Lee Carson there to protect them, there was a distinct possibility that stars like Matt Walsh would be wiped out completely.

The way things stood, Matt's future had never looked brighter. An item in this morning's edition of *The Hollywood Reporter* even went so far as to suggest that maybe the critical tide was turning, and that having stayed the distance, it was high time Matt Walsh was recognised for his services to the motion picture industry. Much to Lee's amusement, the article even had a quote from Jack Nicholson, who defined success by saying: 'The whole thing is to keep on working, and pretty soon they'll think you're good.' The only question was, how good did they think Matt was? As good as Nicholson? Good enough for a Golden Globe? Or was there some greater honour in mind? The author of the article didn't speculate as to what shape the recognition might take, but was it really too much to hope for an Oscar? God knows the Academy had made some surprising decisions over the years. They gave an Oscar to Julia Roberts. Why not Matt Walsh?

Lee pictured Matt up on stage at the Kodak Theatre, delivering his acceptance speech. Then she wiped the thought from her mind. Ultimately, it didn't really matter whether Matt was nominated for an Oscar or not. Likewise, it didn't really matter what the critics thought. All that mattered was the size of his paycheque, and in that respect Matt had very little left to prove. This next deal with Fox could net him a cool twenty million – more if she got her way and they factored in a share of the proceeds. Oscar or no Oscar, Matt Walsh was now one of the highest earners in Hollywood. Finally it looked as if all those years of dedication and hard work had paid off.

Granted, there had always been a certain amount of talent involved too – his as well as hers. And in an industry where good looks mattered far more than good works, a face like Matt's never did either of them any harm. Tall, dark and ridiculously handsome, Matt Walsh had that vital X factor that made women go weak at the knees and had the money men who ran Hollywood seeing dollar signs. But there were plenty of other actors out there who were every bit as photogenic as Matt, and whose careers were over almost as soon as they'd begun. Even that much-hyped 'big break' was no guarantee of longevity. It wasn't so long ago that Chris O'Donnell was tipped to be the Next Big Thing, and who could remember the last movie he made? No, it took a lot more than talent, looks and timing to make a star. It took good management.

Talent was rare enough these days. But the talent to handle talent? That was rarer still. Matt had been one of the lucky ones. When his big break came, Lee was poised and waiting, eager to put all those years of experience to good use and determined that, this time, she and her bright new hope would be rising all the way to the top. It was the late 1980s. The bulk of the so-called 'brat pack' had seen their careers fade along with their youth, and the few surviving members were busy spilling their guts to anyone who'd listen. Previously consigned to a series of underwritten, instantly forgettable supporting roles in movies starring Molly Ringwald in pink or Rob Lowe in a jockstrap, it was fair to say that Matt had never made that much of an impression. But now suddenly here he was in a starring role of his own, playing a cocky young baseball player who embarks on an illicit affair with the mother of one of his teammates while getting his ass whipped on the field and in the locker room. The critics hated *Third Base*, but audiences loved it – so much so that the movie made a significant profit in its first week and Matt made the transition from supporting player to leading man. The image of him bruised and bloodied in his baseball shirt and tight white briefs went on to become part of the iconography of the age.

Lee had several other clients on her books the day she signed Matt Walsh. Some she'd known for as long as she'd been in the business. But as his career took off she let them go one by one. It wasn't a decision she took lightly, but she'd been around long enough to know that this was it, her once-in-a-lifetime, twenty-four-carat golden opportunity. She couldn't afford to be sentimental. If she wanted to get ahead, she would have to trim a little fat. It was that simple. So she dropped the sweet, dumb blonde who had just invested in her starter set of breast implants, but who was still too kooky-looking to ever be considered as anything more than a character actress. She dropped the ageing action hero whose ass had sunk lower than his popularity rating, and who could barely afford a buttock lift since his last three movies had gone straight to video. She dropped the former model who limited her calorie intake by swallowing cotton wool and tried to advance her career by offering blowjobs to casting agents willing to consider her for walk-ons. She dropped every remotely promising, moderately successful minor league player she had on her books, and she staked everything on her rising star, her golden boy, her Matt.

And she hadn't regretted it for a moment. With Lee there to guide him, Matt had made all the right moves, baring body and soul in a string of teen romances guaranteed to satisfy his female fanbase, then demonstrating his versatility and widening his appeal by playing a psychopathic killer in one of the first thrillers to tap into the theme of yuppies in peril. *A Killing on Wall Street* had marked a turning point in many respects. Widely acknowledged as Matt's first grown-up role, it also gave him the chance to show that his charms weren't limited to playing good guys. Displaying a hitherto unseen flair for black comedy, Matt's knowing portrayal of a disaffected college kid who discovers a hidden talent for carving up stockbrokers earned him a Golden Globe nomination and the best critical notices of his career.

Since then he'd shown his sensitive side in a series of domestic dramas, playing the troubled sons of fathers who never learned to say 'I love you'. Movies about men loving men were especially popular in '90s Hollywood, Lee recalled with a shudder. The only proviso, of course, was that it was the kind of man-on-man love that went down equally well in Middle America. Father–son romances were the buddy movies of their day – sensitive, masculine and definitely not gay.

More recently, and in keeping with the demand for simpler stories populated by breathtaking physical specimens, Matt had beefed up for a number of action movies. The settings changed, but the plots were basically the same. In each movie Matt was pushed to the limits of human endurance, stripped of his dignity and the bulk of his wardrobe before coming out fighting in a torn tank-top. He voiced some doubts at first, but as Lee impressed upon him time and time again, there was a price to pay for being as good-looking as Matt Walsh, and movies like *Fire Hazard* and *Whiplash* were designed to give audiences exactly what they wanted to see – their handsome hero roughed up and suffering for their entertainment. The proof was in the box office, and with grosses in excess of a hundred million dollars a movie, nobody could argue that Matt's suffering had been entirely in vain.

None of this had been left to chance. Every step of Matt's career had been planned and executed with military precision. Each role had been carefully weighed up in terms of the financial rewards it offered and the potential it had for satisfying his growing army of fans or backfiring horribly and tarnishing his carefully cultivated public image. Each interview he gave had been stage-managed for months in advance, the interviewers hand-picked, contracts drawn up and copy approval sought. Inevitably, this had led to Matt developing a reputation as something of a control freak, but anyone with an eye on the business knew that the calls for total control came from a higher power. Lee had a hand in every aspect of Matt's life, professional and personal. It was she who decided which roles he should accept, she who negotiated the cost of his services to the studios, she who suggested which starlet he should escort to the latest premiere, she who briefed him on what to say during interviews.

Industry insiders joked that she even wiped his ass when necessary, but who cared what they thought? The public loved him, and in this business that was really all that mattered. It may have taken her a little longer than she'd hoped, but Lee could congratulate herself on a job well done. Her golden boy was the brightest star in Hollywood. And Lee would do everything in her power to ensure that nothing came between Matt Walsh and his fabulous career.

CHAPTER THREE

If someone had told Billy that today his life would change as dramatically as the latest Jerry Bruckheimer blockbuster after a particularly bad audience test screening, he would have smiled politely and told them to spare him the bullshit. Any number of people had promised him all sorts of things over the years, usually in return for some sexual favour or another. 'Sure, I can help find you a better job. Sure, I can set you up in a better apartment. Sure, I can take care of you and love you and see to it that you'll never be lonely again. Now turn over.' Each time Billy had kept his end of the bargain, and each time he'd felt well and truly shafted when his new-found benefactor failed to follow through. So he could be forgiven if, these days, he was wary of anyone who expressed a sudden interest in his welfare, or promised him that a brighter future was waiting just around the corner.

Besides, there was nothing to suggest that today would be remotely different to any other long, hot, manic Monday in LA. He'd spent the best part of the morning working out with Casey at the Crunch gym on Sunset. A popular meeting place for West Hollywood's gay party boys, Crunch was generally far too busy and way too gay for Billy's liking. However, it did boast a stunning view of the Hollywood Hills, otherwise known as 'the Swish Alps'. As inspirational a vision as Cher at sixty or Brad Pitt with his shirt off, this window into a world of international fame and outrageous fortune rarely failed to get the juices flowing, provoking endless speculation about the lives lived in them there hills, and steering the conversation away from the familiar discussions of last night's trade or the next big circuit party. In fact, so intoxicating was the view and so great the thirst for gossip that it was a wonder anyone found time to perform much in the way of exercise. This probably explained why Crunch was the only gym in West Hollywood where male club members spent more time studying the view from the window than they did sizing up the talent in the steam room. Sex was never far from anyone's mind, but when a gym was this popular and this well appointed, it went without saying that certain codes of conduct should be observed.

The greatest gossips by far were the two steroid queens who always hogged the bench press closest to the window, and who spent the first ten minutes of every workout grunting like a couple of pot-bellied pigs with six-packs, before settling into their usual routine and tittering like a pair of schoolgirls as they swapped lurid tales of gay life up in the Hills. Listening to Bruce and his friend Donald, it was clear that they fantasised about living in the lap of luxury and didn't particularly care whose lap it was, provided they had a pool. Fantasy was all it was, of course. Billy knew better than to take their tales of Hollywood pool parties and star-studded orgies too seriously. He'd been invited to a few parties in the Hills, and was aware that a certain amount of homosexual activity went on. He was aware, also, of the existence of a close network of highly influential gay men working within the industry, and often referred to as 'the velvet mafia'. But if half of the conversations he'd overheard at Crunch were to be believed, there wasn't an actor in Hollywood who wasn't secretly banging some muscle boy every night of the week.

Even allowing for the possibility that a small percentage of these tales contained at least an element of truth, Billy thought it highly unlikely that either Bruce or Donald would find their names at the top of any high-powered Hollywood fag's party list. It was well known that the velvet mafia could take their pick of some of the prettiest boys in town, and despite all their efforts at the gym, neither Bruce nor Donald were exactly what you'd call eye candy. Years of steroid abuse had left Bruce with a complexion no amount of micro-dermabrasion or revolutionary new chemical peels could rectify, while Donald was so boss-eyed he wouldn't have looked out of place in the bar scene from *Star Wars*. Aside from making him rather unattractive, this also gave the distinct impression that he wasn't to be trusted. Or as Casey put it, 'You never know where you are with Donald. There's always one eye looking at you and the other eye looking for you.'

Today being an unusually quiet morning by Crunch standards, and one remarkably short on gossip, Billy and Casey completed their workout in record time and were soon showered, dressed and ready to hit the streets.

'Is my hair okay?' Casey asked as they checked themselves one last time in the locker room mirror. Casey's hair was a constant cause for concern. In the past year alone it had been dyed black, bleached within an inch of its life, brutally cropped and carefully conditioned and coaxed back to health. Lately Casey had been experimenting with a hairstyle known as a 'faux-hawk', a kind of mini mohawk that was short in length, heavy on 'product' and extremely popular among the disaffected youth of Beverly Hills.

'Your hair is fabulous,' Billy said, although in all honesty he much preferred Casey's hair the way it had looked two months ago, before the faux-hawk took off and the bleach went back in.

'You don't think it's too young?' Casey asked. 'Too Whitney dressed as Britney?'

Billy grinned. 'Please. Nothing is that scary!'

Casey laughed. 'Yeah, I know. I do feel kinda sorry for Whitney though. All those years as America's sweetheart and then suddenly it's, like, "Houston, you have a problem! It's not right, and it's not okay!" Anyway, how about lunch? There's this great new salad bar just a couple of blocks from here, and they're doing a special deal on wheatgrass juice.'

Billy smiled. 'That last sentence had all the wrong words in it for me. But I guess I can force a salad down. Just spare me the wheatgrass.'

Casey's attempts to wean Billy off his staple diet of junk food had been a feature of their friendship from day one, and might have met with greater success had Casey himself shown even a modicum of restraint where certain other appetites were concerned. Never mind the stories about Whitney. It was hard to take nutritional advice from a man who spent half his waking hours wired on crystal meth, and who'd shoved enough coke up his nose to stun the entire population of a small South American country. But as Billy knew only too well, LA was a town where good friends were hard to find and even harder to keep. Casey wasn't perfect by any means. He was sometimes difficult, and often demanding. But he was always there. In his own messy way, he'd been looking out for Billy since the day they met. If the occasional salad was all it took to keep him happy, Billy figured it was a small price to pay. He could always grab a burger later if he was hungry.

Sitting in the salad bar, munching on a mouthful of raw vegetables, Billy listened as Casey filled him in on the latest gossip from his kick-boxing class. Like many West Hollywood boys, Casey worked out religiously in the belief that, if you're going to abuse your body with large quantities of narcotics, you might as well be in good physical shape for it. In addition to his daily workouts at the gym, he could always find time for at least one other form of regular exercise – usually one which happened to have been endorsed by a famous celebrity. A few years ago, he'd followed Madonna's shining example and signed up for a course in ashtanga yoga. Unfortunately, things hadn't quite worked out as planned and he was left with a sprained groin, the memory of which was so painful, he still couldn't listen to 'Ray of Light' without his eyes smarting. As a rule, Casey tended to stick with something for a few weeks at best. His enthusiasm was impressive while it lasted, but short-lived. If someone questioned his commitment, Casey would argue that he was suffering from attention deficit disorder – a condition he didn't fully understand but liked the sound of, since it seemed to imply that he wasn't receiving enough attention. Lately, however, he appeared to have overcome his affliction. Kick-boxing had been a regular talking point of Casey's since the very first *Matrix* movie, and with each sequel his enthusiasm seemed to have grown in direct proportion to Keanu's fanbase. What few people realised was that Casey's fantasies of becoming a kick-boxer actually started with Jean-Claude Van Damme, whose films were widely considered a joke but whose ass Casey had been admiring for years.

'You should tag along this afternoon,' Casey said as he polished off his wheatgrass. 'Nothing firms up your butt like kick-boxing. I swear I'll be cracking walnuts by Christmas. And you never know when a bit of self-defence might come in useful.'

'My butt is fine, thank you,' Billy replied. 'Besides, I already have plans. There's a rare screening of *The Mirror Has Two Faces* at the Nuart.'

Casey pulled a face. 'The Streisand movie? The movie

otherwise known as *The Diva Has Two Egos*? Are you completely insane? You know, there's a reason they don't screen that movie too often. Something to do with public health.'

Billy laughed. 'Thanks for the warning. I think I'll just take my chances.'

A few hours later, he was wishing he'd taken Casey's warning a little more seriously. The movie was fun for about the first twenty minutes. After that, it went the way of every Streisand vehicle of the past twenty years and provided the leading lady with ample opportunity to show off her nails and be told by some WASPish piece of Hollywood beefcake that she was in fact beautiful.

It did make Billy think, though – and not just about what Barbra Streisand saw when she looked in the mirror, but also about his own face and the trouble it sometimes brought him. His father might have been the first person to make Billy wish he wasn't such a pretty boy, but he was by no means the last. Throughout his childhood, he'd been singled out and bullied by the other kids, who saw his physical beauty as evidence of some kind of character flaw, and tried to beat it out of him on a regular basis. Moving to LA, he soon discovered that looks like his also brought certain advantages, provided one knew how to capitalise on them. The everyday stares of admiration and lust made him feel special where before he'd felt more of a freak.

But lately some of the old feelings had come back to haunt him. Living the lifestyle he did, in a world where youth and beauty were such highly prized commodities, he knew he had a lot to be thankful for. And barely a day went by when he wasn't grateful for the fact that his face and body could still command attention, even in those select places where beautiful boys were in such ready supply they were practically part of the decor. But unlike Casey, who could never fully relax until he was confident that all eyes were upon him, Billy didn't always enjoy the kind of attention his looks tended to generate. Sometimes it was as if his beauty created an invisible barrier between himself and the rest of the world, a window through which every admiring glance was somehow magnified, and viewed with a mixture of gratitude and suspicion. Was it just his imagination, or did people look at him as if they were expecting to hate him, as if they were somehow torn between marvelling at his looks and resenting his good fortune at having been blessed with more than his fair share of them? And even when they were throwing themselves at him, was it him they really wanted, or just a taste of what it would be like to possess such rare physical gifts, preferably for a few hours and without sparing a thought for the person behind the perfectly formed image? It wasn't even as if he could rely on his looks for ever. He might only have been twenty-three, but there were times when he feared that his days of being desired were rapidly running out.

These nagging doubts gnawed away at his self-confidence and left him feeling strangely insecure in a way few of the men who watched him working out at the gym that morning or turned to stare at him as he left the movie theatre that afternoon could even begin to understand. To them he was simply one of the beautiful people.

Whatever traumas he may have endured in the past, and whatever problems he might be facing now, he had never suffered the indignity of being anything less than drop-dead gorgeous. Unlike Barbra, Billy had never known the pain of being an ugly duckling. In most people's eyes, this made him marginally less sympathetic than he might have been had he been found guilty of plotting with terrorists or refusing to recycle. What most people didn't recognise, of course, was that Billy was just as much a victim of his looks

30

as they were of theirs. He simply photographed better, that was all.

He arrived back at his apartment shortly before six. The apartment was nothing to write home about – which was one of the reasons why, on those rare occasions that he did write to his mother, Billy neglected to mention it altogether. Situated in the less desirable east side of West Hollywood, a little too close to the less savoury stretch of Sunset Boulevard, it was a grim, grey two-room rental affair with wall-to-wall carpet, black faux-leather furniture and no real character to speak of. The living room was dominated by a widescreen TV. Next to it was a small shelving unit containing a selection of his favourite movies – *Sweet Charity*, *Breakfast at Tiffany's*, *Pretty Woman* – plus a few rental releases from Blockbuster. Maybe tonight he'd finally get around to watching that Matt Walsh movie everyone was talking about. Apparently, there was a scene in *Whiplash* where, if you hit the freeze-frame button at precisely the right moment, you could actually catch a glimpse of Matt Walsh's cock.

Billy hesitated to call this place home. His third apartment in four years, it was simply the latest in a long line of temporary abodes, a functional living space in which he slept, showered, drank coffee, ate pizza, watched TV and played on his computer. There were a few framed movie posters dotted around the walls, and a photo of himself and Casey at last year's White Party in Palm Springs proudly displayed on a side table. But there were none of the little touches that make a house a home, no air of permanence. Nothing contained within these walls suggested anything even remotely resembling a lifestyle. Everything seemed to indicate that whoever lived here was simply passing through, from the stack of unopened mail on the kitchen table to the pizza boxes littering the living room floor. The empty phone socket spoke volumes.

He took a shower, fixed himself something to eat and was about to settle down in front of the TV when his cell rang. It was a little later than usual, but business was business. He answered the phone, scribbled a few details on a piece of notepaper and wandered into the bedroom, where he changed into a crisp white Hanes T-shirt and quickly packed his black leather briefcase. The briefcase was a gift from Casey, given to him in much the same spirit that a father might grant his only son the funds necessary to put himself through college, or an older brother might advise his younger sibling on the best way to persuade a girl to put out. The briefcase was both a token of their friendship and the summation of everything Casey had learned during his time in LA and wanted to pass on to his friend. Walk into any hotel lobby with a briefcase under your arm, and it didn't really matter how you were dressed. You could have your T-shirt cropped all the way up to your nipples, or your jeans hanging halfway down your ass. Provided you were carrying a briefcase, the last thing anyone would think was that you were a hustler.

To: Michael
From: Lee
Subject: Where's my fucking coffee?

Lee was having a bitch of a day. This was largely the fault of her personal secretary, an obsequious young queen named Michael Rosetti, who'd been on the payroll for all of three months and who practically crawled into the office this morning a full fifteen minutes late, clutching a skinny latte and complaining of a headache so severe it might require a brain scan. To make matters worse, he'd continued to spend the best part of the day complimenting her on her robust constitution in a series of blatant attempts to generate some sympathy for his own, rather less impressive state of health. In Lee's world, efficiency was everything. There was no room for malfunction. From the moment she entered her office, everything was expected to run smoothly, from the automated message service to the remotes that controlled her lights and air-conditioning. Was it really too much to ask that her staff show a little of the same respect?

Lee might have been inclined to humour Michael a little more were she not painfully aware of the fact that this would only encourage him. Michael's short term of employment had brought more than its fair share of medical dramas. Barely a week went by without him complaining of some ailment or other. Given that Michael was both gay and, judging by the look of him, someone who couldn't afford to be too picky about who he slept with, his apparent inability to fend off even the slightest cold might have been cause for concern. But since he was also something of a drama queen, Lee saw no reason to start dusting off the red ribbon just yet. Michael's list of afflictions was no more consequential than the roll-call of friends and supporters certain actresses felt compelled to thank at the Oscars. And as with those interminable Oscars speeches, Lee had decided that the best way to deal with Michael's accounts of all that ailed him was to ignore them completely.

Normally, this had the desired effect of knocking the wind out of his sails before he succeeded in winding her up too much. Like the majority of homosexuals Lee had encountered over the years, Michael was a queen constantly looking for an audience. As soon as he realised that nobody was paying him any attention, he lost confidence and dried up. But for some reason, today he seemed hell-bent on prolonging the agony for as long as possible, referring Lee to a full breakdown of his medical history, as he reminded her of how lucky she was to have been blessed with such a healthy immune system.

Finally she snapped. 'The reason I don't get sick, Michael, is that I don't have the time,' she said sharply. 'And while we're on the subject, neither do you.'

Michael had spent the remainder of the afternoon in a sulk, hunched over his desk in a bid to look busy and occasionally breaking the silence with a highly theatrical cough. Lee was about to haul him into her office and tear him down a peg or two when he buzzed her to announce that Matt Walsh was on the line. The three-minute conversation that followed did nothing to improve her mood. Matt refused to go into the details, insisting that they meet first thing in the morning to talk things over in person. But even before those three minutes were up Lee knew exactly where this conversation was headed. The mere suggestion of it was enough to bring out a physical reaction. Her jawline, normally so firm and proud, began to droop with despair. Nerve endings paralysed by Botox began to twitch ominously. Deep in her stomach, a hunger she'd suppressed for years began to gnaw away at her insides. No amount of cosmetic reconditioning or rigid self-discipline could absorb the shock that ran through her body, playing havoc with her serotonin levels and sending her blood pressure sky high. When Matt uttered those two words 'artistic integrity' it could only mean one thing. Her golden boy was getting dangerous ideas into his head, ideas that could easily put the panic brake on his career and send her skidding back to obscurity.

Shaking with rage as she pictured the fallout from Matt's sudden attack of moral probity, Lee took a moment to compose herself before summoning the one person she knew would lift her spirits.

'I've decided to let you off early today, Michael,' she purred in the sweetest tones she could muster. 'And you needn't worry about coming in tomorrow. You're fired.'

Billy didn't just wake up one day and suddenly decide to become a prostitute. Hustling was a way of life that seemed to creep up on him. It was almost as if the job had chosen him, rather than the other way around. Faced with a number of different choices, he chose the path of least resistance. For Billy, falling into prostitution was a bit like falling in love. Once he began falling, he figured he might as well sit back and enjoy the ride.

It all started back in the days when he was first struggling to find his feet in LA. At the time he told himself that his needs were purely financial, although with hindsight he was willing to admit that it was probably a little more complicated than that. His early treatment at the hands of his father probably had something to do with it. Indeed, there was a part of him that regarded hustling as some kind of sacrificial activity, a form of self-flagellation which would not only pay the rent, but somehow exorcise the memory of the father who had hurt him and then conveniently died before Billy could confront him with the consequences of his actions. From the outset, he approached prostitution almost as a form of personal therapy. It was a nice idea in theory, but as he soon discovered, the practice was rather more prosaic.

Billy probably wouldn't have considered prostitution as a viable career option had it not been for Casey. Always the first at everything, Casey had been hustling since the age of thirteen. The proverbial happy hooker, he took the entirely pragmatic decision that since he was gay and a total slut to boot he might as well make some cash out of it. Casey's work ethic was remarkably straightforward. His motto was 'I'm a human being, not a human doing', and he lived accordingly, working as and when he needed to, in a job which capitalised on his natural abilities without cramping his style. Most of his days were spent at the gym, where he pursued his lifelong ambition to reduce his body fat ratio to three per cent. The closest Casey had ever come to a career move was at the age of sixteen, when he came to LA hoping to break into the gay porn industry. The fact that he couldn't act his way out of a plastic bag didn't bother him in the slightest. In porn movies, nobody was required to act. There were no mere actors in porn movies, only porn stars – as if the medium itself instantly bestowed a level of celebrity most performers could only dream of.

Sadly, any dreams Casey might have had of becoming the next Ryan Idol, or simply of being fucked by him on camera, quickly evaporated when he met a man claiming to be a talent scout for Falcon Studios, who told him in no mean terms that he simply wasn't sufficiently well hung to make it in the highly competitive world of gay porn. 'Sorry, but you're just not up to industry standards' were the man's exact words. Casey's desperate pleas that he was 'a grower, not a shower' had fallen on deaf ears. This, of course, was after he'd been invited back to the man's hotel room and encouraged to perform various sexual acts by way of an audition. His dreams of porn stardom cruelly dashed, Casey soon found his way on to Santa Monica Boulevard, where the rewards weren't nearly as high but the audience was generally more forgiving.

By the time he bumped into Billy one night at Rage, Casey was already a veteran of the local hustler scene. Although only a few years older than Billy, he was experienced enough to know that the Boulevard was no place for a boy hoping to make a decent living out of hustling. With this in mind, Casey had relocated his business activities and was moving up in the world, calling himself a 'personal ego consultant', and swapping the old 'johns' for new 'clients' and the Boulevard for a handful of hustler bars dotted around West Hollywood. The venues weren't particularly glamorous. Nor were the men who lined up at the bar every night, nursing their drinks and waiting for some new prime piece of boy flesh to brighten up their evening. But at least here Casey was protected from some of the tougher elements out there on the street, and wasn't constantly checking over his shoulder for squad cars. The LAPD had better things to do than raid hustler bars, or maybe they just preferred it when these things were kept behind closed doors. Either way, it felt a damn sight safer than hanging around Santa Monica Boulevard.

The first person to pay Billy for sex was an entertainment lawyer called Jeff, who propositioned him one night in Numbers, a smoky, chrome-filled hustler bar where Casey did a fair amount of trade. The decor put Billy in mind of a scene from *American Gigolo*, a movie he considered a triumph of style over content and Casey cited as a major influence. Hunched at the bar in a double-breasted Armani suit Richard Gere wouldn't have been seen dead in, Jeff was clearly nervous, probably married and tended to sweat rather a lot. He had flown in that morning from New York on business, and had a room at the Hollywood Hills Magic Hotel on Franklin Avenue. Billy liked the sound of the hotel far more than he liked the look of Jeff, but the guy seemed harmless enough. It wasn't until they got back to the hotel room that Jeff revealed another side to his character, calling Billy his 'little pig boy' and describing some of the things he'd like to do to him, most of which involved the kind of bodily functions normally reserved for the bathroom. Thankfully, Jeff's imagination was far more active than he was, and within a matter of minutes he had shot his wad and was slumped back on the bed, sweating heavily. As he slipped the roll of dollar bills into his pocket, Billy had a sense that something significant had happened. He had been calling himself Billy for months, but what little remained of Jamie West from Wisconsin finally died that night and was spirited away in a room in the Magic Hotel.

A lot had changed since then. These days, neither he nor Casey had much need of the hustler bars. Proud members of the gay online business community, they each had their own dedicated website, complete with photos inviting prospective clients to take a sneak preview of the goods on offer, a price list, and a number to call if they wanted to close the deal. More importantly, Billy had learned a vital lesson about the nature of hustling. When sex was something you did for a living, you had to find some other part of yourself to hold back, some other way of remaining in control. It wasn't an easy transition to make. For Billy, sex had never been a purely recreational activity. Rather, it had always been a way of getting close to people, a way of achieving some level of intimacy. While others trawled the bars in search of sex, he went out looking for love and willing to offer himself sexually to anyone he thought might provide it. The day he became a hustler, he realised that all that would have to change. From now on, sex was merely a form of currency, something he traded with strangers in return for cold, hard cash. Love and intimacy didn't come into it.

It took him a while, but gradually he learned to put his emotions aside. As time went by, sex and love became so removed from one another in his mind that these days his most private fantasies didn't involve sex at all. Nowadays, whenever Billy imagined himself with that special someone, it could be any one of a series of non-sexual situations he envisaged – walking the dog, having dinner, or watching a movie. Sex rarely entered the picture. And the strangest part was, he actually found this incredibly liberating. By separating his emotional needs from what he did sexually, he discovered that he was finally able to enjoy sex, not for its own sake, but for the pleasure he was able to give others. Hustling was a performance, and he approached it the way an actor approached a live audience. The key was to ensure that each client was completely taken in by the performance, and was left feeling fabulous. Each time Billy closed the door on a client's apartment or hotel room, it wasn't the cash in his pocket that put a spring in his step. It was the satisfaction of a job well done.

Even so, he was feeling mildly apprehensive as he left his apartment, climbed into his car and headed off in the direction of Bel Air. Meeting a client for the first time was always a bit nerve-racking. Regular clients were easy. You already knew what was expected of you, so getting into character wasn't a problem. But first meetings were like first dates. You never knew what to expect. Clearly this guy had money. He was staying in a five-star hotel in Bel Air, which probably meant that he was the kind of person who was used to getting his own way. But Billy knew better than to make too many assumptions. All sorts of men hired hustlers, for all kinds of reasons. Some simply wanted someone to talk to. Some wanted a dumb hunk who would fall to his knees with the stunned, obedient air of a supermarket checkout girl. Others wanted a mean muscle stud who would take charge and fuck them harder than they'd ever been fucked before. And then there were the really freaky ones, like the retired naval officer who liked to put on women's underwear and be spanked, or the district attorney who paid to watch Billy strip down to his underwear and blow up huge party balloons while he jerked off. Billy had been required to play so many parts over the years, he was never sure quite what to expect. The guy he was meeting tonight hadn't sounded like a freak on the phone, but nor had he given Billy any clues as to what he was into, other than to request that he bring condoms and lube. They were safely packed away inside his briefcase, together with a couple of porn videos, some sex toys, a bottle of poppers and the pocket knife Casey insisted he always carry with him in case things ever got out of hand. So far Billy had never had cause to use it, and he doubted he ever would. But as Casey always said, a working boy could never be too careful – even in Bel Air.

He pulled up at the entrance to the hotel, handed his keys to the parking valet, jumped out of his car and marched purposefully through the lobby. A few people turned and stared as he headed towards the elevators, but the look on their faces told him they were staring because they found him attractive, not because they regarded his presence as suspicious. Riding the elevator to the fourth floor, he checked the details on his piece of notepaper and followed the signs until he found the correct room number. Further along the corridor, an older woman in a pink Versace dress way too young for her turned and stared at him for a moment before fishing a key from her handbag and disappearing into her room. From the room opposite, a TV burbled away. Satisfied that nobody was watching, Billy glanced at his watch. He was two minutes early. He took a deep breath and knocked sharply three times on the door. Ready or not, it was showtime.

There was a slight pause before he heard the pad of footsteps and a man's voice call out, 'Who is it?'

'Billy,' he replied quickly, and then the door opened and the man's face appeared.

Billy couldn't believe his eyes. He recognised the face immediately. He must have seen it a thousand times – in magazines, on billboards, on TV chat shows and in countless movies. The thick black hair, the big brown eyes *People* magazine described as 'the sexiest in the business', the lips that had once kissed Julia Roberts and could break into a cocky grin at a moment's notice – it was Matt Walsh! What was more, it was a half-naked Matt Walsh wrapped in a towel, his hair damp from the shower, his bare chest covered in perfect movie-style droplets of water. And as if that weren't enough, at that precise moment Matt Walsh the famous movie star experienced what Janet Jackson's people would probably have described as 'a wardrobe malfunction'. In other words, his towel fell off.

Instantly forgetting everything he'd ever learned about men and the art of hustling, Billy felt the blood rise to his cheeks. The other man smiled – the same smile that had melted millions of women's hearts and was now having a remarkably similar effect on Billy. 'You're blushing,' he said, reaching for Billy's hand and pulling him into the room. 'Don't tell me you're shy. That would totally screw up my plans for the evening.'

CHAPTER FOUR

Casey's head was in a spin. Naked apart from his Calvin Klein briefs, he marched over to the window and turned to face Billy with eyes as glazed as the frame in which he now stood, feet shoulder width apart, palms resting on the window ledge behind him, poised as if he were at the gym and about to perform a set of reverse tricep dips. As the lonely old guy in the building opposite could happily testify, Casey was never one for overdressing, least of all when he was in the comfort of his own living room. Ever since a client complimented him on the improved shape and firmness of his ass, he had taken to parading around in a pair of dazzling white briefs whenever the mood took him – partly out of sheer narcissism, and partly to meet the growing demand for individually signed and soiled items of underwear he was currently receiving from his website. Perhaps it was the vague memory of the same client also telling him that his brains were all in his pants, but something prompted him to reach and gently squeeze his crotch, as if that might somehow sharpen his powers of perception. He felt a familiar stirring in his groin, but other than that, nothing.

'Okay, Billy,' he said finally. 'You've got to help me out here. Is this some kind of wind-up? 'Cos you're not making any sense. No, don't tell me. You're having a *Pretty Woman* moment. I'm right, aren't I? You went and watched that stupid movie again. Shit, Billy, how many times have I told you? It's just a movie. It's not real life. Richard Gere isn't going to walk in here and fall madly in love with you! Things like that don't really happen!'

Casey blinked, and a kaleidoscope of images flashed before his eyes – Billy dressed as Julia Roberts, Billy sharing a bathtub with Richard Gere, Billy bouncing off the walls in a manner Casey was beginning to find rather alarming.

For all his naked virility, Casey wasn't exactly in the best physical shape this morning. He'd been awake all night. This was partly due to business, or rather the lack of it. As a rule, Casey tended to limit the number of clients he did each day to two or three – or as he liked to think of it, a matinée performance followed by two shows in the evening. Only yesterday had been exceptionally quiet. The day had dragged by with no calls for a matinée. The evening had started slowly – so slowly, in fact, that he had considered taking the night off and going out cruising instead. Then at around eleven p.m. his cell phone rang and he was called to attend to the needs of a valued customer. Ralph was one of Casey's regulars, a neurotic little computer technician who wore way too much hair gel and who often took several hours to get off, but who always made up for it by tipping generously, and providing Casey with as much free coke as he could snort without losing his erection – which, since the discovery of Viagra, tended to be rather more coke than Ralph had bargained for.

Two grams, three hours and one very expensive wad of computer technician jism later, Casey took a cab back to his apartment, where he fully intended to go to sleep but was kept awake by the coke coursing through his veins and the couple upstairs fucking so loudly he was convinced it must be somebody's birthday. The tension further heightened by the discovery that he was fresh out of Xanax, he switched on the TV, dug out the drugs he'd bought earlier and was soon happily tucking into the profits from the night's business activities. As usual, he had planned to reward himself with just a few lines, but soon lost all track of time and with it what little self-restraint he possessed. Before he knew it, he'd hoovered up all of the coke and was working his way through the weekend's supply of crystal meth. By the time Billy turned up at his apartment, bright and early and bouncy as a labrador, Casey was so wired he thought he might be hallucinating.

He shook his head again, but the picture remained the same – Billy ricocheting around the room, grinning from ear to ear, babbling on about how he'd spent the night with Matt Walsh. Matt Walsh the famous movie star. Matt Walsh the butch action hero. Matt Walsh the big celebrity closet case.

'Hang on a minute,' Casey said. 'I always thought Matt Walsh was straight.'

Billy looked surprised. 'Really?'

'Sure.' Casey nodded. 'I mean, Matt Walsh is so damn straight, if someone woke me up in the middle of the night and yelled "Straight!" in my ear, I swear the first thing that would pop into my mind would be "Matt Walsh".'

Billy frowned. 'Very funny. So, are you going to listen or what?'

So Casey listened while Billy talked about Matt, about how gorgeous he looked in the flesh, and how generous he was, and how affectionate, and how they'd discussed the possibility of hooking up again, maybe even tonight. It was at this point that Casey decided he'd heard enough. If Billy seriously thought that he was about to embark on a whirlwind romance with one of the biggest stars on the planet, then clearly Casey wasn't the only one who'd gone a bit heavy on the nose candy last night. Of all the crazy shit Billy had come out with over the years, this took some beating.

'Okay,' Casey said slowly, steering Billy over to the couch and sitting him down. 'Let's say I believe you. Let's say this isn't just some crazy story you dreamed up on the way over here, and you did spend the night with Matt Walsh. That still don't make him your boyfriend. He's a famous movie star, Billy. And you, well, you're just a hustler. People like Matt Walsh don't go around falling in love with the likes of you and me. It's just sex. That's what we do, Billy. That's the deal – no strings. Don't you get it? These people don't pay us to go to their hotel rooms and fuck them. They pay us to leave quietly afterwards. It's hush money, Billy. Nothing more, nothing less.'

Casey paused, impressed by his own eloquence. That wasn't a bad little speech for a boy in his condition. Maybe the combination of coke, crystal and sleep deprivation had unlocked a talent he never knew he had. Maybe with a few more grams, a lot less sleep and a little practice he could even turn his hand to writing. He wouldn't be the first sex worker to launch a literary career. Maybe if he found the right agent he could give up hustling altogether and write a book about his experiences. And who knows? Maybe his book would be made into a film. Then he and Billy could hang out with all the movie stars they wanted. But who would he get to play him in the movie? He'd have to be really good-looking. And naturally he'd need to have a great ass, or perhaps they could use a body double for that kind of thing. So who would it be? Ryan Phillippe would have been perfect a few years ago, but these days he looked more like a street person than a movie star. Turning up at awards shows in thrift shop clothes, and with all that facial hair – what was all that about? If celebrities couldn't be relied upon to set a good example, what was the point of them? Besides, Ryan may be cute, but would he be able to play a gay man with Casey's complex emotional makeup and extensive knowledge of narcotics? Would he want to? Most movie stars were so protective of their precious public image, they shied away from anything remotely risky. Even the gay ones were more concerned with acting straight than playing parts a little closer to home. Look at Rock Hudson. Or Matt Walsh.

'You know what,' Casey said. 'If Matt Walsh can fool half the world into thinking he's straight, maybe he isn't such a bad actor after all.'

But Billy wasn't listening. 'I was just thinking about something William Shatner said in a TV interview,' he said dreamily. '"You must always stay open to love."'

Casey frowned. 'William Shatner said that?'

Billy nodded. 'Uh huh.'

Casey looked impressed. 'Wow! That is so Cher!'

Lee tried to imagine how a devoted mother must feel when the child she carried inside her for nine months and has been supporting ever since suddenly turns round and throws all the love she's ever given them right back in her face. It was quite a leap of the imagination, especially for a woman in her position. With no children of her own, and no real experience of love to draw on, she was forced to picture herself in another woman's shoes. And judging by the number of sexy, vibrant women she'd seen reduced to pale, fat, shuffling shadows of their former selves by the drudgery of motherhood, there was one thing she knew for certain – they weren't the kind of shoes she would be seen dead in. Empathy didn't come easily to Lee at the best of times. She only hoped that by imagining herself in some poor breeder's excuse for a life, she could alleviate some of the anger and the frustration she was feeling now. Because whatever else fate had in store for her, it was reassuring to know that at least she'd spared herself the possibility of that particular nightmare ever coming true.

Still, it couldn't be much worse than this. She and Matt were facing one another across the vast pale reception room of her Malibu beach house, and the man she'd devoted the past fifteen years of her life to, staked her reputation on, lost numerous clients and precious sleep over, and finally turned into one of the highest-paid stars around was tossing words like 'truth' and 'honesty' into the conversation with what could only be described as gay abandon. Lee could hardly believe her ears. It was bad enough that Matt had insisted on meeting here, rather than inviting her over to his place in Beverly Hills, the way he usually did when he had something important he wanted to discuss. Even before he walked into the room she had the distinct impression that he was already distancing himself from her. And now she was expected to listen to this crap? At any other point in his career, Matt's sudden attack of conscience would have been cause for concern. Coming now, when all her hard work was finally paying off, it was tantamount to a slap across the face.

'All this talk about truth and honesty is highly commendable,' she said drily. 'But isn't it a bit late in the day to decide that you want to be the next Sean Penn? Trust me on this one, Matt. Tortured introspection isn't your style. Nobody wants to see you playing a retard or some white-trash rapist on Death Row. That's not who you are.'

He laughed. 'So who am I?'

'You're Matt Walsh, star of *Surface Tension*, and one of the hottest names in town. And now is not the time to start

47

chasing after an Oscar nomination. Apart from anything else, it looks undignified.'

He smiled, but he wasn't giving up that easily. 'I take it you saw that piece in the *Reporter*.'

'Yes, I saw it. And I think it's wonderful that the critics are finally recognising your talents. But let's not get too carried away with the whole credible actor thing. The worst thing you could do right now is start pissing away your career on movies nobody wants to see. To be perfectly honest, you could use another hit.'

'You could use another hit' – the words every remotely successful Hollywood player feared hearing more than anything. Lee hoped that would knock some of the wind out of his sails, and she wasn't disappointed.

'Another hit?' he said, faltering. 'But you just said I was one of the hottest names in town.'

'And you are, Matt. You are. You're right up there with Cruise, Travolta – all the Scientologists. But if you want to stay up there, you have to play safe. Stick to what you do best. Stick to what you know.'

Matt clenched his jaw. 'I don't remembering signing up for any religious sect. Seriously, I'd sooner stick pins in my eyes than make another dumb-ass action picture. I'm tired, Lee. I'm tired of running around film sets with my shirt off. I'm tired of playing safe. Surely you can understand that?'

'As a matter of fact, Matt, no, I can't. Right now I'm a little confused. See, I thought we already had this conversation. I thought we'd agreed—'

He cut her off. 'That was a long time ago, Lee. A very long time ago. I made a lot of decisions back then, some of which I've lived to regret.'

The space between Lee's eyebrows twitched slightly, indicating that she was attempting to frown. 'I hope you're not referring to the gay thing. Remember, Matt. There's only so much truth this town can take.'

He paused. 'No, I wasn't referring to "the gay thing". Although come to mention it, maybe coming out wouldn't be such a bad idea. It would certainly make life a lot less complicated.'

Lee flashed him a warning shot. 'You don't mean that.'

Matt glared back at her. 'Don't I?' he asked, holding her gaze for a moment. Then he faltered. 'No, I guess I don't. But it's tough, Lee. You've no idea how tough it is sometimes. I just feel so . . . trapped.'

Lee narrowed her eyes. 'Have you been smoking pot?'

Matt frowned. 'What? No.'

''Cos there's no shame in admitting you have a problem. Nobody will think any worse of you for it.'

'And they will if they know I'm gay?'

'We both know the answer to that.'

'Well give it to me again, just to be sure.'

Lee's tone was that of a kindergarten teacher addressing a small child. 'What you do in your private life is your own affair. But not during business hours. Nobody wants your private life shoved down their throat.'

Matt glared at her. 'That's a crock of shit and you know it. Look at Ian McKellen. Coming out didn't do his career any harm.'

'That's a totally different situation,' Lee said patiently. 'Ian McKellen doesn't have your fanbase. No one gives a flying fuck who Gandalf sleeps with. Nobody has ever mistaken him for a sex symbol.'

Matt looked wounded. 'So is that all I am now, a sex symbol?'

His tone was playful, but Lee wasn't taking any chances. Backtracking like the true professional she was, she tried a little flattery. 'Of course not. We both know you're a serious actor. All I'm saying is—'

He cut her off mid-flow. 'Then give me the opportunity to prove it,' he said earnestly. 'Find me something I can sink my teeth into. If I can't be true to myself, at least I can be true to my craft.'

Lee bit her tongue. Actors talking about their 'craft' usually provoked an outburst of scornful laughter, but in the present circumstances she thought it best to play safe.

'Fine,' she said briskly. 'But let's not rush into anything just yet. There's already talk about a sequel to *Surface Tension*, and with your stock riding as high as it is right now, I reckon we're good for twenty million plus a share of the profits. And you know what they say, Matt: "If they liked it once, they'll love it twice." Then, as soon as the deal is signed, you can have your passion project. We'll find you a nice juicy role in some small independent movie. You can grow a beard, slurp your soup. Hell, you can even play gay if that makes you happy. And you needn't worry about it damaging your reputation. Play gay these days and everyone automatically assumes that you must be straight.'

Suddenly Matt exploded. 'You're not listening to me,' he said, his voice taking on a tone and quality she hadn't heard before and didn't much care for. 'You haven't listened to a single word I've said. Christ, Lee. I'm reaching out to you here. Is it too much to ask that you shut up and listen for a moment?'

Lee smiled through gritted teeth. 'Okay, I'm listening.'

'Thank you,' he said, his tone calmer but still distinctly chilly. 'First off, I'm not interested in making a sequel to *Surface Tension*. Not now, not ever. I don't want to be part of some franchise. That's not why I became an actor. And this isn't about me suddenly wanting to play gay roles. Apart from anything else, I wouldn't want to deprive Dean Cain of the work. I just want to dig a little deeper, that's all.'

Try as she might, Lee couldn't contain herself any longer. 'What the hell's got into you, Matt?' she said, eyes blazing. 'People aren't paying you millions of dollars to dig a little deeper. They're paying you to put asses on seats. Listen to yourself. Next you'll be asking me what your motivation is. Well, let me remind you. It's the cash, Matt – the best damn motivation there is, and don't let anybody tell you differently.'

No sooner were the words out of her mouth than a terrible thought entered her mind and lodged there, like a piece of shrapnel in an untreated wound. She paused, eyeing him suspiciously. When she spoke again her tone was teasing, jocular, but with a distinct undercurrent of menace. 'Is there something you're not telling me? Someone else you've been talking to? If I hear you've been discussing this behind my back you know I'll be mortally wounded.'

Matt sighed. 'I haven't been discussing anything with anyone. That's part of the problem. I've been bottling this up for a long time. The last few movies I've done – they made a lot of money, but they weren't remotely rewarding for me as an actor. I feel like I've lost sight of why I got into this business in the first place.'

'Well, I'm sorry you feel that way,' Lee said testily. 'I had no idea you were so unhappy with the way I've been running things. I don't remember you complaining when Fox stumped up twenty million dollars for *Surface Tension*. Deals like that don't come easy, y'know. I've worked my ass off for you. I believed in you when nobody else did. You'd have been screwed without me.'

Having played her trump card, she turned her back on him and considered squeezing out a few tears as she waited for her words to sink in.

Matt's voice weakened. 'I know, and I'll always be grateful to you for that. I'm grateful for everything you've done. Christ, Lee. You make it sound like I was suggesting we part company. All I'm saying is that I want to explore some different avenues for a change. I still want you there with me to manage things. We're still a team.'

'You're damn right about that!' Lee said, and turned to face him. He was surprised to see that she was actually smiling.

He looked at her guardedly. 'So we're still okay?'

'Sure we are,' she replied, still flashing that Hollywood smile. 'Like you said, we're a team. Now, how about some coffee?'

'Great,' he said, and followed her into the butcher-block kitchen. Lee's kitchen had recently been featured in *World of Interiors*, where it was duly noted that she never cooked, making her choice of style an affectation at best, or at worst something more sinister.

But Matt wasn't thinking about that. As he watched her pour the coffee, he decided that the tightness of Lee's smile was probably due to her recent facelift. He might have been a sex symbol to millions of adoring female fans, but the truth was, he was never any good at reading women.

CHAPTER FIVE

Michael Rosetti studied his reflection in the bathroom mirror. There was a pimple developing on his left cheek, flaming red and swollen with pus. He poked at it with a Q-tip and it responded by flaring up even more angrily and stubbornly refusing to release even a drop of putrefying liquid.

It was the stress that had brought it on, of course. The job had been stressful enough, and now to top it all he had to suffer the rejection of being fired without so much as a thank you for all his hard work. Michael didn't take rejection well. Considering the amount of practice he'd had, one might have assumed that he'd be used to it by now. But for some reason he had never developed the thickness of skin required by those destined to deal with rejection on a regular basis.

Skin problems weren't his only cause for complaint. Nature hadn't been very kind to Michael. Lacking the distinction of being either extremely good-looking or hideously ugly, he was saddled with the kind of face usually dismissed as plain – high forehead, weak chin, significant acne scarring on both cheeks and little else in the way of distinguishing features. In any other part of the world, this might have been a little easier to live with. Here in LA, it rendered him practically nonexistent. In Hollywood terms, Michael wasn't exactly leading man material, but nor did he have what it took to be a character actor. He wasn't like Kevin Bacon, whose porcine nose and pock-marked face made such an indelible impression in movies like *Hollow Man* and *The Woodsman*, and whose ass was one of the perkiest and most overexposed in the business. Michael's ass was nothing to write home about. As for his face, the best it could have hoped for was a non-speaking part as a supporting player.

Had he at least grown up with the advantage of being straight, there was the distinct possibility that Michael might have come to terms with his physical disadvantages rather more easily. But to add to his problems, he was gay. Whether nature or nurture was to blame for this particular misfortune, Michael didn't care to speculate. But it certainly grieved him to think that, having been given so little to work with in the looks department, he was forced to compete in a world where youth and beauty were the only virtues deemed to be of any value. In many ways, he was living proof that the religious right had got it horribly wrong, and that being gay was not in fact a choice. One look at him and it was clear that Michael had had no part in the decision-making process.

Alas, one look was all the interest he tended to generate. Had someone taken the time to look beyond his physical defects and get to know him properly, they would have discovered that he possessed many fine qualities, among them a deep attachment to his mother, whom he phoned regularly despite her stubborn refusal to loan him the twenty thousand dollars he desperately needed for extensive cosmetic surgery. But the gay process of natural selection being what it was, he'd reached the ripe old age of twenty-seven never having been in a relationship that lasted longer than it took for the other guy to shoot his load and suddenly remember that his presence was urgently required someplace else.

Luckily for Michael, nature hadn't let him down completely and he had developed certain coping mechanisms, notably a profound sense of his own martyrdom, coupled with an unerring ability to pass himself off as just another one of life's losers, lacking the instinct for survival or the stomach for revenge. In fact, Michael was far more resourceful than people gave him credit for. Life had given him lemons and he'd made his own special brand of lemonade, laced with a poison so subtle it was virtually undetectable. To this day there wasn't a single surviving soul in Blairstown, New Jersey, who suspected that young Michael Rosetti had had anything to do with the fire that ripped through his high school one Friday after recess, leaving several students pursuing compensation claims for post-traumatic stress disorder and resulting in poor Mr Cunningham, the supply teacher on whom young Michael had developed quite a crush, being slowly burned to a crisp after failing to return Michael's affections and foolishly locking himself inside the staff washroom.

Mr Cunningham's tragic death had a profound impact on Michael, not least because it was the first time he'd seen the consequences of his actions played out as popular drama on the early evening news. Like Nicole Kidman's ruthlessly ambitious weathergirl in the movie *To Die For*, Michael firmly believed that TV had the power to transform people's lives. The evidence was paraded across the screen every night. Lowly checkout girls touched by the magic of TV and turned into fairy-tale brides. Lumbering straight guys given the 'Queer Eye' and taught the value of personal hygiene. Rooms redesigned. Bodies reshaped. Dirty laundry aired in public, secrets shared and problems solved. And since part of the magic of TV lay in its power to absolve all personal responsibility, it didn't really matter what you did to get there. At the end of the day, the medium justified the means. Watching the local news reports on Mr Cunningham's death, Michael's only regret was that his own name wasn't mentioned in connection with the day's events. But since the rest of the population hadn't caught up with his and Nicole's way of thinking, he was left with no choice but to forfeit his moment of glory and enjoy the buzz that came from fooling his friends and family into thinking he was every bit as grief-stricken as the rest of his classmates.

It was a stunning performance – a little hammy perhaps, but correct in every detail and ultimately rather moving. He may have lacked the physical qualities necessary for a career as an actor, but when it came to faking emotions, Michael was already something of an old pro. This wasn't the first time he'd been called upon to put his talents to the test. Unbeknownst to those around him, his teacher's untimely demise was merely the latest in a long line of retributive actions cunningly disguised as unfortunate coincidences. When Michael was five and his parents suddenly transferred their affections to his baby brother Anthony, it was only a matter of weeks before the newborn baby was rushed into hospital with a piece from Michael's favourite jigsaw mysteri-ously lodged in its throat. When Michael was twelve and his best friend Todd betrayed his confidence by telling the other boys that Michael had tried to kiss him, it was only a matter of time before Todd found himself the subject of similar gossip, made all the more plausible by the fact that Michael had found himself a girlfriend and the other boys had found a gay porn mag hidden inside Todd's locker.

For many troubled teenagers, the shift into adulthood brought with it the promise of better things to come, of a new position in life, well out of range of the slings and arrows that had been their misfortune until now. Michael had hoped that this would be his fate too, but sadly it wasn't to be. If any-thing, the transition only served to drive the arrows even deeper into his too, too tender flesh. St Sebastian had nothing on Michael, not when you considered the pains he went to trying to find his rightful place in the gay firmament. He had hoped that coming out would have alleviated some of the suffering. Instead, he had felt more victimised than ever before. Never popular, and not yet in a position to boost his fragile ego by entertaining pretty boys on company expenses, he was painfully aware of his lowly place in the gay pecking order. He dealt with it the only way he knew how, venting his frustration by pouring scorn on anyone who showed the least sign of weakness. Never short of a quip or two, he made up for his physical failings by lashing out at those less vicious than himself. To the casual observer, his verbal assaults may have appeared indiscriminate and unprovoked. But there was method in his madness. To Michael, every social encounter came weighted with possibility, and with it the potential for further rejection. The tougher the opponent, the greater the challenge. The prettier the challenger, the stronger the desire to annihilate.

By the time he left New Jersey and moved to his small apartment on the edge of West Hollywood, Michael was well practised in the art of revenge. He could serve it a million ways – hot, cold, one small portion at a time, or a full banquet in one sitting. And bearing in mind that his most daring plot had resulted in him literally getting away with murder, the cut and thrust of the movie industry held little fear for him. With his instincts, he was certain to make a killing in no time.

Unfortunately, Michael's Hollywood career hadn't quite gone according to plan. His first attempt at writing a screenplay, heavily influenced by the early works of Stephen King and drawing on episodes from his own life, took three months to complete and was rapidly passed over by every studio story department in town. Michael couldn't understand it. Any fool could see that a movie about a poor downtrodden kid with a talent for starting fires was a surefire hit, yet nobody was willing to give him a break. Calls weren't returned. Doors didn't open. It was the exact same story with his second script, and his third. Finally, when the thought of four rejections in a row became too awful to contemplate, he decided it was time for a quick rethink and applied for a job at one of the studios, composing press releases for the publicity department. It wasn't quite the glittering writing career he had in mind, but at least it would give him a foot in the door. Only it didn't. His job application was rejected. No interview. No letter thanking him for his interest or offering condolences. Nothing.

Still Michael didn't give up. Furiously energised by his recent run of bad luck, he threw himself into a frenzy of activity, brushing up on his secretarial skills, faking a few references and polishing up his resumé until he was too attractive a proposition to pass over – at least on paper. His aim was simple. If he couldn't find a job suited to his talents, he would at least find one where he could rub shoulders with celebrities. In Hollywood, personal dreams of stardom were rarely fulfilled, but there was always the compensation of working in close proximity to those who'd succeeded where others had failed. His secretarial career began inauspiciously, with a junior position at a minor talent agency few people had heard of and even fewer took seriously. But with growing confidence and a new sense of direction, it wasn't long before Michael was brown-nosing his way towards bigger and better things. It was almost as if this was the job he was always destined to do. Suddenly finding himself in a world where oily charms were no hindrance to promotion, Michael's rise through the murky waters of Hollywood's press and public relations divisions left an impression of slick professionalism that couldn't fail to get him noticed. Soon he emerged as a prime candidate for career advancement, reaching for a place among the upper echelons of his profession, where the pressures of work were rumoured to be far greater but the opportunities for star-fucking were little short of legendary.

And so it was that Michael came to work for Lee Carson. It wasn't the greatest job in the world. The hours were long, the pay wasn't all that good, and the perks weren't all they were cracked up to be. While Michael dreamed of power lunches with the Hollywood elite at Morton's, the best his expense account could stretch to was a chilli dog with some wide-eyed kid at Pink's. It wasn't in Lee Carson's nature to take new employees under her wing or show them a good time. On the contrary, Michael's new boss was every bit the tough, demanding bitch people said she was. Nothing he did was ever good enough. Every unreasonable demand was expected to be met, every little chore done better, faster, by yesterday. Michael had tried playing for sympathy, faking every illness he could think of, but to no avail. Lee Carson didn't have a sympathetic bone in her body.

On the other hand, she did have a close working relationship with Matt Walsh, and for that reason alone Michael was happy to be working for her. The rest of the business he could take or leave. He hated the Hollywood types with their precision suits and their goal-achieving hairdos almost as much as he hated the West Hollywood boys with their hardened self-confidence and cruel good looks. But just to answer the phone and hear Matt Walsh's voice was enough to make Michael's day. He'd fantasised about Matt for years, seen every movie, bought every magazine, watched every TV appearance, never dreaming that one day he and his idol would actually be on speaking terms. These past few months had been among the happiest Michael could remember. It didn't matter that his boss was an ungrateful bitch who wouldn't know a kind word if it smacked her in the mouth. It didn't matter that his personal life was still an endless merry-go-round of meaningful looks and meaningless encounters, as cold and empty as his boss's heart. It didn't even matter that the cosmetic surgery he craved so desperately was still only a pipe dream. Matt Walsh knew that he existed, and that made Michael's life worth living.

Or at least that was how it used to be, until Lee Carson decided to go and ruin everything. All Michael had left now was the memory of those phone calls and the stash of promotional materials he'd stolen from the office before clearing his desk. It wasn't much. A few movie posters. A press release or two. Some glossy ten-by-eight publicity shots individually signed by Matt himself and intended for the wives and daughters of studio heads and other industry bigwigs. There was one taped to the bathroom wall next to the mirror. Michael had put it there earlier to remind himself of everything he aspired to be, of everything he'd lost, of everything Lee Carson had taken from him.

Well maybe it was high time someone taught that bitch a lesson. If she thought she could cross Michael Rosetti and get away with it, she was sorely mistaken.

CHAPTER SIX

Billy knew it was time to head home when Casey, delirious with sleep deprivation but evidently convinced that Billy was telling the truth, suddenly demanded a detailed description of Matt Walsh's dick. Embarrassed, and feeling strangely protective of a man he'd only just met, Billy made his excuses and left, promising to call Casey later. Physically tired and feeling somewhat deflated, he strolled across to Santa Monica Boulevard in search of a quick caffeine fix.

The Starbucks on Santa Monica was one of the busiest, most happening coffee houses on the Westside. Today there were even a few faces Billy might have recognised, had he not been so lost in thought. The moment he entered the room, a couple of older queens with blond highlights and other hair issues looked up from their skinny lattes and flashed bleached grins, privately hoping to move up a few notches in the gay pecking order by establishing, very publicly, that they were on smiling and nodding terms with one so young and so very beautiful. Sadly, any attempts to impress the present company failed miserably as Billy ordered a double espresso to go and stood waiting for almost two minutes without so much as a glance in their direction – much to the amusement of a journalist from *Circuit Noize* magazine who had just returned from a party in Palm Springs, and who derived as much satisfaction from the public humiliation of his fellow gay men as some people derived from the bloodiest of spectator sports. On days like these, a little sadistic pleasure was just the tonic he needed to take the edge off his comedown.

Billy, of course, was oblivious to all of this. Without Casey there to help keep things in some kind of perspective, Billy was lost in a world of his own, barely conscious of his surroundings and happy to follow his train of thought wherever it might take him. The more he thought about it, the more he realised that, deep down, he wasn't that surprised to discover that Matt Walsh was gay. He'd heard the rumours, even if the majority of Matt's straight fans hadn't. And while he wasn't someone who regularly scoured the tabloids for the latest celebrity gossip, he'd be lying if he said that the sex lives of the rich and famous was a subject that held no interest for him. How could it not? Like most of the gay men he knew, Billy had grown up without any real role models to speak of. Even today, if someone asked him to name a gay movie star, his thoughts immediately turned to the boys who worked their tight little butts off shooting gay porn movies in the San Fernando Valley. They might not be movie stars in the traditional sense, but as Casey was fond of reminding him, they had their own fan clubs and awards ceremonies, and they gave pleasure to millions of viewers around the world, so what difference did it make?

Billy was aware that not everyone was a fan of gay porn. And secretly he was grateful for the fact that Casey had never fulfilled his dreams of becoming a porn star. With his appetite for drugs, he'd probably have ended up like Joey Stefano, the beautiful bottom who appeared in Madonna's *Sex* book before lucking out and dying of an overdose at the ripe old age of twenty-six. But whatever else people said about the gay porn industry, at the very least it had produced a handful of stars people like he and Casey could call their own. Hollywood, on the other hand, still had trouble accepting that gay people even existed. Even character actors like Nathan Lane took years before finally confirming what most people had suspected all along. There were always those excessively butch action stars people had a few doubts about, but they seemed to spend as much time denying they were gay as they did shaving their chests or showing the world their armpits. To this day, Billy couldn't name a single Hollywood leading man who was gay and didn't care who knew it.

Which was precisely why, when someone as famous and as physically attractive as Matt Walsh was rumoured to be a big closet case, the stories spread through the bars and clubs of West Hollywood faster than an outbreak of hepatitis. Billy could still remember the first time he heard someone say they knew for certain that Matt Walsh was gay. It was five years ago, and Matt had just appeared in the first of a string of hugely popular but instantly forgettable action movies. Billy couldn't recall the name of the movie, but the main talking point was that the once boyish star had undergone a complete physical transformation and was suddenly boasting the kind of ripped, buff body that made him look as though he'd wandered in off a gay porn set. One of the hustlers who hung out at Numbers claimed to know the personal trainer who had helped Walsh achieve this new look, who in turn claimed to have intimate knowledge of the star and some of the tricks he could perform with that hot new body of his.

Had this been the only story Billy had heard concerning Matt Walsh and his secret gay life, he might have put it down to wishful thinking. But over the past few years, the stories had come thick and fast, and it did seem rather strange that a man as successful and as attractive as Matt Walsh had never met the right girl.

So no, it didn't really surprise Billy to learn that Matt Walsh was gay. What did surprise him was that someone in Matt's position would be willing to take the risk of hiring a male escort. Billy had been with a handful of Hollywood clients before, but they were always those faceless industry types few people outside the business could put a name to. Who cared if some balding studio exec liked nothing better than to bugger pretty blond boys on the back seat of his Porsche and was willing to pay handsomely for the pleasure? Prostitution was a time-honoured tradition in Hollywood. It was just another service industry feeding the demands of the film business. And whatever anyone thought about it, the bottom line was that nobody was paying to watch some studio exec kiss the girl and save the day. But Matt Walsh – that was a different story entirely. For him, image was everything. So why risk it all for a night of passion with a male hustler whose photo he found on the internet? Surely there were other ways of satisfying his needs, other people he could call on, people he was certain he could trust?

According to Casey, it was precisely because hustlers were seen as so untrustworthy that people in Matt's position thought it safe to use them. Or as Casey himself put it, 'Who're most folks going to believe? Some guy who sells his ass for a living? Or some famous movie star who's the envy of every bitchy fag in West Hollywood?'

Billy could see the logic of Casey's argument. Still he found Matt's behaviour a little hard to understand. Matt could probably take his pick of hundreds, if not thousands of men. So why pick someone he knew absolutely nothing about? Why take the risk?

'How do you know I'm not going to run to the papers?' Billy had asked as he packed his things into his briefcase and prepared to leave Matt's hotel room that morning.

'I don't,' Matt had replied. 'What I do know is that I'd really like to see you again. So I guess the ball's in your court. Sell your story, or join me for dinner tonight. The choice is yours. But I should warn you. I may be a lousy cook, but my lawyers are the best in the business.'

The invitation to dinner had sounded genuine enough, though Billy was reminded that clients often fell for his charms on first meeting and insisted on seeing him again the next night and maybe even the night after that, only to tire of him a few days later. But it was what Matt did next that really made an impression on him, and left him entertaining the idea that maybe this time it would be different. Apologising for the fact that they couldn't be seen leaving together, Matt Walsh the world famous movie star suddenly grabbed Billy and held him tighter than he could remember anyone holding him in a very long time. As they parted, Matt had blushed slightly before regaining his usual composure. In less time than it would have taken for someone to shout 'Action!' the famous charisma and the cocky charm were switched back on, radiating around him like an electric forcefield. But for one brief moment, Matt had dropped his defences, and Billy thought he saw a man not so very different from himself.

Walking along Santa Monica and turning up Crescent Heights, Billy played the scene over and over in his head. His night of passion with Matt had only ended a few hours ago, and already it was beginning to resemble one of those dreams that was as clear as day the moment you woke, but slowly faded as time wore on. Determined to keep the memory of last night alive for as long as possible, he forced himself to focus on the details – the rise and fall of Matt's chest, the unfamiliar but distinctly expensive smell of his hair, the hardness of his back, the musky warmth of his body as he slept. Remembered this way, he was no longer Matt Walsh the famous movie star. He was just a man. A very rich, very generous man who had insisted on paying Billy double what he normally charged for an overnight stay. An exceptionally sexy man, obviously – probably the sexiest man Billy had ever spent the night with. But a man nonetheless, with the same basic needs and desires and responses as other men. In his present frame of mind, Billy found this idea immensely comforting.

Sadly, the image was shattered as soon as he hit Sunset Boulevard and was confronted with a forty-foot-tall billboard advertising Matt's latest contribution to the art of Hollywood motion pictures. The movie was called *Surface Tension* and appeared to be set aboard a nuclear submarine. The billboard showed Matt looking particularly mean and moody in the tattered remains of a naval officer's uniform. Clinging to him, and desperately trying to convey the idea that she was in dire need of protection despite her immaculate hair and makeup, was a skinny blonde woman with tits so pneumatic they would be considered positively dangerous on a nuclear sub. Billy didn't recognise her face, but thought her surprisingly plain for an actress starring opposite such an obvious heart-throb as Matt Walsh. But what really caught his attention was the tag line. Emblazoned across the bottom of the billboard in bright red letters was the simple warning: 'Trust No One'.

To: gary.koverman@foxstudios.com
From: lee.carson@leecarsonassociates.com
Subject: Matt Walsh

Gary, I still haven't had a reply to my last email. It's been a long day and I'm in no mood to play games. This is Matt Walsh we're talking about, not some glorified soap star who

couldn't carry a movie if his life depended on it. I'll expect
to hear from you first thing tomorrow morning.
Lee

When Lee was still in high school, undecided about what to
do with her life but determined never to repeat her mother's
mistakes, her mother floated into her room one night, sat
down at the foot of the bed and gave her a piece of advice she
remembered to this day. Maybe it was because, despite being
an only child, Lee had never enjoyed a particularly close relationship with her mother, so anything resembling a cosy
maternal chat was bound to leave a lasting impression. Maybe
it was because, in the family home where Lee was incarcer-
ated for the first eighteen years of her life, the strange, adult
world of physical love and emotional violence was rarely
alluded to, except in the most oblique way possible. Maybe it
was simply the smell of alcohol on her mother's breath.
Whatever the reason, the brief exchange that took place
between mother and daughter that night had been ingrained
in Lee's memory ever since. 'Never trust a man with a beard,'
her mother announced after one of her heated rows with Lee's
father and a few too many martinis. 'It means he's hiding
something.'

Georgina Carson was a hopeless old soak who married the
first eligible bachelor who came along and had been quietly
regretting it ever since. Her life story read like the script for a
Southern-fried family drama which, were it ever made into a
movie, would probably star either Ellen Burstyn or Gina
Rowlands. The daughter of a Baptist preacher who taught her
that a woman's place was in the home, she had no career of her
own and few resources to fall back on when her looks faded
and the cracks in her marriage began to show. Incapable of
standing on her own two feet even when sober, she recognised

that her options were limited and resolved to repress her emotions as best she could, turning to the bottle with greater frequency as the years dragged by and disillusionment gave way to despair. Holed up in her Florida mansion, quietly pickling in her own juices, her life these days was extremely comfortable but without purpose and ultimately rather sad. Confined to her bed for the best part of the day, she filled the long, lonely evenings by throwing cocktail parties for local doctors' wives while her highly paid, oversexed gynaecologist husband was out conducting intimate examinations of women in whom he had absolutely no professional interest.

Despite the overt theatricality of her daily performances, which seemed to suggest at least a passing familiarity with the fragile heroines found in the works of Tennessee Williams, Lee knew her mother well enough to rule out the possibility of her ever having forged a deep emotional attachment with a real-life homosexual. This could only mean that her words of advice were utterly devoid of double entendre and were intended to be taken purely at face value. In other words, when Lee's mother warned her against men with beards, she was referring simply to men with an abundance of facial hair. What she almost certainly wasn't referring to was the practice, often seen in Hollywood, of prominent male stars disguising their homosexuality by escorting beautiful women to film premieres and parading them before the world's press. 'Red carpet camouflage' was the way most people referred to this particular type of arm candy, but in less polite circles they were known simply as 'beards'.

Considering the number of blonde, buxom, generally brain-dead but undeniably photogenic beards she had personally procured and vetted for Matt over the years, Lee didn't doubt for a moment that her mother would have disapproved most strongly of her actions. But that wasn't what bothered her. What bothered her now was the nagging suspicion that the old girl might still have the last laugh. Lee didn't know what had gotten into Matt lately, but given the strange way he was behaving, she couldn't rule out the possibility that, beard or no beard, he might turn out to be one of those men her mother had always warned her about. The irony of this wasn't lost on her. It was even conceivable that, in time, she would look back and laugh. But right now time wasn't on her side. She needed answers, and like every remotely powerful person in an industry where everyday megalomania was part of the job description, she needed them yesterday.

First she needed to rule out the possibility that Matt was looking for a new manager, or that he'd been talking to someone at William Morris or one of the other big agencies in town. He'd denied it, of course, but then he was hardly likely to own up to such a blatant act of betrayal. Still, Lee's instincts told her he was telling the truth. When he wasn't playing straight for the cameras, Matt Walsh was a lousy liar. But despite his insistence that his little speech this morning was all his own work, Lee remained convinced that somebody, somewhere must be putting ideas into his head. Matt had always been the kind of actor who took direction well. And when it came to making important business decisions, people in Matt's position rarely thought for themselves, not when they had agents and managers to do their thinking for them. If it wasn't some other manager or agent he'd been talking to, then maybe the source was a little closer to home. Maybe it wasn't professional advice he'd been receiving, but guidance of a more personal kind. The more Lee thought about it, the more convinced she became that her hunch was right. When you knew someone as well as she knew Matt, and they suddenly started behaving in a way that was totally out of character, it usually transpired that there was a new special someone in their life. Either that, or they had a drug problem.

Lee hated drugs with a passion. It was thanks to drugs that most Hollywood parties these days were split into two camps. There was the party downstairs, full of recovering alcoholics with hair plugs and willing young starlets eager to make a good impression. And there was the party upstairs, with six people to every bathroom and no one willing to spare a thought for some poor woman dying for a pee. Drugs were divisive, destructive and deadly dull. They made people lose control, and turned them into selfish, unthinking bores. But given the choice, Lee would sooner be told that Matt had a major crack addiction than discover that he was in love. Admitting you had a drug problem wasn't the career suicide it once was, not if you handled it correctly. And given the amount of networking that went on at NA meetings these days, it was quite possible to turn a taste for narcotics to your advantage. If Matt came to her with a drug problem, Lee would know exactly what to do – check him into rehab, book that coveted spot on *Oprah* and wait for the great wave of public sympathy to come flooding in.

But if love was the drug, then Lee feared she might be out of her depth. As a rule, she wasn't remotely interested in affairs of the heart. In fact, there were few topics of conversation she found less stimulating than other people's love lives. Only this was different. If her suspicions were correct, and some boy or other was muscling in on Matt, steering him in directions that were clearly bad for his career, it could make her job extremely difficult. In fact, it could possibly even spell the end of their working relationship. Because this definitely wasn't what they'd agreed. This wasn't part of the deal. Matt had known the score right from the word go. His private life was his own business. All Lee asked was that he keep his personal affairs to himself, and leave the public relations to her.

That was what he paid her for after all. And experience told her that Matt should keep his private life firmly under wraps. Under no circumstances should he go public about the fact that he wasn't quite the ladies' man he appeared, and at no time should he allow his sexual proclivities to interfere with his career. It was a small price to pay for such a golden opportunity, and as she explained to him at the time, this was simply the way these things were handled in Hollywood. It was okay to be queer, just never during business hours.

Lee had known that Matt was gay even before they'd met. She'd made it her business to know, the same way she made it her business to know if a client was having an extramarital affair, or had developed a drink problem or a drug habit. Anything that might end up splashed across the papers, she wanted the lowdown on first. In Matt's case, digging the dirt had been easy. He was young, ambitious, still fairly new to Hollywood, and so bad at covering his tracks it was a wonder he hadn't ruined his chances of a career before it had even begun. Discretion wasn't something Matt seemed to know the value of, at least not in those days. It didn't take Lee long to discover that he'd used his boyish charms to persuade a certain director to cast him in his first movie, or that a certain maverick studio exec had taken the up-and-coming young actor under his wing and over his desk one night when the office was empty and it was too late to be considered business hours.

Thankfully, Lee had been able to teach Matt the error of his ways and tame that reckless streak of his. She'd trained him well – so well that, all these years and all these movies later, the mere fact of his homosexuality didn't present anyone in Hollywood with too much of a problem. Studio execs, producers, directors, casting agents – they all knew about Matt Walsh and his secret life. What was more, they couldn't give a damn. Nobody cared less what Matt got up to behind closed doors. Half of them were gay themselves. That was why Lee laughed whenever she heard people accuse the industry of homophobia. Hollywood was crawling with homosexuals! Take away the Jews and the gays and there'd be no industry left. The truth was, this was a liberal industry, full of liberal people. Some were so damn liberal they even bought Asian vegetables! Personal politics didn't enter into it. All that mattered in Hollywood was making money, and when it came to making money on this scale it didn't matter how liberal you were – big money was always conservative. Lee hadn't met one person working in the industry who didn't understand this one simple equation. This was a liberal industry catering to a conservative market, and this meant that certain rules had to be observed. If you were an actor and you happened to be gay, rule number one was that you kept your personal life firmly under wraps. Play by the rules, and the industry would do everything in its power to support and protect you. Break the rules, and they'd drop you like a hot brick. That wasn't homophobia. That was just taking care of business.

For as long as Lee could remember, Matt had played by the rules. Sure, there'd been boys, but never anyone he'd grown too attached to or allowed to get close enough for Lee to consider them a liability. And when it came to press interviews, Matt could thank his lucky stars that he enjoyed the kind of fame that allowed him to be stingy with the personal details and still make the front cover. The important thing was, he always confided in her. He warned her when some blast from his past was threatening to sell their story to the tabloids, or when some minor indiscretion at a sauna in San Diego had the potential to provoke further speculation about his sexuality. And when Lee advised him to play it cool for a while or to suddenly start dating some young starlet, he always followed her advice to the letter. Because whatever else happened, Matt had always assured her that what mattered most was his career.

But what assurances did she have now that he hadn't changed his mind, or that someone hadn't changed it for him? Once, Lee had teased Matt about his weakness for pretty blond boys. 'It's not a weakness,' he told her, grinning. 'It's an interest.' Well, that was a matter of opinion. Harmless pastime or fatal character flaw, it all depended on the circumstances. One thing Lee was certain of – the Matt Walsh she had talked to this morning wasn't the Matt Walsh she knew. There had been a strange look on his face, a look that unsettled her deeply. It was the look of someone whose head had been turned. Lee's mother had had that look once. It was captured in the wedding photo she kept on her dressing table. And what had it brought her? Nothing but a lifetime of misery.

Love could do terrible things to people, and Lee had been around long enough to know that movie stars were no more immune to its devastating effects than those poor saps who paid their ten bucks to watch Julia Roberts faking it for a few hours. How many failed marriages and broken engagements did Julia have under her belt? Three? Four? And she wasn't the only one. Brad and Jennifer were supposed to be Hollywood's golden couple, until Angelina came along and Jennifer was left sobbing her heart out to *Vanity Fair*. And what of the other Jennifer, she of the perfect cheekbones and ample posterior? The two-headed monster known as 'Bennifer' no longer roamed the tabloids, not since the allegedly inseparable Ben Affleck and Jennifer Lopez went their separate ways. And how long did it take poor Jennifer to find herself a new husband? Six whole months. In

Hollywood, that was longer than some marriages. Just ask Britney Spears.

And was it any wonder so many relationships were doomed to failure, considering the egos involved? Lee hadn't met an actor yet who didn't constantly crave attention, or wasn't desperately trying to compensate for the lack of love they felt they received as a child – a subject they were more than happy to discuss with you for hours at a time, provided of course that you didn't offer too much in the way of advice. Most were driven to succeed by the belief that fame and fortune would somehow fill the void inside and make them complete, although you only had to look at the way some of them coped with the pressures of life in the spotlight to see that this was rarely the way things worked out. In Lee's experience, some of the biggest, most successful stars in the world were also the most needy. It didn't matter how big their trailer was, or how many Lear jets they owned. They remained every bit as dependent on the empty love of the masses as many of their associates were dependent on the ego-boosting properties of cocaine.

It was a terrible thing for Lee to have to contemplate, but contemplate it she knew she must. Matt may have given her the impression that he was above this kind of thing. He may even have convinced himself that love was something he could happily live without. But what if they were both wrong? What if, even now, he was embroiled in a torrid love affair that could leave him open to blackmail, destroy his career and possibly even break his heart into the bargain? If that were the case, then clearly Matt needed saving from himself. She wouldn't let him down.

CHAPTER SEVEN

By late afternoon, Casey had more or less recovered from his night of overindulgence in drugs and was feeling sufficiently motivated to squeeze himself into a pair of indecently low-rise jeans and a vintage Madonna 'Who's That Girl?' tour T-shirt, venture outside his apartment and indulge himself in another of his favourite pastimes – shopping for porn videos. For someone who'd seen his dreams of porn stardom so cruelly dashed at such a tender age, Casey's continued interest in the gay adult film industry was touching, if a little hard to understand. Indeed, some might have considered the depth of his loyalty somewhat weird, possibly even masochistic. Billy certainly seemed to think so, and would regularly take Casey to task over the vast amounts of time and money he spent tracking down the hottest new titles and adding them to his collection. Casey, of course, never took a blind bit of notice. For him, a day without porn was like a day without sunshine. And since he happened to live in LA, where both porn and sunshine were in such ready supply, to take advantage of one and not the other struck him as positively perverse. Besides, what Billy failed to recognise was that Casey's gay porn collection actually held many positive benefits. It inspired him to work even harder at the gym, and it gave an element of order to an otherwise fairly chaotic existence.

Casey's porn collection wasn't just a bunch of dirty movies

he'd thrown together willy-nilly. It was a serious collection he'd built up over many years, with the same degree of dedication and painstaking attention to detail that a music fan might devote to their CD collection, or an avid reader might put into creating their very own library. Indeed, so extensive was Casey's porn collection that he felt it more than made up for the shortage of books in his apartment. In this respect, as in so many others, Casey was something of a trailblazer. All across West Hollywood there were plenty of openly gay men who kept their porn movies hidden from view and their bookshelves piled high with books they had absolutely no intention of reading. Not Casey. He wasn't the least bit embarrassed by the lack of reading materials on his shelves, and was more than happy to put his porn on permanent display for all to see. From Casey's perspective, it all made perfect sense. After all, people were always saying how LA was a movie town. If they liked books so much, they should try moving to New York.

Today Casey was looking for two new DVDs featuring his current favourite porn star, Chase Young. Still relatively new to the business, Chase was a pretty, blond, all-American quarterback type with an exceptionally cute ass and a vague expression which made him a natural in scenes where he was cast as a dumb farm boy, caught feeding the chickens with his dick hanging out. Like every good farm boy who ever found himself bent over a bale of hay on a gay porn set, he squealed like a prize pig each time he was rimmed, but had never been fucked and swore that it would never happen, what with him being straight and all. Like many gay porn stars before him, Chase was 'gay for pay', meaning that while he was paid to perform certain homosexual acts for the delectation of gay audiences, a large part of his appeal was that he was supposedly only in it for the money and had no real interest in gay sex beyond what was required of him by the script. While his enthusiastic vocal performances may have led some fans to conclude that there was rather more to Chase Young than he was letting on, there were no shortage of porn directors willing to testify that Chase was as straight as a die, and that what audiences were tuning into was simply the sound of a man who took great pride in his work.

Chase lived in Palm Springs with a woman he claimed was his girlfriend, performed at gay clubs all across the country and was regularly nominated for a whole host of awards at the annual Gay Erotic Video Awards show right here in LA. The closest Casey had ever got to meeting the object of his affection was one night after the show, when Chase and a bunch of prize-winning porn stars caused a minor riot by turning up unannounced at Mickey's. Drunk on champagne and high on crystal, Chase evidently enjoyed all the attention he received that night from a roomful of gay men who seemed to regard him as some kind of god. Whether the rumours were true, and some humble bartender had been touched by the hand, lips and throbbing nine-inch cock of this particular god long after the club had closed, Casey couldn't say for certain, but he sincerely hoped not. He preferred to think of Chase as the hot-blooded heterosexual he always claimed to be. Knowing that he was unattainable did nothing to diminish his sex appeal, and made his failure to spot Casey's face in the crowd that night a little easier to bear.

Inspired by Chase's polysexual approach to life, Casey decided to give his usual gay video store a miss and check out the merchandise at Hustler Hollywood – part of Larry Flynt's adult entertainment empire, and the kind of emporium where gay and straight customers were encouraged to spice up their sex lives in perfect harmony. The store's motto was 'Relax, it's just sex', which Casey thought eminently sensible, although clearly some people weren't quite as convinced. Arriving at the storefront on Sunset, Casey noticed that his movements were being monitored by a couple of old ladies out walking their dogs, who exchanged disapproving looks and glowered at him from across the street. He responded by flashing them a smile, knowing that this would wind them up far more than showing them the finger. He'd come across their type before. Even in a city where pretty much everything and everyone was up for grabs if the price was right, there were still those who insisted on seeing the sex industry as the devil's work. God knows, Casey had tried reasoning with these people. But after several years and many heated rows he'd decided that, rather like Scientologists or gay men who voted Republican, theirs was a way of life he would never fully understand.

Before entering the store, he paused to examine the concrete forecourt with its handprints of porn stars past and present and was saddened to see that Chase hadn't made the grade. Still it was encouraging to know that someone, somewhere took these things seriously. Hollywood had its Walk of Fame. Why shouldn't the porn industry have its own hallowed ground? Smiling to himself, he stepped through the door, headed past the displays of chiffon panties and novelty vibrators and located the gay video section. Dotted around the store, a small selection of older, less attractive male customers suddenly began fingering the dildos and exchanging furtive glances. Conscious of the effect he was having, but determined to let nothing come between him and his beloved porn, Casey continued scanning the shelves. Even when he knew exactly what he was looking for, he could never resist the lure of the display copies with their cover shots of naked men with improbably pert butt cheeks and impossibly large penises. He knew from experience that the movies themselves were often disappointing – poorly acted, roughly edited and so badly dubbed that he could barely decipher the moans of pleasure and growls of 'suck that big cock' over the cheesy soundtrack. But that didn't stop him from fantasising about the covers. With their tantalising images and teasing titles they promised a world free from complications and utterly devoid of disapproving old women, where seducing unsuspecting delivery boys was as easy as ordering a pizza and straight sex was something cute college studs and hunky prison cellmates discussed briefly before they sucked each other off.

To the casual observer, the range of titles currently spread out before Casey's adoring eyes might have appeared to be rather limited. It was certainly true that the cover photos were pretty generic. But what the packaging lacked in originality, some of the titles more than made up for with their cunning wordplay and sly references to other, more famous and far less controversial forms of filmed entertainment. As a true porn aficionado with extensive knowledge of the market, Casey was always quick to spot new trends. What was more, he felt he had a moral duty to support those working within the industry who regularly rose to the challenge of taking risks and pushing the medium in exciting new directions. There would always be a place in Casey's affections for classic gay porn movies with straight-talking titles like *The Bigger the Better*, *A Matter of Size* and *Every Last Inch*. There was a place, too, for movies with a certain sense of humour and more imaginative titles like *Jack Hammer*, *The Fireman's Hose* or *Nine Inch Males*. But when a gay porn director had the courage to pitch his work against some of the biggest talents in Hollywood and name his latest opus *Position Impossible*, *Bareback Mountain* or *Shaving Ryan's Privates*, that was when Casey knew he was in the presence of greatness.

It took Casey well over an hour to select his purchases,

finally deciding on three new DVDs from Falcon's ever-popular *Jocks* series, a couple of European imports featuring what were described as 'Hungary men', plus the two all-important Chase Young movies – *The Thrill of the Chase* and the enticing *Chase's Tail*. As he approached the cashier, the thought of Chase's tail had a predictable effect on Casey and he felt a stirring in his groin. The cashier was a snot-nosed college kid with a lip ring and an overly familiar manner who blatantly checked out Casey's crotch as he rang up his purchases. Feeling generous, Casey pretended not to notice, casually stretching his arms above his head and treating his admirer to a tantalising glimpse of his washboard abs.

The bill came to just over two hundred dollars. Some people might have considered this an excessive amount to spend on porn in one afternoon. But as Casey always said, some people were happy to squander their cash on Fabergé eggs or tickets to see Celine Dion at Caesars Palace, so what the hell did they know? Reaching into his pocket, he gave his crotch one last provocative squeeze before handing over his credit card.

Billy's heart was beating so fast he thought it might explode, and come bursting out of his chest like the creature in *Alien*. Considering that he was one of the estimated thousands of gay men living in West Hollywood without the luxury of health insurance, this was a matter of some concern. But what could he do? It wasn't as if his present condition was self-inflicted, brought on by a recent drugs binge or a night without sleep. Unlike Casey, Billy rarely felt the need to push his body beyond the limits of all endurance. Judging by the number of muggings, car-jackings and drive-by shootings reported each night on the local TV news, life in LA was fraught with enough dangers without him tempting fate and adding a few health hazards of his own. Besides, no amount of health insurance could have prepared him for the emotional upheavals of the past twenty-four hours. He was a hustler after all – affairs of the heart were as alien to him as tax returns or the mating habits of people who only had sex on Sundays. If he was left feeling fragile, and entertaining thoughts of a messy death, it was only to be expected. Given the circumstances, keeping calm simply wasn't an option.

He'd started the day on such a high, still buzzing from the excitement of his encounter with Matt Walsh and the memories of what had happened in that hotel room. It seemed silly now, but for a brief moment he'd even convinced himself that it had been more than just a simple business transaction, that somehow, against all the odds, he and Matt had made some kind of special connection. Then seeing that billboard with Matt and his female co-star looking so cosy together had brought Billy back down to earth with a bump. Suddenly his night of passion with Matt hadn't seemed so special after all. He consoled himself with the thought that he wasn't the first person in LA to fantasise about falling in love with someone famous, and he probably wouldn't be the last. Living in a city like this, surrounded by so many celebrities, the opportunities for forming deep and meaningless attachments were endless. When stars were this thick on the ground, and in such close proximity, people were often inclined to mistake them for friends, talking about them in familiar terms, or referring to them by their first names only. Seeing Julia shopping at the Beverly Center, spotting Keanu at Orso's, even breathing the same car fumes as Cher, it was easy to get caught up in the illusion that their lives weren't so very far removed from your own. But as Billy now knew, there was nothing quite like a giant billboard towering over the streets of West Hollywood to remind you that, really, they were worlds apart.

Seeing Matt up there on that billboard, where only the chosen few could ever hope to see themselves, he seemed so remote, so larger-than-life, so utterly untouchable that whatever little intimacies he and Billy had shared the night before paled into insignificance in the full glare of his fame. A single billboard was all it took to spell out the full meaning of Matt's celebrity status, whisking him away into a world of velvet ropes and limousines, and shattering any illusions Billy might have had that their lives might somehow become entwined. The distance between them was insurmountable. He'd be kidding himself if he thought otherwise. By the time he arrived back at his apartment, he'd made a firm resolution to forget all thoughts of romance and put the entire episode behind him. Matt's moment of awkwardness, his flattery, his invitation to dinner – they were just his way of showing Billy what a nice guy he was, and reducing the risk of him running to the papers. The last thing Billy expected was that he would hear from Matt Walsh again. He had spent the afternoon sorting his laundry, updating some of the information on his website and generally trying to establish some order in his life in the hope that this would take his mind off last night. He was doing a pretty good job of it too until his cell phone rang and a familiar voice said: 'I forgot to ask – how do you like your steaks?'

That was over two hours ago, and still it hadn't completely sunk in. Dinner for two with Matt Walsh, at his place in Beverly Hills. Billy couldn't remember the last time someone had invited him to their house for dinner – not unless he counted the night Casey invited him over to watch the MTV Music Awards and they ordered in a pizza. And with his work schedule, even dining out was rare. Most of Billy's clients preferred the anonymity of hotel rooms to the flashiness of restaurants, and few were willing to waste valuable time and money on dinner when the only thing they really had an appetite for was sex. Billy knew this wasn't true of everyone in his situation. He'd met plenty of hustlers who were regularly wined, dined and sixty-nined by generous clients with large expense accounts. But for some reason he always seemed to miss out on the wining and dining and skip straight to the last item on the menu. And because it had been such a long time since he'd really dated anyone, the mere thought of sitting down to dinner with a man he was actually attracted to was daunting enough. The fact that tonight's dinner was with Matt Walsh only added to the pressure. Matt the world famous movie star, and him a mere hustler. What could they possibly have in common? What on earth would they talk about?

Last night had been different. Billy had been called out to the hotel on business, and once he'd recovered from the initial shock of finding a major Hollywood star lurking behind the door, he'd slipped into his designated role with comparative ease. But tonight the roles weren't so clearly defined. Billy didn't know what was expected of him. Had he been invited to dinner simply as a hustler, by a satisfied customer willing to invest a little extra time and money in the hope of a repeat performance? Or was this actually some kind of date? Matt hadn't brought up the subject of payment, and Billy, still reeling with surprise at the sound of his voice, hadn't thought to ask. He sorely wished he had. At least then he might have some idea of what to wear. Dressing for work was easy. Nobody expected him to keep his clothes on for very long anyway, so unless a client specifically requested that he arrive dressed as a traffic cop, a marine or a pizza delivery boy, Billy tended to wear the same basic butt-hugging jeans and muscle tank/T-shirt combo favoured by every hot-bodied homosexual this side of the Santa Monica Freeway. But when it came to dressing for a date, he was a little out of practice, as shown by the bewildering array of clothes spread before him.

The entire contents of his wardrobe were laid out across the bed, some items piled together in a chaotic heap, others arranged in a series of potentially pleasing combinations. It was a bit like that scene from *American Gigolo*, except that Billy didn't look nearly as confident as Richard Gere and his clothes weren't by Armani. The labels were those no self-respecting gay party boy could possibly live without – everything from Abercrombie & Fitch to Whitall & Shon, with some vintage Levis for that slightly nostalgic '70s street hustler feel, half a dozen pairs of cargo pants in various shades of beige and a splash of Versace thrown in for fun. There were T-shirts in every colour, tank-tops with various sporting logos and a collection of extremely small, extremely white outfits first unveiled at circuit parties in Palm Springs and South Beach and seldom worn since. If there was one single, unifying theme to Billy's wardrobe, it was that every item was designed to draw maximum attention to his ass, crotch, pecs or biceps. Pants were either tight at the crotch or worn so low they invited people to draw bets on where his abs ended and his pubic hair began. T-shirts were bought a size smaller than recommended and sometimes cropped to reveal a tantalising glimpse of taut flesh at the waist. Sleeves were either torn off at the seams or shortened to within an inch of his armpits. Nothing was worn for comfort. It was all about packaging.

Surveying the contents of his wardrobe, Billy was still no closer to deciding what to wear. In the past two hours he had tried on every item of clothing he owned, studied himself in the full-length mirror and then promptly discarded it as either too slutty, too subtle or too physically restricting for a dinner date. The one thing he had finally reached a decision about was his underwear, but then the toss-up between Calvin Klein and 2Xist briefs wasn't such a tough call to make, and if the truth be told he'd already changed his mind about the 2Xist briefs he was currently wearing – twice. At this rate he'd be dressed in time for breakfast and his relationship with Matt Walsh would be over before it had even begun. On those rare occasions when they mixed with mere mortals, stars could be as late as they liked. It was expected, which explained why some even acted as if their reputations depended on it. But if there was one thing Billy had learned from repeated viewings of Madonna's *Truth or Dare* documentary, it was that nobody kept a celebrity waiting – not even another celebrity. Anyone could see that Warren Beatty's relationship with Madonna was doomed the moment he left her pacing her hotel room, cursing the man who'd been keeping her waiting for almost ten minutes!

Billy checked his watch. Just over an hour to go. The time for floundering from one fashion crisis to another was rapidly running out. Important decisions had to be made. Remembering some words of wisdom imparted to him by a male model who once appeared in a Gucci ad ('Black is always the new black'), Billy peeled off his dazzling white 2Xist briefs and immediately swapped them for a pair of Calvins – black, of course.

CHAPTER EIGHT

Casey had been walking the leafy back streets of West Hollywood for almost ten minutes before it finally dawned on him that the men trailing a few yards behind him weren't simply admiring his ass. On a good day, Casey prided himself on being extremely streetwise. When you made your living as a hustler, it paid to keep your wits about you. But the excesses of last night meant that his wits were operating a little further afield than usual. And with his mind currently preoccupied with thoughts of getting home, stripping off his clothes, putting on one of his new porn movies and enjoying the uncomplicated pleasure of watching other people have sex, this was one of those rare occasions where Casey's hustler instincts had let him down.

Three young Latinos dressed in homeboy denims and displaying all the jewellery-encrusted machismo of rap stars had spotted him leaving Hustler Hollywood and had been following him ever since, the level of their banter gradually rising as the streets became less busy and their intentions towards him became more obvious. Had this been a scene from a gay porn movie, they would have followed Casey all the way back to his apartment before exchanging a few words of clumsy dialogue, rubbing their crotches in a provocative fashion and inviting themselves in for a gang bang. But since life rarely lived up to the promises of gay porn – even in West

Hollywood – Casey was forced to consider the possibility that, right now, the chances of him getting fucked weren't nearly as high as the chances of him getting mugged. A quick glance over his shoulder confirmed his suspicions, and he began to walk a little faster.

'Hey, faggot!' the biggest and by far the most attractive of the Latinos shouted after him. 'You wanna suck my dick?'

Tempting though it was to take this as a sign that things were looking up, Casey could tell the offer wasn't serious. Still he couldn't help wondering what would happen if he said yes, or what the guy's dick looked like. He'd seen Latin guys in porn movies, flaunting their body hair and playing with their foreskins like they were something special – which, in a world of shaved pubes and cut dicks, maybe they were.

'Sure,' Casey said, throwing caution to the wind and turning to eye up his tormentor. 'You want to whip it out here, or were you thinking of someplace more intimate?'

Taken aback, and possibly haunted by the memory of some shameful childhood episode, the Latino blushed. He wasn't prepared for this. There was an awkward silence, suddenly broken when both his buddies fell about laughing – not because they found his loss of face funny, but because they were picturing him getting his dick sucked by a faggot and they found the picture disturbing. Exposed and alone, he did his best to hide his blushes, swallowing hard, staring at the ground and shifting his feet like a kid caught with his pants down. Casey found it all rather touching. For all his macho bravado, this dumb hunk of Latin muscle was clearly no match for a faggot with such sharp wits and finely tuned defences. For a moment it looked as if the unexpected boldness of Casey's remark had thrown him completely off balance, forcing him to stop, reconsider and finally decide to end this now rather than risk further embarrassment. Then his body stiffened and his face darkened.

'You'd like that, wouldn't you?' he snarled, staring Casey straight in the eye. 'You dirty cocksucker! Filthy faggot!'

Still hovering at a discreet distance but clearly encouraged by this unambiguous expression of contempt for all things homosexual, his two sidekicks wiped the smiles from their faces, furrowed their brows and concentrated on exuding as much testosterone as possible. Reassured that nobody was about to get their dick sucked, not even in a fag-bashing, power-tripping sort of way, they immediately lost their inhibitions and felt compelled to take a more active role in the scene unfolding before them. Eager to make their voices heard, but let down by a strictly limited vocabulary, they racked their brains for some fresh insult to throw at the faggot, before finally recognising the futility of their efforts and flailing around for some other way of demonstrating their worth. Suddenly the one in the red bandanna had a brainwave.

'Hey, faggot,' he spat, pointing at the plastic carrier Casey held in his right hand. 'What you got in the bag?'

Casey flinched. By now, alarm bells were definitely ringing. Only a few weeks ago he'd heard about a couple of gay guys who'd been beaten to a pulp in broad daylight, right here in the supposedly safe haven of West Hollywood. But this wasn't the only cause for alarm. There was also the porn to consider. Casey being the dedicated aficionado he was, the thought of some gay-bashing Latino homeboys getting their thieving hands on his precious porn movies affected him more profoundly than any threats to his personal safety. There were times in every man's life when he had to stand up for what he believed in, and for Casey this was one of those times. He could already feel the adrenalin pumping. But now something deep within him stirred, sending a rush of blood to his brain and filling every fibre of his being with a sense of injustice so intense it gave him a whole new insight into Larry Flynt's brave crusade against the forces of conservatism. Nostrils flaring, Casey gritted his teeth and gripped the bag tightly in his hand. The odds might be stacked against him, but he was damned if he'd give in without a fight.

'Okay, guys,' he said, butching up his act as best he could while wearing a vintage Madonna 'Who's That Girl?' tour T-shirt. 'Here's the deal. I may be a faggot, but I'm the kind of faggot who'll happily rip you a new asshole, and then fuck you up it. And as much as I'd love to stand here and shoot the shit with you, I have things to do. So why don't you just fuck off back to South Central before I lose my cool and somebody gets hurt?' Then, staring at the guy in the red bandanna, he gave a cocky grin. 'And honey, what's with the headscarf? It may be ghetto, but it sure isn't fabulous.'

There was a long silence, punctuated by a short burst of nervous laughter. The atmosphere was still tense, and as the seconds ticked by Casey could feel the pressure mounting. Try as he might, he couldn't keep this act up for much longer. But for now it seemed to have done the trick. The worried looks on the faces of the three Latinos told him that his threats of violence and sexual assault were not only completely unexpected but were actually being taken seriously. Unless he was very much mistaken, they'd bought his butch act and were beginning to doubt the wisdom of taking this any further. Swelling with pride, Casey congratulated himself on a towering performance, the likes of which was seldom seen on these queer streets and might even go down in history as a major breakthrough in the battle to reduce hate crime in the city. After all, punks like this didn't target gay men just because they hated them. They did it because they saw them as easy pickings, passive victims who wouldn't fight back. Maybe after today they'd be inclined to see things rather differently. Or maybe not.

'You don't scare me, faggot,' the first guy said, though Casey could sense that he wasn't too sure of himself. Clearly his two friends sensed it too, because suddenly they both moved forward, until they were standing so close Casey could smell the Double Mint on their breath.

'C'mon, faggot,' the third one growled. 'Show us what you got!'

Casey's pulse raced. So much for brazening it out. Now he was left with two choices – flight or fight. Faced with such a tough decision, Casey applied the same logic many Hollywood studio executives applied every day of their working lives. He considered the risks involved and weighed them against the expectations associated with a certain type of movie. But unlike most studio executives, Casey acted quickly. A nanosecond was all it took for him to decide on a course of action based on a rapid assessment of the dangers now facing him and his prolonged exposure to Jean-Claude Van Damme movies – which, since they contained significant amounts of gratuitous male nudity, were viewed by Casey in much the same way as gay porn, with one hand on his penis and the other on the remote. He'd seen Jean-Claude kick-box his way out of situations like this a thousand times. How hard could it be? Turning as if to run, Casey paused before swivelling on the ball of his foot and delivering a devastating combination of spinning kicks, back fists and angle jabs that took his attackers completely by surprise, knocking the ringleader to the floor and sending his two accomplices scurrying off into the distance, terrified of the fate awaiting them if they hung around and the faggot was as good as his promise.

With only the biggest and the best-looking of the Latinos

left to contend with, and one dazzling display of kick-boxing faggot power already under his belt, Casey stopped to catch his breath, confident that the worst was over. His moment of triumph was immensely gratifying, but extremely short-lived. Unfortunately for Casey, the Latino sprawled before him was not only the biggest and best-looking of the three, but was also the one carrying a knife. In the split second it took for this to register, he lunged forward, and before Casey had time to react, the blade had sliced clean through his Madonna T-shirt and was buried deep in his stomach, somewhere between his lower right rib and the six-pack he'd been work-ing on for years and had only recently achieved through a combination of punishing exercise, strict dieting and regular drug binges.

Feeling no pain, but sensing that he should probably call for help, Casey watched the Latino scramble to his feet and beat a hasty exit before reaching into his jeans pocket for his cell phone. The inside of the pocket felt warm and sticky, and as he raised his hand he panicked at the sight of blood. Dizzy with shock, he fell to his knees. He felt the sun on his face. He smelt the scent of orange blossom. He heard the distant sound of a car alarm. Gradually his vision cleared and he spotted the bag of porn videos lying a few feet in front of him. Smiling contentedly, he leaned forward and felt a sudden shooting pain in his stomach. He stared down at the piece of metal protruding from Madonna's mouth with a look of mild astonishment. Moments later he lost consciousness, slumping to the ground with his precious porn videos just out of reach and his blood slowly soaking on to the sidewalk.

Michael Rosetti removed his Oliver Peoples sunglasses and stepped into the darkened recess of the grand old building on

Main Street. Inside, the cool air soothed his skin as his eyes slowly adjusted to the flickering light of candles. The drive downtown had been every bit as gruelling as expected, and it was a relief to leave the modern world behind him, if only for a short while.

It had been a trying day. He'd spent the best part of the afternoon going over his finances, realising with horror that he barely had enough cash to cover his living expenses for another month and becoming all the more determined that, one way or another, that bitch Lee Carson was going to pay – and sooner rather than later. Michael knew, of course, that revenge was a dish best served cold. What scheming queen didn't? But sometimes you had to strike while the iron was hot. Soon he'd need to find himself a new job. That could take weeks, possibly even months. And once the job-hunting was over, he'd be too busy sucking up to his new boss to concentrate on anything else. Revenge was a demanding business. It required imagination, determination and as much undivided attention as one might devote to one's career, or possibly even a relationship. All things considered, it was far better that he get on with it now, while there was nothing to distract him.

In fact, he doubted if anything could distract him now, he was that angry. And anger, as Michael knew only too well, was a great motivator. Anger focused the mind. It made you strong. It could even offer hope. While many Angelenos built their hopes on a daily dose of false optimism, quietly kidding themselves that the smog was just a heat haze and that the daily tremors were no indication that 'The Big One' was on its way, Michael had always been a firm believer in the power of negative thinking. He'd seen enough daytime TV to know that anger management was all the rage these days, and had even been shown to change people's lives, enabling them to control their anger in ways they'd never thought possible. But

Michael wasn't one of those people. He didn't want to control his anger. He didn't want to rein it in. He wanted to unleash it, and watch it destroy his enemies like the great plagues sent by the vengeful God of the Old Testament. It was on days like these that Michael wished he lived in less complicated times, when good men trembled before God and sinners were struck down by lightning bolts. Fuck anger management. What he really needed was a God who would happily open up the ground beneath Lee Carson's feet.

But since divine intervention was hardly an exact science, Michael knew better than to waste his time with prayers. He'd done enough of that to last him a lifetime. Like every good Catholic boy, young Michael Rosetti had spent a large part of his childhood on his knees, praying for the things that would have made his life more bearable. He prayed for a new bike. He prayed for his parents to pay him more attention. He prayed for his brother Anthony to catch some deadly disease, for his friend Todd to stop telling everyone he was queer, and for his teacher Mr Cunningham to fall madly in love with him. His prayers were never answered, and each time Michael was left to find the only consolation he could. It would have been nice to discover that somebody up there really did like him, that someone was watching over him, that some almighty entity cared enough to make amends for some of the terrible injustices he'd been forced to endure all his life. At least then he might have been spared the added burden of taking the law into his own hands. Deep in his heart, young Michael had always known that what he did was wrong, that his actions were not those of a good Catholic boy. But when even God had failed him, what was he supposed to do?

Of course that was all in the past. The Church didn't have the same hold on him now that it had when he was a boy, and for that Michael was eternally grateful. Looking back, it was probably fair to say that the Church rejected him long before he rejected it, but either way the loss of faith Michael experienced during his late teens was a blessing in disguise. It alleviated some of the guilt he felt over previous misdeeds and made his unclean thoughts and violent mood swings far easier to live with. How much easier only became apparent some years later, when Michael watched *The Sopranos* on HBO and saw for the first time what a lucky escape he'd had. He didn't know how those Mafia guys managed it. Practising Catholics up to their necks in organised crime, balancing their religious convictions with their work commitments, taking Holy Communion one minute and spilling the blood of innocents the next. It was all so complicated.

Thankfully, since he was no longer a practising Catholic, there was no reason on earth why Michael should be troubled by such matters. Of course there were those who insisted that, like herpes, Catholicism was something you were stuck with for life. But since he'd been a lapsed Catholic for so long, and had lapsed so often and to such spectacular effect, Michael was confident that all those years of guilt and sacrament were firmly behind him. So if he sometimes burned incense or crossed himself, this was merely force of habit. If he regularly visited leather bars in Silver Lake and took part in ritualistic scenes of sexual role play, conducted in hushed tones of almost religious reverence and invested with all the pomp and circumstance normally associated with pronouncements by the Pope, this was simply the way he liked to spend his evenings. And if he occasionally drove to the La Placita church in Downtown, the way he had this afternoon, it was only because it was the oldest religious structure in LA, and like anyone with a proper sense of occasion, he'd come to admire the building with its grand old architecture and many fine modern additions.

Standing before a tiled mosaic of the Annunciation, created by the artist Isabel Piczek back in 1981, Michael felt a familiar stirring in his chest and immediately attributed it to a highly developed appreciation of the arts. Irrespective of how it might have appeared to the outside world, in Michael's mind there was nothing to suggest that the spiritual hopes and religious convictions of his childhood were anything but a distant memory. He didn't feel the need to confess. He wasn't plagued by self-doubt or riddled with guilt. And he certainly wasn't looking for salvation, either in this life or the next. He would make his peace his own way, with or without the promise of redemption. The way Michael saw it, justice was its own reward, and a person as hell-bent on revenge as he was right now could ill afford to have their judgement clouded by religious sentiment. All that mattered were the practical considerations – the hows, whens, whys and wherefores. The rest was between a man and his conscience. And as far as Michael was concerned, conscience was simply a question of perspective.

There was never any question of why he should exact revenge on Lee. After the way she'd treated him, the woman was lucky to be alive. And he'd already decided on the when – as soon as possible. But after several hours of frenzied brainstorming, he was still no closer to deciding how to go about it. He wanted to hit her where it would really hurt, but since she was a woman apparently devoid of any real feelings it was hard to imagine where her weak spot might be. He'd thought about tarnishing her professional reputation, but since she appeared to thrive on the fact that everyone regarded her as a vicious bitch, there didn't seem to be much scope. He'd considered the possibility of targeting her at home, but since her personal life was practically nonexistent, the chances of anyone witnessing her untimely demise were negligible, and for Michael no redemptive action would be complete without that vital element of public humiliation. He'd even toyed briefly with the idea of setting fire to her offices, but the security system at Lee Carson Associates was far more efficient than anything he'd had to contend with back at his high school, and in any case he was reluctant to relive former glories when deep down he knew he should be striving towards bigger and better things.

Like many of his more admirable qualities, Michael's refusal to rest on his laurels was the result of a childhood trauma. When he was twelve and still competing with his brother for his parents' approval, he'd rushed home from school one day, bursting with pride at having come top of the class in a spelling test. By the age of twelve, Michael was well aware that there were some talents his brother possessed in such abundance, it was pointless him even trying to compete. The nine sporting trophies engraved with the name 'Anthony Rosetti' and displayed above the fireplace were ample proof of that. But this was one occasion where Michael had achieved something Anthony never could, and although he didn't have a trophy to show for it, he arrived home confident of a hero's welcome. His mother was in the kitchen, preparing dinner. If she was proud of his achievement, she had a funny way of showing it. Rather than shower him with praise, she took her eye off her spaghetti sauce, turned to him and smiled sadly. 'You're only as good as your last achievement,' she said. 'You did well today, but now you must concentrate on tomorrow and the next test. Your brother already has nine trophies on the wall, but it's the tenth trophy that matters. Never forget that.'

As harsh as it sounded, Michael had never stopped to question the wisdom of his mother's advice. Her words had echoed in his ears all his life, and they echoed again now. It didn't matter that his mother abhorred violence and would probably die of shame if she knew what her own son was capable of. All Michael heard was her voice urging him to improve on his past performance, to do better and to make someone proud. Tempting though it might have been to give Lee Carson a taste of the same fiery fate that befell Mr Cunningham, Michael knew it would be a Pyrrhic victory. He needed to push himself, to set himself new challenges and explore new ideas. Anything less would be an admission of defeat. He was aware, of course, that this way of thinking was out of synch with the methods of the movie industry. The majority of people in Hollywood thought nothing of repeating the same tired formula over and over again. But then Michael had always considered himself a cut above the majority of people in Hollywood. The paucity of imagination in this town was nothing short of criminal. Most people would sooner play safe and squander what little talent they had than risk sticking their necks out and coming up with a single original thought.

Well, not Michael Rosetti. Sitting here in the oldest church in LA, he felt the spirit of invention descend upon him, and with a blinding flash he knew exactly what he had to do. He stepped out of the church and ran back to his car.

The short drive out of the walled city of West Hollywood and deep into the heart of Beverly Hills took even less time than Billy had anticipated. Still it felt as if he'd entered another world. If West Hollywood was most people's idea of a gay theme park (and Billy had never met anyone who would dispute that), then Beverly Hills was the closest thing to a theme park for the rich and famous. As he steered his red Volvo along the lushly planted, heavily monitored streets, Billy gazed in awe at the endless succession of lavish mansions, expensively manicured lawns, elaborate sprinkling systems, deep blue pools and high electric fences. Policed to the point of sterility it might have been, but there was still an air of romance about Beverly Hills that no amount of security measures could spoil, a particular kind of opulence that harked back to the golden days of Hollywood pool parties, silver screen goddesses and 'all those wonderful people out there in the dark'.

These days, of course, a large number of the local residents were rich immigrants from Iran and Israel who, unlike previous generations of Jews who'd come to Hollywood, weren't remotely interested in changing their names and becoming movie stars. Rumours abounded that some of these people had actually made their fortunes through business interests totally unconnected with the movie industry, which rather begged the question of why they should feel so at home in Beverly Hills. Still Billy didn't need a Stars' Homes Map to know that there were enough celebrities in them there hills to keep a little of the old magic alive. Not wishing to dilute the fantasy any further, he reminded himself that the first movie stars to move into Beverly Hills were Mary Pickford and Douglas Fairbanks, and tried not to think too much about Steven Segal and Anna Nicole Smith.

Driving down these sacred streets, past giant nodding palms and mansions the size of his apartment building, Billy hoped he didn't look too out of place. After much agonising over what to wear, he'd finally settled on a pair of black Gucci pants, teamed with a tightly tailored white Versace shirt. Even with his shirt collar open and his nipples accentuated by the cunning cut of the fabric, the overall look was rather more formal than he was used to. Billy couldn't remember the last time he'd worn real leather shoes with socks, let alone an outfit that concealed far more flesh than it revealed. But it wasn't as if Matt didn't already know what lay beneath those layers of crisp white cotton and shiny black acetate, and given the circumstances Billy felt it was probably a good idea to dress up a little. Maybe after dinner he would unbutton his shirt and see what effect that had, but for now he thought it best to err on the side of caution. He wanted to make a good impression, and he somehow doubted if showing up at Matt Walsh's private residence looking like a hustler would do much to endear him to a man so famously protective of his public image.

Endearing himself to Matt Walsh was what tonight was all about. Tonight there would be no cheap hustler routines. Men like Matt didn't have time for games, and for Billy this was a rare chance to prove that he wasn't just some rich guy's plaything. It was a dinner date after all. The stakes were already raised. And there would be plenty of time for sexual athletics later. But first he would lay his cards on the table, or the kitchen counter, or wherever they happened to be sitting as they tucked into their steaks. He would show Matt that he had far more to offer than simply a repeat of last night's performance. He would show him that he was more than just a great fuck, that he was someone to be trusted, someone worthy of love, someone a man in Matt's position might even consider spending the rest of his life with. Of course he wasn't going to come right out and ask if he could move in straight away. He wasn't going to rush things. But if the signs were there, Matt would find that Billy was more than willing to go the distance. And if everything went according to plan, by tomorrow morning Matt would have no option but to insist on never letting him go.

Partly out of respect for Matt's privacy, and partly for fear of ruining his hair, Billy had resisted the temptation to drive through Beverly Hills with the top down. Huddled inside his Volvo convertible, shielded from the prying eyes of passers-by and the damaging effects of the elements, he was probably no different from the majority of Angelenos who saw their cars not simply as a means of transport, but as a place of refuge. But as he approached the two-storey Spanish colonial-style mansion Matt Walsh called home, Billy experienced a level of paranoia few people were likely to experience, whether battling their way through rush-hour traffic on the busiest freeway or snorting another line as the sun came up at a beach party in Malibu. Suddenly he felt as if everybody was looking at him, and not in a good way. Suddenly his own anxieties about being the focus of attention seemed small and inconsequential. Suddenly he had a taste of how it must feel to be Matt Walsh.

Matt had warned him not to drive too slowly lest he attract the attention of the Beverly Hills cops, whose vigilance was nothing short of exemplary but who were sometimes a little overzealous in the way they exercised their duty to protect movie stars' homes. It wouldn't be the first time a young man had been stopped on his way to visit Matt Walsh, and there were only so many excuses a man could make for the number of attractive male visitors he received before his private affairs were plastered all over the papers. Scanning the street for squad cars and seeing no moving vehicles other than his own, Billy pulled up to the wrought-iron gates. As if things weren't stressful enough already, a floodlight came on and a security camera whizzed into action. Feeling more tense than ever, Billy lowered the driver's window and spoke into the entry-phone. Suddenly tempted to make light of the situation and order a Big Mac and fries, he thought better of it and simply gave his name.

There was a moment's delay, then the gates slowly opened

and he drove through. Checking his hair in the rearview mirror and finding it every bit as immaculate as when he'd left his apartment, he stepped out of the car, adjusted his crotch and walked up to the door. Nervous with anticipation but relieved to have made it this far without being arrested, he took a deep breath and rang the doorbell. As the door opened and he stepped across the threshold into the air-conditioned comfort of Matt Walsh's private world, Billy was finally able to relax.

Little did he know that, even now, he was being watched.

PART TWO

Simon

CHAPTER NINE

As British Airways flight 283 began its slow descent over the airbrushed expanse of LA, Simon Fowler surveyed the view from the window and turned to the woman seated next to him. 'Is it always this beautiful?' he asked.

The woman, who'd been in a sedative-induced sleep since Heathrow and was now busy inspecting her makeup, snapped her compact shut and blinked at him through enormous false eyelashes. 'Beautiful?' she snorted. 'Are you kidding me? LA is just Miami with smog. Only don't tell the locals I said so. Most of them are convinced it's only a heat haze.'

Laughing politely, Simon held her gaze for a moment. There was something vaguely familiar about her. For a moment he had the feeling that maybe they'd met somewhere before, though where on earth he would have come across such an extraordinary creature he had no idea. She certainly wasn't the sort of woman you were likely to forget in a hurry. The Pucci print pantsuit was awfully dated and the enormous black hair was almost certainly a wig. Judging from her accent, he'd have put her down as a New Yorker, although he couldn't be a hundred per cent sure. She had a slight mid-Atlantic twang that suggested a life of international travel and made her precise origins a little harder to pinpoint. Looking past the heavy eye makeup he guessed that she was probably around the sixty mark, although again he couldn't be certain.

Cosmetic surgery could take years off people, and with her fashion sense it wouldn't have surprised him to learn that she was well into her eighties and was flying into LA for her seventh facelift.

'I'm Simon,' he said, offering her his hand.

'Jackie,' she replied quickly. 'So, this your first time in LA?'

He nodded.

'And what brings you here, Simon? Don't tell me you're one of those poor unfortunates hoping to break into the movies.'

He laughed. 'Not exactly. I'm a writer.'

'Really?' she said, her eyes lighting up. 'What kind of books do you write?'

'I don't. I mean, I haven't. Not yet, anyway. I'm a journalist.'

At the word 'journalist', Jackie's eyes glazed over and she began rooting around in her handbag. 'Well, it was nice talking to you, Simon,' she mumbled, none too convincingly. 'Now you'll have to excuse me while I try to find my travel documents. We'll be landing any moment, and immigration is a bitch.'

Yeah, well, it takes one to know one, Simon thought, but said nothing. He was just being oversensitive. The old trout probably didn't mean any harm. How was she supposed to know that she'd touched a raw nerve, the one with the word 'book' stamped all over it? The truth was, he had always planned to write a book one day. It was what most young journalists did, particularly those who were keen to be taken seriously. Only Simon wasn't quite so young any more. He was thirty-five next birthday, and still that elusive book deal hadn't materialised. He'd always assumed that his first book would just come to him – one sudden flash of inspiration and it would write itself. It was something of a shock to discover that a book was usually something you planned for and laboured hard at. For all his natural gifts, Simon had never been much of a grafter. Maybe it was time he accepted the fact that books, like babies, simply weren't part of the game plan. (He could still remember the look on his mother's face, the day he finally plucked up the courage and confessed to his parents that he was gay and had no intention of impregnating a lesbian purely in the hope of producing grandchildren. His mother was crestfallen, sobbing into her Marks and Spencer woolly cardigan over the little booties she would never be required to knit. Meanwhile, his father tried to hide his disappointment by turning his attention to the garden and the prize rose bush he'd been meaning to cut back for months and was suddenly compelled to attack with a brand-new pair of pruning shears and a vigour his wife hadn't witnessed in years.)

To make matters worse, the publishing world wasn't exactly waiting with bated breath for Simon Fowler to make his literary debut. After years of gentle prodding, his agent appeared to have finally given up hope of him ever producing so much as an idea for a book proposal. Had she been the kind of woman inclined by nature to wear a woolly cardigan, Simon could have imagined her sobbing into it, though picturing her in anything but the haziest of detail was becoming increasingly difficult. Like his mother, she hardly ever called these days, and the invitations to lunch that were once a fairly regular feature of their working relationship appeared to have dried up. Maybe she didn't want to pressure him. Or maybe she was too busy lunching with other, more important clients, writers with serious literary ambitions and book proposals coming out of their ears. He could see them now, hanging out at Soho House or the Groucho, surrounded by hordes of adoring acolytes, cracking open the champagne and toasting six-figure book deals that would make them rich beyond their wildest dreams.

Not that Simon was doing too badly, financially speaking. In fact, he'd never had it so good. All those years of scratching around for work as a freelancer had finally paid off and he enjoyed the security of being contracted to several newspapers and magazines, some of whom paid the kind of word rates most first-time authors could only dream of. He was employed primarily as a features writer, though when required he could also turn his hand to the occasional book or film review. The bulk of his income came from interviewing famous celebrities. It was a job he enjoyed for a whole host of reasons, and given the unprecedented amount of public interest in anyone even remotely famous, it was one he could easily picture himself doing for the rest of his working life. In fact, it was largely because he was so successful a journalist that he hadn't fulfilled his dream of writing a best-seller by the time he was thirty. The ambition had always been there, but the rewards of journalism had been so great, and had come to him so easily, he could hardly be blamed for failing to drop everything and lock himself away in solitary confinement for the best part of a year. Writing a book was a major commitment. And when it came to commitment, Simon had always been a bit on the phobic side.

Besides, there was no shame in being a humble hack, particularly when you were as good a hack as Simon. Of course he was aware that not everyone shared this opinion. To the general public, journalism wasn't exactly the most noble of professions, not by any stretch of the imagination. And in the grand scheme of things, his own contribution probably mattered less than most. Simon Fowler didn't risk life and limb reporting from the world's trouble spots. His brand of journalism didn't bring down governments. Nobody had ever been required to hold the front page in anticipation of Simon's latest dispatch. It was doubtful that anyone would be tempted to make a film based on his professional achievements, and even if they did, he certainly wouldn't be played by either Robert Redford or Dustin Hoffman.

But what Simon did, he did exceptionally well. Put him in a room with a famous celebrity and you could pretty much guarantee that he would come away with a fresh insight, a new angle, a killer quote. His interview with Madonna, conducted in New York around the time of her *Bedtime Stories* album, showed a woman convinced that the whole world was out to punish her and was widely considered a classic. His famous run-in with Hugh Grant, in which the world's favourite Englishman took great exception to the suggestion that his acting was perhaps a little limited, was breathtaking in its daring and infinitely more entertaining than the film Grant happened to be promoting at the time – the one where he went up a hill, came down a mountain and failed to do anything half as interesting as meeting Divine Brown.

And there were plenty more where those came from. Simon Fowler was the man who prompted a former Spice Girl to say the word 'cunt', and Boy George to reveal the true depths of his bitterness at no longer being 'Top of the Pops'. He was the first British journalist to get the inside story on Jude Law's split with Sadie Frost, and the last to be granted an audience with London club legend Leigh Bowery, a month before he succumbed to an AIDS-related illness.

Extracting private confessions from public figures was part of Simon's job description, and was helped in part by his shabby appearance. Simon had never been anyone's idea of a good-looking man. From his mother he'd inherited small green eyes and a weak chin. From his father he'd inherited a long narrow nose, thinning hair and a permanently worried expression, as though any moment now he was expecting to find himself summoned back to the family home and forced to weed the garden. Put together, his features were pale, pinched and really rather plain. But rather than try to disguise them with expensive grooming products or dress them up with designer clothes, Simon had taken the brave – some might say foolhardy – decision to simply work with what he'd been given. Like most journalists in his position, he had a regular supply of promotional T-shirts donated by various film and record companies eager to plug their products. Unlike most journalists, he actually wore them – and not just to bed. The day he met Madonna, Simon was sporting a rather fetching T-shirt for a film entitled *Money For Nothing*.

The remains of his wardrobe showed a similar disregard for the vagaries of fashion, consisting as it did of crumpled jackets with ink-stained pockets and several pairs of jeans in various shades of blue, none of which could be described as 'designer'. The overall effect was unstructured, dishevelled, scruffy even, but in Simon's case it had proved far more successful than plain old-fashioned power-dressing. Maybe the stars he interviewed were thrown off balance by his apparent lack of vanity, or maybe they simply felt pity for him. Either way, they tended to open up to him far more readily than they would for some slick individual with a sharp suit and a killer grin.

Still the job was often far tougher in practice than Simon's casual appearance and breezy writing style suggested. Friends often remarked that he was lucky to meet so many famous people in his line of work, and he was forced to admit that, yes, there was a certain amount of luck involved. There weren't many professions where you were paid good money to spend time in the company of bona fide icons like Debbie Harry and David Bowie. But what Simon's friends failed to appreciate was that time spent in the company of such people was always time spent under pressure. There was no such thing as a cosy chat with a famous celebrity, despite some journalists' attempts to persuade their readers otherwise. Saying you'd enjoyed a glass of chardonnay with Julia Roberts at the Dorchester Hotel might lead some readers to think that you'd struck up some kind of friendship, but it was hardly an accurate reflection of the truth. A more honest account would have mentioned the months it took to set up this meeting, the conditions laid down by Julia's people, the way the apparently cosy chat was carefully orchestrated and the queue of journalists waiting patiently outside her suite for their own special stage-managed moment with the Oscar-winning actress.

Contrary to what Simon's friends and the readers of certain gossip magazines thought, the whole business of interviewing celebrities was fraught with hidden dangers, and was becoming more hazardous all the time. For one thing, PRs wielded more power now than at any time Simon could remember. Somewhere along the line, they'd gone from being the people who ordered the lunch and poured the wine to being the new gatekeepers. It wasn't unusual for PRs to brief journalists on what could and couldn't be discussed during a potential interview, or to blacklist those who refused to play ball. Simon could still recall the days when PRs were committed to keeping journalists sweet. These days they were more likely to bully you into submission with thinly veiled threats or subject you to a torrent of abuse. It was like *The Stepford Wives* in reverse – friendly, compliant females (most PRs tended to be female), suddenly transformed into cold, scheming bitches. Not surprisingly, it was a phenomenon first identified in Hollywood, where agencies like the mighty PMK were reputed to have a virtual stranglehold on the media. But gradually the disease had spread to most parts of the world, and every corner of the entertainment industry. All across

London, vast armies of PRs were battling for control of the written word and making Simon's job increasingly difficult. Where some of the bigger names were concerned, just being considered for an interview was an achievement in itself.

Of course the situation wasn't helped by the fact that large numbers of hacks were only too happy to sell their souls in exchange for an opportunity to worship at the altar of modern celebrity. Celebrity journalism had never been famous for its clear-eyed devotion to the truth, and there were plenty of journalists out there whose genuflection to the demands of pushy PRs regularly went beyond the call of duty. Deals were made and controversial topics dutifully avoided. Pertinent questions were struck from interviews and quotes edited to ensure that no unnecessary embarrassment was ever caused. Profiles were written and PRs invited to check for errors and confirm that their client really had been shown in their best possible light. And with growing numbers of editors willing to hand over complete copy approval to egocentric celebrities or only employ writers who were pre-approved, it was no wonder that most celebrity profiles weren't worth the paper they were written on.

Luckily for Simon, he was employed by the kind of editors who prided themselves on their independence and usually had the balls to back their journalists when the going got tough. This was especially true of the women. No female editor ever made it to a senior position in the British media without displaying some balls along the way. And since publications like *The Sunday Globe* were among the most respected in the business, and regularly sold enough copies to guarantee the kind of publicity few celebrities could afford to turn down, even the pushiest PRs were obliged to play nicely. Still it wasn't all plain sailing. Even assuming you made it past the first hurdle and were granted the interview you so desperately wanted, you were still required to jump through hoops. More often than not, an interview slot these days was exactly that – a narrow opening in some busy celebrity's tightly packed schedule, a small window of opportunity in which you were expected to put the subject at ease, allow them to plug their latest venture and then, if you still had any time remaining, move the conversation on to more interesting topics like their first major crush or their last major fallout. It was hard enough back in the days when you were guaranteed a full hour in which to win them over. These days, interviewing world-famous celebrities was the professional equivalent of speed-dating. The last time he interviewed Beyoncé, Simon was given precisely eleven minutes.

Despite all this, nothing gave Simon such a buzz as interviewing a world-famous celebrity. He had very little interest in profiling talented newcomers, and none at all in identifying the stars of tomorrow. Struggling actors and hungry musicians were sometimes good for a quote or two, but it was only when they'd been around for a while and had achieved a certain degree of fame that Simon found them truly worth the trouble. He loved stars – not in a sleazy, starfucker kind of way, but with a passion that put even his closest personal relationships into the shade. He loved the tension between the public image and the private person. He loved the fact that most stars had egos the size of small planets, and IQs that were rarely above room temperature. He loved the ridiculous way they lived, and the ridiculous lengths they went to trying to convince the world that they were just regular Joes. He loved the fact that these were people who'd been interviewed hundreds of times before, who knew the drill, and who were determined not to give too much away, no matter how charming you were or how hard you pushed them. In short, he loved the challenge.

And now here he was touching down in LA, tired, jet-lagged, but ready to face what could well be his toughest challenge yet – an audience with the newly appointed king of Hollywood action heroes, the extremely famous and notoriously private Matt Walsh.

Casey spent a total of sixty-three hours in hospital. The first day he was mostly unconscious, only coming round after the anaesthetic wore off to discover that he was still alive and hadn't died and gone to heaven together with the entire cast of *ER*, before being administered a mild sedative to help him sleep and to give the nurses a break from his constant badgering. The next two days were spent adjusting to his new lease of life and wondering how on earth he was going to pay for it, especially now that he was sporting a scar which, small though it was, totally ruined the appearance of his abs, spoiling their beautiful symmetry with an ugly red gash and thereby reducing his market value by a considerable margin. The doctors had assured him that the scar would disappear eventually, and that they were only keeping him in 'for observation'. But Casey didn't care. The way he saw it, he'd been stitched up in both senses.

To make matters worse, he'd been instructed to steer clear of the gym for at least a few weeks, avoid kick-boxing and generally limit his physical activity as much as possible. For all their medical certificates, it was clear that the good doctors at Century City Hospital had absolutely no comprehension of the amount of work required to maintain a working body like Casey's. Follow their advice and pretty soon he'd be too fat to hold his head up in West Hollywood and would have to retire to a trailer park somewhere. After that, it would be downhill all the way. So far as Casey was aware, trailer parks didn't come equipped with personal gyms. Nor were they the natural stamping ground for talent scouts from the gay porn industry. The best he could hope for would be an appearance on *Jerry Springer*, by which time he'd probably weigh something in the region of four hundred pounds and would have to be air-lifted off his couch and into the studio where he would suffer the ultimate humiliation of being branded a loser by an audience of Tennessee truck drivers and single mothers on welfare. All things considered, the long-term prospects weren't looking good.

But for now there was the more pressing question of how he was going to pay his medical bills. Casey had heard horror stories involving people with no medical insurance actually being turned away from emergency rooms in LA. While his doctor had assured him that in the case of genuine emergencies such practice was, in fact, illegal, he also left him in little doubt that the hospital would do everything in its power to recoup any costs incurred during his stay. He smiled as he said it, of course, but the smile did nothing to disguise the determination in his voice. It was at times like this that Casey wished he'd found himself a rich sugar daddy, preferably one with a few million in the bank and a heart condition. In some parts of LA, treatment for a simple allergic reaction could set you back something in the region of a thousand dollars. A broken finger was valued at five thousand, while a broken leg came in at twenty-five thousand. It was for this reason that Casey trusted in the quality of medical and dental care provided at the LA Free Clinic. He could think of far better things to squander his cash on. Porn, for example.

Try as he might, Casey couldn't stop thinking about his missing porn. Considering that it was part of the reason he'd ended up in hospital in the first place, he might have been forgiven for never wanting to watch another porn movie again. But Casey was made of sterner stuff. He'd gone down fighting for his precious purchases from Hustler Hollywood and he was damned if he was going to let them go so easily. Unfortunately, nobody he'd spoken to over the past two days seemed to share his concern. If they had any information concerning the whereabouts of his porn movies, they certainly weren't letting on. The police who came to interview him about the assault seemed more interested in establishing the motive for the attack than in apprehending his attackers or tracking any personal items reported missing from the crime scene. As for the hospital staff, the story he'd been given was that no such items were found on his person when he was admitted to the emergency room. All they'd found was his cell phone. The phone was small enough to slip into the front pocket of his jeans, and since it didn't boast the latest features, probably wasn't worth much on the street.

While Casey was willing to entertain the possibility that the Latino had stolen his cash and credit cards, it did strike him as highly unlikely that he'd have left the cell phone and made off with the porn instead – unless of course he was as big a closet case as Matt Walsh and as devoted a fan of Chase Young as Casey himself. Tantalising though it was to picture his attacker jerking off to Chase's latest exploits, Casey couldn't really see it somehow. A more likely explanation for the disappearance of his porn was that one of the ambulance crew or possibly even one of the male nurses had taken a shine to it. Either that, or the queen who first found him lying unconscious on the sidewalk wasn't quite the Good Samaritan he made out. It was nice of him to call 911 and wait for the ambulance to arrive and take Casey to the hospital, but the fact that he hadn't been to visit did suggest that maybe he had a guilty conscience.

For the past three days, doctors and nursing staff had done

their best to talk Casey around, impressing upon him time and time again that, really, he was lucky to be alive. Traumatic as the experience undoubtedly was, the worst he'd suffered was a flesh wound. Apparently, the knife that tore through his Madonna T-shirt entered his body at just the right angle, narrowly missing a number of vital internal organs. It was almost as if Madonna herself had been watching over him. True, the wound did require more stitches than one might expect. And yes, he did lose a fair amount of blood, hence the decision to keep him in for observation. But it could have been a lot worse. Thanks to the timely intervention of a fine young gay man who happened to be out stretching his legs in preparation for next weekend's big AIDS charity walk, Casey wasn't left to bleed to death on the sidewalk like the latest casualty in some crack dealers' turf war. He was bundled into an ambulance, rushed to the emergency room and patched up in no time. All things considered, he had a lot to be thankful for. In fact, it wasn't unusual for people in his position to experience a kind of euphoria, an emotional high brought on by the sudden realisation that, somehow, they had succeeded in cheating death.

Casey wasn't convinced. Comforting though it was to be told that he hadn't suffered any serious damage or been left to bleed to death, he still felt that life had dealt him a pretty shitty blow. A few days ago he'd been in prime physical condition, the proud owner of a six-pack, with a body fat ratio most queens would gladly die for and a bunch of new porn movies to enjoy. Now here he was, three days behind with his fitness regime, with a visible layer of fat already developing around his midriff, half a dozen stitches and a scar that not only prevented him from jumping straight back on the treadmill, but would probably send half his clients running for the hills. So no, he wasn't exactly jumping for joy. In fact, he was downright miserable. And when Casey was miserable, he saw to it that everyone around him was miserable too. He snapped at the nurses. He complained about the food. And for the best part of forty-eight hours, he sulked.

Whether his distemper contributed in any way to the speed at which he was declared fit enough to go home Casey couldn't say, but on the morning he was discharged from hospital he did have a sneaking suspicion that certain members of staff were glad to see the back of him. He consoled himself with the thought that he probably made more in a week than most of these people made in a year, and was immediately reminded that, at this precise moment in time, his earning potential wasn't quite what it could be. Right now he didn't even have the cab fare home. He would have called Billy and asked him to come collect him, only Billy's number was stored in his cell phone and his battery was dead. Obviously nobody these days was expected to commit friends' phone numbers to memory, not when they had cell phones and Palm Pilots to do the brain work for them. He'd call Billy as soon as he got home and could check the address book on his computer. Luckily he was still in possession of the keys to his apartment. He tapped his pocket just to be sure, and made his way out of the hospital.

Outside was another bright sunny morning, the kind of morning that generally made a person happy to be alive, unless that person happened to be a not-so-happy hooker who'd spent the past three days in hospital. The sky was cornflower blue, with tiny white wisps of cloud that would soon melt away or fade to orange with the smog. In the parking lot, rows of shiny black SUVs glinted in the morning light, reminding Casey of the time he attended his uncle's funeral. Uncle Roy was a pillar of the community, a family man with a taste for bourbon and a keen interest in his young nephew's physical development. Barely a day went by when Uncle Roy wasn't moved to comment on Casey's expanding chest or tempted to squeeze his thighs. Casey didn't mind. At thirteen, he was grateful for the attention, and as time went on became quite attached to his eccentric uncle with the whisky breath and the wandering hands. So it was a shock to learn that his uncle had hanged himself. A shock, but hardly a surprise. His family might have feigned bewilderment as to why a man like Roy would take his own life, but Casey wasn't taken in by their pained expressions and baffled looks. They knew the reason why, as surely as they knew that Roy's interest in his nephew was more than a little queer. Aunt Sarah probably knew more than most, but she kept it to herself. If she was bitter, she didn't let it show. The funeral she gave her late husband was every bit as grand as a man of his position demanded, and every bit as theatrical as a man of his tastes would have appreciated.

A siren screamed, snapping Casey out of his flashback. Moments later an ambulance pulled up and a man was carried out on a stretcher. Judging by the look of him, he'd just got off the set of the latest slasher movie, where he was employed as a stunt corpse. His face was messed up pretty bad, and his arms hung limply by his sides, hands practically clawing the ground as his lifeless body was carried past the spot where Casey stood and disappeared into the building. Watching him go, Casey wondered if it wouldn't be quicker and easier to just dump him in the back of one of those shiny black SUVs. That was one dude who definitely wouldn't be renewing his gym membership.

CHAPTER TEN

The Regent Beverly Wilshire was the hotel where *Pretty Woman* was shot. According to local legend, it was the only five-star hotel in the zipcode that would allow the film-makers to point their cameras there. The others insisted that nobody ever brought hookers to their hotels – not even privileged guests like Richard Gere. If Simon's memory served him correctly, the original script for *Pretty Woman* ended with Gere's kerb-crawling millionaire kicking Julia Roberts back out on to the streets, only the studio got nervous and drafted in director Garry Marshall to sweeten things up with a fairy-tale ending in which the two stars hooked up on a non-profit-making basis. Then of course the movie became a massive hit, and the Regent Beverly Wilshire enjoyed a boom in business as a result. How much of that business came from known hookers wasn't something they told you in the welcome pack, but if the present guests were anything to go by, Simon suspected it wasn't a great deal. The hotel was positively crawling with pink, corpulent middle-aged couples, the majority of whom had already signed up for the coach tour of Universal Studios and were busy discussing which movie star's home they would most like to see after breakfast. Most looked as if they hadn't had sex in years.

Simon had been in LA for less than twenty-four hours, but already he was getting a feel for the place. It was remarkable the extent to which the character of the city could be gleaned from the movies, even a silly menopausal male fantasy movie like *Pretty Woman*. Especially a silly menopausal male fantasy movie like *Pretty Woman*. After all, the vast majority of movie moguls were both male and menopausal, so it was hardly surprising if most of the movies that came out of Hollywood reflected their particular fantasies and somewhat narrow world view. Unlike the British film industry, which seemed to squeeze all the joy out of film-making, fretting over worthy literary adaptations or agonising over grim tales of life up north, there was something unashamedly shallow and narcissistic about Hollywood that Simon found rather refreshing. Movies about middle-age spread, marital breakdown and earthquakes might not be to everyone's taste, but in a strange way they were more honest than films featuring southern toffs with northern accents or Helena Bonham Carter in a corset and yards of antique lace.

The level of sentimentality attached to the British film industry was one of the reasons Simon avoided becoming a full-time film critic. That, and the occupational hazard of listening to his fellow critics harp on about Woody Allen. If he'd been told once that Allen's oeuvre was a love letter to New York, he'd been told a thousand times. It was generally assumed that LA didn't inspire nearly as much devotion as the Big Apple, although Simon was beginning to suspect that this was a myth perpetuated by New Yorkers in an effort to deny the curious attractiveness of the West Coast. Certainly LA appeared to have more than its fair share of admirers, many of whom could be described as successful film-makers, if not auteurs. Driving from the airport yesterday, watching the landscape unfold from the back seat of a yellow cab, Simon experienced a powerful sense of déjà vu. You didn't need to take a tour of Universal Studios for that movie theme park experience. It was all around you. Familiar sights loomed at every corner, from the Hollywood Walk of Fame where generations of stars were immortalised to the famous sign where frustrated starlets plunged to their deaths. There was the building where Bruce Willis flexed his muscles in *Die Hard*, and the rooftop where Tobey Maguire fought Alfred Molina in *Spider-Man 2*. This was the city celebrated in *LA Story* and *Short Cuts* and lovingly recreated in *LA Confidential*. And after twenty-four hours in Beverly Hills, even movies like *Bride of Frankenstein* and *Forever Young* took on a whole new meaning. What better way to reflect the obsessions of a town where surgeons were regularly called upon to perform miracles and nobody ever appeared to grow old? The more Simon thought about it, the more it seemed to him that, somehow, he'd been here before.

The fact that he hadn't might have struck some people as rather odd. Twelve years in the job, and never once had he been flown out to LA for the big Hollywood interview. But really there was no great mystery. For many years, Simon had specialised in interviewing stars of a very British calibre – those grand old thespians and hip young pop singers who made the West End great and encouraged successive generations of *Smash Hits* readers to part with their pocket money. And since most Hollywood stars were now in the habit of visiting Britain on press junkets, there really wasn't a great deal to be gained from jetting off to LA for what would probably turn out to be a standard thirty-minute interview. Even allowing for the fact that you might buy yourself a little more time, when all was said and done a hired room at the Dorchester probably wasn't all that different from a hired room at the Chateau Marmont. Both were equally anonymous settings in which to conduct an interview. Both offered little in the way of local colour, or special insight into the person sitting in front of you. Both required that you be equally fastidious in your research and fearless in your approach if you held out even a glimmer of hope of coming away with more than a couple of half-decent quotes. The only real difference was that one was right on your doorstep while the other was located halfway across the world.

That said, in the case of this particular interview there was never any question that Simon should just drop every-thing and catch the first available flight to LA. Matt Walsh hadn't been spotted at a press junket in years. Nor was he the kind of movie star who granted interviews every day. At a time when many celebrities built their careers on the illu-sion of unlimited access, spilling their guts about their eating disorders or feeding the press stories about their coke habits, Walsh preferred to keep his mouth shut and his nose clean. He'd probably given fewer interviews over the past decade than some stars gave in a week. All things consid-ered, this was one assignment worth flying halfway across the world for. Just being granted an audience with Matt Walsh was a major coup, regardless of whether the photo shoot actually came off or Simon got the kind of access he was hoping for. Of course it helped that he was writing for *The Sunday Globe*. A title like that still opened doors, even in this age of kiss-ass celebrity magazines and tabloid tittle-tattle. Negotiations had been going on for months. Emails had been sent and requests acknowledged. Calls had been placed and messages taken. Arrangements had been made and remade. The last thing Simon heard, an email from the offices of Lee Carson Associates had been sent to his editor, suggesting that he may have more time with Matt than previously thought.

Still, Simon wasn't counting on it. When you were dealing

with a star of Matt's magnitude, arrangements could change at a moment's notice. It happened all the time. One minute you were being invited to hang out with everyone's favourite movie star at home, the next you were conducting your interview over the phone with three lawyers listening in for good measure. Or better yet, you were reciting your questions on to an audio tape and FedExing the tape all the way to Bermuda, where Catherine Zeta-Jones was busy enjoying some quality time with her husband and would be only too happy to answer your questions at her earliest possible convenience.

Simon knew better than to rely on the kindness of that strange breed of people known as Hollywood publicists. Most of them didn't have a kind bone in their bodies. And if half the stories he'd heard about Walsh's manager were true, lawyers were the least of his worries. By all accounts, Lee Carson ate journalists for breakfast. In Hollywood folklore, her reputation was exceeded only by Harvey Weinstein, head of Miramax, whom Bernardo Bertolucci once described as 'a little Saddam Hussein of cinema', which would probably put Lee on a par with Eva Peron. There were tales of her ripping phones from walls, tearing strips off editors and forcibly ejecting journalists from interviews that weren't going quite the way she planned. One story even had her grabbing some guy's dictaphone and tossing it into the pool. His crime, apparently, was to suggest that Matt Walsh wasn't exactly the most versatile actor the world had ever seen – an observation which, however unwelcome it was to her ears, could hardly be described as controversial.

Why a woman of Lee's temperament had agreed to let a journalist with Simon's track record within a mile radius of Matt Walsh, he really had no idea. Maybe he was flattering himself that his reputation extended as far as Beverly Hills.

Still it seemed pretty inconceivable that Carson hadn't done her homework. The woman lived and breathed the Matt Walsh business. She was also famously overprotective of her client, and if Simon's instincts were correct, she would do everything in her power to ensure that Matt Walsh survived this brush with the media with his precious public image intact. So it seemed pretty safe to assume that she'd have gleaned as much information as possible about the man whose interview skills she would be putting to the test.

If so, there were at least three things she would have learned about Simon, none of which was likely to endear him to her or particularly meet with her approval. One, he was pushy. Two, he was gay. Three, while he wasn't a fan of that infantile form of gay terrorism known as 'outing', he was someone who regarded a star's sexuality as a suitable subject for enquiry.

His motivation wasn't political. Simon certainly didn't think of himself as a gay activist. He didn't even see himself as a gay journalist. Though he made no secret of his sexuality, he had always regarded himself as a journalist first and a gay man second. For him, one didn't necessarily inform the other. He was far more pragmatic than that. Unlike the advocates of outing, Simon wasn't interested in naming and shaming famous people in the vain hope that they might somehow see the error of their ways and suddenly become positive role models. But as a journalist he found it extremely frustrating when someone he'd been entrusted to interview spent the whole time pussy-footing around something as fundamental as their sexuality. He didn't particularly wish to force anyone out of the closet, but nor was he willing to compromise himself or his readers by listening to a pack of lies and writing them up as fact. If someone was prepared to lie about who they were and who they slept with, the chances were they would happily lie about other things too. And what was the point of publishing an article composed entirely of lies? You might as well just cut out the middle man and print the press release.

Besides, the sex lives of the rich and famous were plastered all over the media all the time, be it Britney's wedding photos or Jude's affair with his children's nanny. It was only when a celebrity was rumoured to be gay that media pundits suddenly discovered they had a conscience, or waxed lyrical about a person's right to privacy. Why was it in the public interest to know the intimate gynaecological facts about Angelina's pregnancy, but beyond the realms of decency to suggest that someone might be homosexual? Saying that someone was married with children actually revealed far more about them than simply stating that they were gay. It told you who they were sleeping with and what kind of sex they were having – i.e. the unprotected kind. Saying someone was gay merely suggested that they were unlikely to appear in a sex tape with Paris Hilton any time soon.

Of course, not everyone shared Simon's point of view, least of all the stars themselves. For many, all personal questions were strictly off limits. The trick was knowing how to talk them round. And even when they could be persuaded to open up a little, you could be certain you'd be treated to a little discourse on the evils of the modern media. That was the trade-off. You got your story, they got to lecture you on the ethics of your profession. These days, invasion of privacy was every pampered celebrity's favourite moan. What most of them tended to forget was that, unlike the rest of the population, they were actually paid according to how much attention they received. Few saw any contradiction in the fact that they were just as likely to open their hearts to *Oprah* and their doors to *Hello!* magazine as complain about their latest violation by the tabloids. One minute they were throwing punches at the paparazzi, the next they were talking hormone shots and miscarriages with Barbara Walters. Privacy was a quaint old-fashioned notion they fell back on whenever the precious publicity they spent half their lives courting suddenly backfired and left them with egg all over their surgically enhanced faces.

It took some temerity, but since when were celebrities short on front? Height maybe, front never. So Madonna could compare herself to poor Princess Diana, hounded to death by the paparazzi, a few short years after she was photographed masturbating in a conical bra and inviting the world to explore the inner workings of her vagina with her *Sex* book. Or how about poor old Catherine Zeta-Jones, claiming she'd been personally violated because *Hello!* ran a perfectly flattering photo of her wedding when she and husband Michael Douglas had already signed an exclusive million-dollar deal with a rival publication.

When it came to making a spectacle of himself, Matt Walsh wasn't quite in these ladies' league. But nor was he known for giving the media an easy ride. What few press cuttings Simon had managed to put together only went to confirm his initial impression that Walsh would be a tough nut to crack. Matt Walsh had never leapt up on *Oprah*'s sofa or broken down on Barbara Walters. He'd never made an embarrassing sex tape or entered into a slanging match with a fellow celebrity. He'd never had a drug or drinking problem, or been treated for 'nervous exhaustion'. He'd never bitten anyone. It seemed unlikely that he would ever be found naked and babbling in a bush in Beverly Hills or caught speeding along the Pacific Coast Highway, wild-eyed and bearded like Nick Nolte on a bad day. In an industry where people regularly crashed and burned within their first few years of becoming famous,

Walsh had survived almost two decades in the spotlight without putting so much as a foot wrong. In a town where people regularly feasted on one another's failures with glee, he remained hugely successful and enormously well liked. Mention the name Matt Walsh and people would immediately comment on how polite he was, how utterly charming, how totally professional. Testaments to his all-round niceness were a recurring theme of the Matt Walsh story, together with his parents' messy divorce when he was eight and a childhood so impoverished it was positively Waltonsesque in its hard-grit homeliness – which, presumably, was precisely the effect he was going for.

And that was about all anyone really knew about him. His face had graced a million magazine covers. His movies had grossed more than a billion dollars at the box office. His personal fortune was estimated at a hundred million dollars. But what really impressed Simon was that Walsh had achieved all this, and cultivated such an enormous fanbase, while at the same time remaining virtually unknown. People didn't actually know who Matt Walsh was – not really, not in the way that they knew the intimate secrets of a hundred other celebrities. Almost twenty years in the public eye and he remained, if not a total enigma, then certainly something of a mystery. And judging by the way he conducted his affairs, he was determined to keep it that way.

Walsh didn't bleat on about press intrusion the way many of his contemporaries were prone to do. He didn't lash out at photographers, or waste valuable time in interviews complaining about the pressures of being famous. He was never moody or difficult. He was far too smart for that. But at the same time he was always somewhat guarded, a little distant. Anyone who'd ever interviewed him came away feeling flattered, charmed, but really none the wiser. That was Matt

Walsh's greatest talent – to create the illusion of intimacy while at the same time revealing very little about himself.

For Simon, Matt Walsh represented the ultimate challenge. This could well be the interview of his career, bigger and even more widely discussed than his interview with Madonna. By the mid '90s, it was clear to anyone with half a brain that Madonna didn't harbour any deep, dark secrets. For her *Sex* book and the accompanying *Erotica* album, the poor woman was even forced to invent an alter ego and fake a few personal perversions, just to get tongues wagging. If Madonna had anything left to hide at all, it was probably the fact that there was actually far less to her than met the eye. As Simon suggested at the time, that was the reason why she kept changing her hair colour every few months. Madonna's thirst for reinvention wasn't the restless artistic endeavour some people claimed. It was just that if she stayed still long enough, she was sure to be found out.

Matt Walsh was a different story altogether. With him there was the distinct possibility that there were a few skeletons lurking in the closet. At this precise moment in time, Simon couldn't say for certain if the rumours about Walsh were true or not. But he certainly intended to find out.

Casey arrived back at his apartment to find his computer in sleep mode and his mailbox bulging with offers inviting him to add inches to the length and girth of his penis, together with half a dozen requests for soiled underwear. (There were no actual letters waiting to be opened – non-electronic mail being, like, so last century!) He took a few minutes to reply to his emails before searching through his address book for Billy's number and setting his cell phone to recharge.

The light on the answering machine was blinking away, indicating that while Casey and his cell phone had been out of action, the machine had lived up to its responsibilities and recorded a grand total of six new messages. The first had been left two days ago at 6.07 a.m., suggesting one of two possibilities – either someone he knew had just died or someone he didn't know had just got home from the clubs, high on crystal and horny as hell.

'Hi there, Casey,' said a slurred voice. 'I guess it's kinda late, or maybe it's kinda early. Anyway, I already tried your cell and your ad did say twenty-four hours. I was calling to see if you could get yourself over here so I can fuck your beautiful ass. Or maybe you can fuck me. Whatever. Are you there? Casey? Christ, what is it with you guys? You never answer the fucking phone. Well, fuck you. Fuck you all to hell.'

The following three messages had been left at roughly ten-minute intervals, and featured the same slurred voice repeating 'hello' a few times before muttering something about 'lousy fucking hustlers' and hanging up. Casey swore that if this asshole ever called again, he'd tell him where he could stick his two hundred dollars. Hustler or no, he was entitled to a bit of respect.

Next up was a message from Snakeman. A long-standing aquaintance and occasional client, Snakeman lived over in Silver Lake, in a one-bedroom apartment he shared with three boa constrictors and a shih-tzu named Mr Shit. Recently dubbed 'the coolest neighbourhood in Los Angeles' by the leading cultural barometer known as *Vanity Fair* magazine, Silver Lake was where bohemian types turned their backs on the excesses of West Hollywood, developed facial hair and generally enjoyed a far gentler pace of life than that experienced by the majority of the city's gay inhabitants. Unfortunately, nobody appeared to have explained this to

Snakeman, whose commitment to facial hair was question-able at best, and who found it extremely difficult to relax as he lurched from one personal crisis to another, only pausing to take stock of his situation and wind himself up some more. He made a living dealing drugs and divided his time between the dog park, the gym and the local record store, where he could usually be found browsing the punk selection in search of the latest releases by Nick Name and other angry men with guitars and mohawks.

To say that Snakeman had 'issues' would be putting it mildly. A recovering alcoholic with all the pent-up aggression of a man constantly at war with himself, he refused to go into therapy on the grounds that therapists were part of some grand capitalist conspiracy, designed to turn everyone into happy, compliant little consumers. Never one to appear too compliant (or too happy), Snakeman wore his neuroses with pride and signalled his refusal to conform with a blue mohawk and a face that had never known the wonders of exfoliation or the benefits of a good moisturiser. His skin was so dry and flaky, it wouldn't have surprised Casey to discover that he'd adopted the same skincare routine as his scaly com-panions, waiting for his epidermis to split and peel away in its own time rather than investing in expensive skin products.

Casey had seen enough documentaries on the Discovery Channel to recognise a cold-blooded vertebrate when he saw one, and despite his high blood pressure, there was something distinctly reptilian about Snakeman. For one thing, he hardly ever blinked. One slight flutter of the eyelids at the point of orgasm and that was about it. And like the many snakes and lizards who abandoned their young the moment they hatched, Snakeman seemed to have a bit of a problem with intimacy. Sure, he was happy to invite someone over to his place and have them drip hot candle wax on to his scrotum or insert an enormous dildo rather a long way up his ass. But make the mistake of asking him how he was feeling or what name was printed on his driving licence and he totally freaked out. Not that Casey was particularly bothered. Too much intimacy with a client was never a good idea. Besides, there was more than one way to skin a snake. Snakeman could be as mysterious as he liked. It hadn't stopped Casey from making a few enquiries and establishing that his real name was Julian.

Casey hadn't heard from Julian in a while, so the sound of his voice immediately lifted his spirits. 'Hey, Casey,' the message began. 'Whassup, man? It's your old buddy Snakeman here, over in sunny Silver Lake. I haven't seen you in a while, so I was kinda hoping you could come on over, have a few laughs, get ripped, maybe have us a bit of a party. I'll make it worth your while. Plus I've got some crystal that's gonna blow your mind, man. Call me.'

Casey was about to pick up the phone and do just that when the machine beeped one last time and Billy's disembodied voice echoed around the room. 'Casey, where the hell are you? I tried calling your cell but you must be out of range or something. Anyway, guess what? I'm at Matt's place, lying in his bed. Christ, listen to me! I'm inside Matt Walsh's house! It's kind of weird actually. Marble floors for miles, and rooms full of antique chairs that nobody sits in. But he's the perfect host. He's downstairs right now fixing me breakfast. Matt Walsh – fixing me breakfast! Can you believe it? Anyway, I'm dying to tell you all about it but I'd best keep this short. I don't want him to walk in on me talking to you like this. You know how these movie star types are about their privacy! Okay, gotta go. Call you later.'

Casey played the message back one more time before punching in the number for Billy's cell. An automated voice told him that all calls were being diverted. He left a brief message informing Billy of his visit to the emergency room, and requesting that he call him back as soon as he came up for air. 'And don't forget who your friends are,' he added, only half jokingly. 'I know you're moving up in the world, but some of us could still use some personal attention.'

Michael Rosetti strolled into Koo Koo Roo exuding as much quiet self-confidence as he could possibly muster. This in itself was no mean feat. Part of a chain of chicken restaurants with branches throughout the city, Koo Koo Roo was where LA's gay party boys went for their daily protein fix (carbs, of course, were strictly off the menu). One local gay food critic had likened the ambience at Koo Koo Roo to the cast catering on a gay porn set, and there was certainly something vaguely pornographic about the way the meat was served up and whipped out before a crowd of hungry men with blond highlights and barely any body fat. Standing among them, Michael felt like a swine before pearls.

Mercifully, the man he'd arranged to meet was already seated at one of the tables, sipping a large Diet Coke and staring unashamedly at a particularly fine specimen of manhood he had absolutely no hope of seducing. Ted Chalmers was a minor league player in the Hollywood pecking order and a major cause of concern to his cardiologist, who saw him as a heart attack waiting to happen and warned him repeatedly that if he didn't lose weight soon he could kiss his medical insurance goodbye. Everyone else saw Ted for what he was – a deeply unhappy man in his early thirties, fighting a losing battle against an ever-expanding waistline, clearly gay and inclined to hide his pain behind a wall of self-deprecating humour. His favourite quip, repeated ad nauseam, was that he suspected he was suffering from anorexia, 'because each time I look in the mirror I see a fat person'.

All things considered, Ted Chalmers was a pretty sad excuse for a Hollywood homosexual, which was one of the reasons Michael had remained in touch with him after they were introduced at an AIDS charity dinner two months previously. Men like Ted made Michael feel better about himself. Plus, there was the small matter of Ted's position at Universal Studios. Staff copywriters weren't the most powerful people in town, not by any stretch of the imagination. Writers generally didn't rate very highly on the Hollywood totem pole. There was a famous joke, often trotted out by movie producers, about a starlet so dumb that she actually slept with the writer. And there was another joke, usually repeated by writers, that the reason so few Hollywood executives read books was because their lips grew tired after ten pages. In actual fact, very few executives even bothered to read scripts these days. They had assistants to do that for them. And if a script couldn't be summed up in ten words or fewer, it didn't warrant further consideration. That was how highly writers were regarded in Hollywood. If you really wanted to make your mark as a writer, Hollywood was the worst place on earth in which to do it. You'd be better off putting a message in a bottle.

Ted wasn't even what Michael would call a proper writer. Despite their somewhat lofty-sounding job titles, staff copywriters were little more than publicists. They spent their days drafting press releases for the studios and dreaming of the day when they would have a screenplay of their own to shop around or maybe even a book deal under their belt. The chances of a man with Ted's build ever getting anything under his belt seemed pretty remote. Even so, Michael figured that Ted Chalmers was a man worth knowing. In Hollywood, it was all about who you knew, and Michael didn't know many people who could be counted on to return his calls, never mind meet him for brunch. And besides, right now Ted might be in a position to help Michael with a little project he'd been working on.

'Ted,' Michael said, walking over to the table and sliding into a chair. 'Good to see you again. Is it just my imagination, or have you lost weight?'

Ted's smile seemed a little brittle. 'Michael, you know me better than that. Sorry to hear about you losing your job. And so suddenly too. That must have hurt.'

Now it was Michael's turn to force a smile. 'Not especially. It was only ever meant as a stopgap. I have plenty of other irons in the fire.'

But Ted wasn't listening. His attention was directed at a gay couple who had just walked in, one blond, the other dark, both with thirty-one-inch waists and pecs to die for. 'Don't you just hate the way some people walk into a room looking as if they've had sex this week?' Ted asked bitterly. 'Which reminds me, how are the sex addiction meetings going?'

'They're not. I only went once. There wasn't a single hot guy, so I quit.'

Ted laughed. 'Well, that's the price you pay for going downtown. You should try the meetings in Hollywood. No shortage of hot guys there.'

'Maybe I will, Ted. Maybe I will. Now, shall we get down to business? I don't suppose you've had a chance to read my script?'

'Sure I did. I liked it.'

Michael's eyes flashed. 'Really?'

Ted nodded. 'Absolutely. Very visual. Very filmic. Not sure about the title, though. *Starfucker* – it's a bit aggressive, don't you think? But the overall tone is good. Producers are always asking for something a bit more muscular these days, and this certainly fits the bill. I mean, it's practically apocalyptic. Kind of *Sunset Boulevard* meets *The Day After Tomorrow*. I particularly liked the scene where the hustler's car smashes through the Hollywood sign. Very poetic. It's not a bad script, Michael. Not bad at all. But of course you know it'll never get made.'

Michael frowned. 'Why not?'

Ted laughed. 'Why not? Well, for starters there's the main character, the movie star guy. He sounds a lot like Matt Walsh.'

'So?'

'So everyone in town knows Walsh is a big fag. But that doesn't mean you can have him swishing about in your movie, not when he's alive and well and very likely to sue. There are laws against that kind of thing.'

Michael sneered. 'So I've heard.'

Ted went on. 'And then there's his manager. Any fool can see that's supposed to be Lee Carson.'

Michael nodded. 'Well, you know what they say, Ted. Write about what you know. Or in this case, who you know.'

'I don't think it's meant to be taken quite so literally, Michael. You are permitted to make stuff up. It's what's known as artistic licence. You should give it a try sometime.'

'Believe me, Ted. Nothing I could make up would be half as interesting as the truth. So tell me, is there anything else I should look at before we take this to the next level?'

Ted looked confused. 'Well, there's a couple of pieces of dialogue I'd cut, a few scenes I'd do differently. But it really doesn't matter. There is no next level. There's no way anyone is going to touch this script. Not a chance. Matt Walsh has a lot of friends in this town. He keeps a lot of people off unemployment. And the moment she gets wind of this, Lee Carson will be gunning for your ass. You'll be lucky if you can get a job in the mailroom at one of the smaller agencies. Believe me, you'll never eat lunch in this town again.'

Michael laughed. 'To tell you the truth, I'm getting pretty tired of Cobb salad anyway.'

'I'm serious, Michael. This is a total non-starter.'

Michael smiled knowingly. 'Well, I have to say I'm very disappointed in you, Ted. Really I am. I had you down as a man of vision. But since this may be the last lunch I ever eat, I suppose we might as well order. Then I can tell you all about the hustler.'

Ted's face showed a mixture of surprise and excitement. 'The hustler? What about him? He's not based on anyone in particular, is he?'

Michael grinned. 'Well that's the million-dollar question, isn't it, Ted? Now, shall we order?'

CHAPTER ELEVEN

To: gary.koverman@foxstudios.com
From: lee.carson@leecarsonassociates.com
Subject: Your laughable offer

Gary,
You are joking, of course. You should know by now that my
client won't get out of bed for less than $20 million. Call
me when you're ready to talk business.
Lee

Lee was busy putting her new personal secretary through his
paces. 'Run and fetch me some coffee, Chad,' she snapped.
'Skinny latte, hold the sweetener. And when you've done that,
haul your ass into my office so I can run through my schedule. Things are going to be pretty tough around here for the
next couple of weeks. If you know what's good for you, you'll
see to it that I'm not let down by your performance. My last
secretary was a great disappointment to me, and I'm not the
kind of person who takes disappointment well.'

If Chad was intimidated by her stern words or leopard-
print safari suit, he didn't let it show. 'Absolutely,' he said, his
face the picture of earnestness. 'I mean, this is a great opportunity for me, Ms Carson. I won't let you down.'

Lee fixed him with one of her coldest stares. 'Then what are you waiting for? I don't pay you to stand there looking pretty. I want to see some action. Show me how much this opportunity means to you and maybe you'll still have a job at the end of the day.'

Watching as Chad scuttled off with his tail between his legs, Lee allowed herself a little smile. Still haunted by the memory of that sickening queen Michael Rosetti and his failure to go a single day without complaining of some mystery ailment, she'd hired Chad on account of his glowing resumé, robust health and thrusting heterosexuality. Chad was solid Ivy League stock, the kind of square-jawed, wholesome hunk who scored just as highly on the football pitch as he did in the classroom. His hair alone was an advert for the kind of All-American equestrian lifestyle regularly promoted by the likes of Ralph Lauren and Tommy Hilfiger. Blond and thick, it moved in heavy waves like fields of ripened corn. Lee couldn't imagine Chad ever being sick, or afraid of a hard day's work. There was a golden glow about him, a certain sheen that guaranteed a peak performance at all times. Coupled with his poster-boy looks, he had the eager demeanour of a labrador and the fashion sense of a frat boy. For his job interview, the kid had even turned up wearing a Brooks Brothers suit. Such sartorial oversights might not have gone down too well on *Queer Eye for the Straight Guy*, but for Lee the effect was strangely reassuring.

Right now, Lee could use all the reassurance she could get. Her recent dealings with Matt had left her with a profound sense of her own vulnerability, the likes of which she hadn't felt in years. First there was his sudden attack of conscience, all that talk about turning his back on the Hollywood mainstream, exploring new directions, staying true to his craft and 'digging a little deeper'. It made Lee wince just thinking about it. Did Tom Cruise turn his back on the mainstream when he came over all hip and started mouthing 'respect the cock' in *Magnolia*? Did Brad Pitt worry his pretty little head about staying true to his craft? Did Ben Affleck lie awake at night, wondering if he should dig a little deeper? Did Matt have any idea just how self-indulgent he sounded? If every major Hollywood player suddenly woke up one day and decided to dig a little deeper, the effects would be nothing short of catastrophic. Profits would fall, foundations crumble, and pretty soon an industry built on big ambitions and powerful market forces would lie in ruins. Movie audiences weren't interested in exploring new directions. They liked to know exactly what they were getting, and it was the job of every bloated producer, hotshot director and overpaid actor in Hollywood to give it to them. And whatever she may have told him in the past, Matt Walsh hadn't got where he was today by stretching himself as an actor. People didn't pay to see Matt Walsh act. They paid to see him being Matt Walsh. Preferably with his shirt off.

And as if all this weren't bad enough, there was the nagging suspicion that he wasn't being entirely straight with her, that there was something, or more likely someone, he'd neglected to mention. Lee had made a few discreet enquiries, but short of hiring a private detective to monitor his every move, there was no way of knowing what Matt got up to when she wasn't around. Not that Lee had ruled out the possibility of hiring a private dick. She even had a particular dick in mind for the job. Joe Nelson was a retired cop with an office over on the sleazier stretch of Sunset. Lee had called on Joe's services several times before and was confident that he could be trusted not to go spilling his guts to the tabloids. But she wasn't ready to put that particular plan into action just yet. Her relationship with Matt was strained enough already. The last thing she needed was for him to stumble on the fact that she'd hired someone to spy on him. Joe being the seasoned professional he was, she knew the risk was minimal. Still it was a risk she wasn't willing to take. If Matt was entertaining even the slightest thought of finding himself a new manager, a move like that would give him just the excuse he was looking for.

No, if Lee wanted to stay on top of the situation, she'd have to play her cards extremely close to her chest. Keep Matt sweet and his career on track. And most importantly of all, keep the rest of the blood-sucking Hollywood scum in the dark. The last thing she needed now was for someone at Fox to get wind of the fact that Matt Walsh was having some kind of mid-life crisis. It wouldn't make a blind bit of difference to them that the profits from Matt's movies had already paid for their kids' school fees and their condos in Malibu. In this business, show the least sign of weakness and pretty soon the buzzards would come circling. They came for everyone eventually. One day they were just tiny dots on the horizon, then before you knew it your luck had run out and they were picking over the corpse of yet another Hollywood career. Matt had done well to outrun them for as long as he had. His luck had lasted a lot longer than most. And he wasn't getting any younger. His position wouldn't remain unchallenged for ever. But Lee was damned if she was willing to give it all up just yet. Matt might have forgotten what it was like to have doors slammed shut in his face, but she certainly hadn't.

So for now she'd just have to play it safe. Act as though everything was normal, keep things ticking over and hope that by the time the new deal was on the table, Matt would have come to his senses. And in the meantime, if he asked her for a progress report she would just have to lie and say that she was busy tracking down some of those edgy, independent new projects he had his heart so set on. Luckily for her, Matt wasn't in the habit of asking too many questions. For years he'd been happy to leave the business decisions to her, confident that she knew what was best for him. And if his recent behaviour suggested that he was beginning to develop some ideas of his own, there was still no reason to suppose that he didn't trust her to follow his instructions to the letter. For all he knew, she'd already come around to his way of thinking and was every bit as excited at the prospect of exploring new directions as he was.

Besides, for the next few weeks Matt would be too tied up with the business of being a movie star to keep constant tabs on his manager. Soon the final round of publicity for *Surface Tension* would be in full swing. The movie opened in under two months, and with a budget of over a hundred million and everything riding on the opening grosses, even a star of Matt's magnitude was required to show willing and fake a little humility for the world's media. Television slots had been booked, including a much-publicised appearance on *The Late Show* to keep the older fans happy and an earlier slot on MTV to target the younger demographic. Recent polls suggested that teenagers these days were more inclined to get their kicks from state-of-the-art computer games than traditional action movies, hence the decision to give *Surface Tension* the look and feel of a computer game, complete with cartoon violence, a hero capable of performing superhuman feats without putting a hair out of place, and a leading lady replete with blonde hair, improbably large breasts and other physical attributes commonly associated with the sexual interests of adolescent boys.

First and foremost, however, *Surface Tension* was a Matt Walsh vehicle, and it was with his hordes of adoring female fans in mind that much of the press coverage had been generated. *Vanity Fair*, *Premiere* and *Entertainment Weekly* all had their 'exclusive' interviews and location reports sewn up months in advance of course. But recently it was the women's magazines which had suddenly found themselves enjoying unprecedented access to one of Hollywood's hottest stars. *Cosmopolitan* led the way with an in-depth profile spread over six pages. In it, Matt spoke out about the responsibilities of making action movies in the aftermath of 9/11, the pressures of approaching forty in a world obsessed with youth, the reasons he would never consider having cosmetic surgery and the truth behind those ugly gay rumours.

'I have nothing against gay people,' he told a swooning *Cosmo* reporter over a bottle of Pellegrino water at the Chateau Marmont. 'I bought George Michael's latest CD. I watch *Will and Grace*. Christ, some of my friends are gay. Working in this business, it's inevitable that you're going to be exposed to that kind of lifestyle. But it's not the way I choose to live my life.'

Matt had always handled himself well with journalists, and whatever her concerns about his future ambitions, this latest round of interviews left Lee in little doubt that he could still be relied upon to work the press. This month's *Glamour* magazine contained a four-page profile, revealing Matt's personal likes and dislikes, his favourite ways to unwind (playing tennis and horse-riding were both mentioned, smoking pot and butt-fucking were not), and the qualities he looked for in a woman (intelligence and independence were high on the list, leading most readers to the somewhat erroneous conclusion that what Matt Walsh really wanted was the love of a good strong woman). Due to hit the news-stands next week was an even more intimate profile in *People* magazine. Here Matt opened up about his troubled childhood, revealed the painful truth about his involvement with a charity devoted to helping children with Down's syndrome, and shared his hopes for a family of his own one day, when the pressures of the job eased off a little and he was confident that he could juggle the demands of his career with the responsibilities of parenthood.

None of this had been left to chance. Each encounter with the media had been orchestrated with military precision, and surrounded by a level of security normally reserved for the development of the latest stealth bomber. Naturally, Lee had played a major part in all of the necessary arrangements. Matt had his role to play, and she had hers. It was she who negotiated with the TV stations, she who vetoed the various publications, she who briefed the producers and editors, she who ensured that individual journalists were made fully aware of the sanctity of their 'time with Matt'. And her work wasn't done yet. There were still a handful of magazine editors desperately waiting to discover whether they'd made the grade, and a select few journalists eagerly awaiting further instructions. She'd call the editors first. Nothing gave her greater pleasure than the anguished cries of editors at having their requests denied. Then she'd firm up the arrangements for the coming week's interviews. That dizzy blonde from *In Style* was waiting to hear if Tuesday's lunch at the Ivy was still on. And she mustn't forget that guy from *The Sunday Globe* who'd just flown in from London. Simon something-or-other. He'd already left half a dozen messages. Enjoyable though it was to leave him sweating, she should probably put the poor thing out of his misery and touch base.

Lee reached for the phone and was about to start dialling when she caught sight of Chad hovering at the door, a package in his hand, his face a peculiar shade of puce. Maybe she'd misjudged him. Barely a day into the job and already that golden glow was gone. Even his hair looked stressed. 'Well don't just stand there,' Lee barked. 'Come in. And what the hell happened to my coffee?'

'This just arrived,' Chad said, and held out the package as

if it were a bomb waiting to explode. 'I wouldn't have opened it, only I wasn't sure if it was important or not, and, well . . . Anyhow, I think you should take a look.'

With Billy otherwise engaged, it didn't take Casey long to decide to return Snakeman's call and drive out to Silver Lake. Considering that he had just checked out of hospital, it was debatable as to whether he should be driving at all. But the painkillers appeared to be doing the trick, and provided he didn't get too carried away and wasn't too athletic, Casey figured he was better off shaking his money-maker at Snakeman's apartment than sitting home alone, waiting for his wound to heal and his sutures to dissolve, counting the days until the agony was finally over and he could return to the gym.

He could certainly do with the cash. Today was Friday. The rent was due on Monday, and much as he liked the idea of putting something aside each month in case of emergencies, the grim reality was that good ideas didn't always work out in practice. It didn't seem to matter how much he made. Whatever funds he had at his disposal were always whittled away on weekly essentials like drugs and porn. Besides, a boy had to eat, and with the fridge empty and a trip to Ralph's too awful to even contemplate, it was either phone for a pizza or avail himself of Snakeman's hospitality and the possibility of some free drugs. Doing a quick cost-benefit analysis, and weighing up the potential fat content, fun quota and financial rewards of the two options, Casey followed his natural instincts and climbed into his car.

It was a little after midday, the sun was high in the sky, and as he drove up to Santa Monica Boulevard he was surprised by the lack of traffic and the almost total absence of smog.

Everything in LA was always so predictable – the weather, the tailbacks, the steady build-up of auto emissions – it was easy to forget how beautiful it could be. On a day like today, so clear that you could see, if not for ever, then certainly as far as the mountains, the beauty took your breath away as effectively as a lungful of car fumes. People who complained that LA was completely fake were missing the point. For Casey, that was the key to its charm. What did people mean when they said that something was fake anyway? That it wasn't real? That it couldn't be appreciated? Or simply that it hadn't occurred naturally, that it required a little help along the way, a little encouragement, a little effort? Was that such a terrible concept? Natural beauty was so totally overrated in any case. All too often, the things people tended to think of as beautiful were simply an accident of nature – a stretch of water, a range of mountains, a pretty face. Natural wonders were all very well, and Casey enjoyed a pretty face as much as the next man. But when there was no real effort involved, was it really something to get so het up about?

The truly wonderful thing about LA was that it was all about effort. There was no point coming to LA and complaining that it was unnatural. If things had been left as nature intended, there would be no city to complain about. No movie studios. No freeways. No imported palm trees. No gyms, or juice bars, or restaurants serving grilled chicken and forty-five-dollar salads. No Crunch. No Jamba Juice. No Koo Koo Roo. No shopping malls, or supermarkets, or cute little boutiques selling discounted designer wear. No Beverly Center. No Pavilions. No Abercrombie & Fitch. No bathhouses, or beaches, or cruising areas frequented by world-famous celebrities. No Hollywood Spa. No Venice Beach. No Will Rogers State Historic Park. No clubs, or coffee houses, or bars with beer bashes and go-go boys. No Abbey, or Mickey's, or Mother Lode. No Rage, or Spike, or Revolver. No West Hollywood. No Beverly Hills. No Santa Monica or Marina del Rey. And certainly no Silver Lake. Just a vast expanse of desert, as bleak and as unforgiving as some of the religious fanatics currently employed by the city's talk radio stations.

Casey's decision to move to LA had been largely inspired by a documentary in which it was explained that, by rights, the city shouldn't have existed at all. LA had none of the natural features common to so many big cities across the world. It hadn't sprung up alongside a great river or developed next to a deep-water harbour. It didn't have a natural water supply, the biggest river being little more than a storm drain. Even the ground it was built on was considered unstable. But that hadn't prevented it from becoming one of the greatest cities in the world. Mountains had been levelled, deserts paved, rivers channelled and a great concrete island created virtually out of nothing. The only natural influence left was the weather, and even that was subject to the powers of air-conditioning. LA was living proof that nature could not only be tamed but improved upon. It was no wonder so many of its inhabitants chose to perform similar acts of revenge on their faces and bodies.

Maybe it was delayed shock from the events that had landed him in hospital, or maybe it was the sight of all the male hustlers lining the road, but as he drove east along Santa Monica Boulevard, Casey began to wonder if the life he'd carved out for himself was all it could be, or if there was the possibility, however small, that he wasn't maximising his potential. He may have left the Boulevard behind, but apart from the manner in which he advertised his services, his lifestyle really hadn't changed all that much since he arrived in LA almost a decade ago. Much like the migrants who first laid the foundations for this great city, Casey had come to LA with a few dollars in his pocket and very little in the way of natural assets. By the age of sixteen, it was clear that he was never destined to be a great beauty. But careful dieting, controlled exposure to the sun, meticulous grooming and a dedicated gym routine enabled him to make the best of what he'd been given. Back then, he was bursting with optimism. He was young, dumb and full of cum, and pretty soon there wasn't a gay man in West Hollywood who hadn't seen some evidence of the fact.

But more importantly, Casey had a dream – the dream that, one day, he would become a world-famous porn star. It was the dream that kept him going, the dream that kept him warm at night and cool in the days when clients were constantly trying to rip him off. And then one day he was told that his dream would never come true, and despite himself he began to lose faith. He tried to fight it, of course. But the more time passed, the harder it was to keep the dream alive. Regular movie stars could be discovered at any age. Look at Morgan Freeman. But porn stars had to make it while they were still young. In the big, bad, buffed-up world of gay porn, there were no second chances, no golden opportunities for late developers. Either you made it by the time you were twenty-five, or you gave up and resigned yourself to a life of hustling.

Casey was one of those who didn't make it. His twenty-fifth birthday came and went, and slowly the dream died, until now the only reminder left was his precious porn collection. The movies still gave him some comfort, of course. But without the burning ambition, what did it all amount to? Just a load of cheesy dialogue and some cum-shots. Fine for a bit of light relief, but hardly the stuff that dreams were made of.

Of course he still enjoyed the work. For Casey, there had

never been any question of resigning himself to a life of hustling. How could he resign himself to a job he loved? And unlike the boys who still worked the Boulevard, Casey at least had the comfort of knowing that he'd gone up in the world. But the simple truth was that he couldn't go on turning tricks for ever. Hustlers had more time on their side than porn stars, but even they were advised to take early retirement if they wished to avoid becoming tragic. A couple of years ago, the obvious solution would have been to find himself a rich sugar daddy. But with so many gay men choosing hustling as a viable career option and planning for an early retirement, the competition was stiff and getting fiercer all the time. It was becoming increasingly obvious that there were no longer enough rich sugar daddies to go round. He could always try looking for another career, but when the only skills you'd ever really mastered were for hot fucks and blowjobs, the options tended to be rather limited. Employers weren't exactly queuing up to offer top positions to retired hustlers, and he'd sooner sell his ass for a living than get fucked over in some lousy job pumping gas or waiting tables. Maybe it was time to admit defeat and move to Miami.

Casey had always assumed that, one day, he would move back down south – obviously not all the way to Memphis, but certainly as far as Florida. In many ways, it made sense. The Sunshine State had some of the best weather, and Miami's South Beach had everything a party boy could wish for – sand, sea, salad bars and plenty of opportunities for sex. It wasn't called the Sodom of the South for nothing. Plus it was the spiritual home of the White Party – the biggest, boldest, most spectacular event in the circuit party calendar, the party all others aspired to. Casey would carry the memory of his first White Party with him for ever. Dancing on the bay at Viscaya, high on a combination of ketamine and crystal meth, mouthing the words to 'Love Is in the Air' by John Paul Young, Casey had one of the best nights of his life. The only problem was, once the party was over and love was no longer in the air but lying vomiting in a hotel room somewhere, he wasn't sure what you were supposed to do exactly. Wait for Donatella to invite you over for dinner at the Versace mansion? Or start planning your outfit for the next big circuit party? South Beach was the perfect place to hang out for a week or two, but he couldn't imagine actually living there. Florida was where people went when they were waiting to die. Moving to Miami would be like giving up. At least here in LA he felt like he was still alive.

Feeling the need for a little driving music, Casey turned on the car radio and took a sharp intake of breath as some tuneless piece of gangsta rap assaulted his eardrums. He quickly changed stations and was soon singing along to Beyoncé and 'Crazy in Love'. Casey himself had never actually been in love, crazy or otherwise. He'd been on dates. He'd had plenty of sex. He'd even been known to enjoy the odd sexual encounter without the promise of cold, hard cash. But he'd never really been in love – not in the way that Beyoncé sang about, or that Billy dreamed about. Casey had never understood the appeal of Billy's dream, his big romantic fantasy that some day his prince would come – and not just with a sac full of semen, but with a heart full of love and a head full of plans for the future. It was all such an alien concept. Casey had always worked on the assumption that love was strictly for losers. People in love always seemed to have so much excess baggage, and he preferred to travel light.

But what if he was wrong? What if, all this time, he'd been missing out on something wonderful? What if his ideal man was out there right now, waiting to sweep him off his feet, shower him with tokens of his affection and prove to him that however unlikely it sounded, even a hardened hustler with an impressive porn collection and a spiralling drug habit could fall crazy in love? Stranger things had happened. A week ago, nobody would have suspected that Billy was about to embark on an affair with one of the biggest stars in Hollywood. But judging from his message, and the fact that he still wasn't answering his cell phone, Billy's romance with Matt Walsh was not only real but was really beginning to hot up. Casey could just picture the scene – Billy and Matt lounging together in the hot-tub, quietly sipping champagne, casually fondling one another in a way that suggested sex might raise its head at any moment, but nobody was expected to perform and nobody was watching the clock. For all Casey knew, they were even kissing – the one act of intimacy most hustlers were loath to throw in for free, and the final proof, if it were needed, that this was a different arrangement altogether.

Try as he might, Casey couldn't picture himself falling in love with a world-famous celebrity. Stars' egos were too big, and frankly, who'd belong to any club that would have David Furnish as a member? Dressing in floral prints and sleeping with Elton John simply wasn't an option. But the rest of the picture Casey could quite happily live with. Maybe Billy had had the right idea all along. Maybe love was the answer. Wasn't that what his favourite female vocalists had always said? Whitney with 'My Love Is Your Love', happy to be homeless on the streets and sleeping in Grand Central Station so long as her lover was sleeping by her side. Cher with 'Believe', wounded by love but still looking fabulous and determined to live and love another day. Madonna with 'Drowned World', finally tired of chasing her own fame and deciding that all the sex and all the trinkets in the world were no substitute for love. Beyoncé with 'Crazy in Love', shaking her booty over some man who clearly knew the way to a woman's heart, even an 'independent woman' like Ms Knowles.

As he headed into Silver Lake and turned into the street where Snakeman lived, Casey finally found the inspiration he'd been looking for. He wasn't willing to go homeless on the streets (certainly not the mean streets of LA!), but from now on, he would stop substituting the various substances he consumed on a weekly basis for the love that was clearly missing from his life. He would follow Cher's shining example and dare to love, with or without the benefits of extensive plastic surgery. He would find his inner Beyoncé and get his own rather impressive booty into gear. He wasn't about to fall crazy in love – not today, and certainly not with Snakeman. And he couldn't afford to quit hustling – not yet, not until he found himself a rich sugar daddy or someone offered him an alternative form of employment. But he could cut out some of the bullshit that came with the job. He could clean up his act, stop numbing himself with drugs, open himself to the possibility of love and significantly reduce the risk of either growing old alone or dying of a heart attack by the time he was forty. It wouldn't be easy, and it wouldn't solve all his problems overnight. But at the very least it would be a step in the right direction. From this moment forward, Casey resolved to start living his life the way the divas were always urging him to, and to risk feeling something for a change.

Pulling up outside Snakeman's apartment, he jumped out of the car, took a deep breath and rang the doorbell. Five minutes later his host laid out two massive lines of crystal and Casey's resolve was pronounced missing.

CHAPTER TWELVE

Simon was hunched over the desk in his hotel room, flicking through a copy of *Variety* and waiting for the phone call that would confirm when and where he would finally be introduced to the man he'd flown all this way to meet. Outside, the midday sun was blazing down and the temperature, like the film that first launched Matt Walsh on an unsuspecting public, was in the eighties. Inside, the air-conditioning was playing havoc with Simon's sinuses and the mini-bar was tormenting him in ways only a borderline alcoholic with all the guilt of a middle-class upbringing could even begin to comprehend. The desire for a drink so early in the day would have been bad enough back home in the media dens of London, where borderline alcoholism was widely accepted as something of a character quirk. Here in LA, where drinking before dinner was generally frowned upon, and drinking before lunch was seen as a sure sign of moral decay, such cravings were probably on a par with a passion for kiddie porn or coffee enemas.

Simon had already had more than his fill of coffee – administered in the traditional manner, not via a rubber tube inserted up his back passage. He was very particular about what went up his back passage. Indeed, it had often been said that his sphincter was so tight, he barely qualified as a gay man at all. Personally, Simon had never really seen the appeal of anal sex. Regardless of the way such things were presented in the fantasy world of gay porn, the reality of anal intercourse had always seemed such a painful, messy business, and the thought of laying himself open to another man's penetrating desires was about as appetising to him as being reamed out with a red-hot poker. If called upon, he could just about summon the will to insert his own penis into another man's anus, although in all honesty the act gave him very little in the way of gratification. Condoms were such a nuisance, and even with the proper application of water-based lubricant there was always the underlying anxiety about the condom splitting, or slipping off, or suddenly disintegrating through contact with some as-yet-unidentified bodily secretion. Similar hang-ups limited his enjoyment of oral sex, especially when he was the one whose oral skills were being put to the test. It didn't matter how many flavoured condoms the manufacturers came up with. Chocolate, cherry or mint, they all tasted of rubber and they all carried the same risk of making him gag before the first drop of semen was spilled. This probably explained why Simon was the only gay man in his immediate circle of friends who wasn't reputed to be out enjoying sex with a different man every night of the week, and whose sexual history was largely restricted to periods of mutual masturbation which in recent years had given way to occasional wrist-jobs which weren't so much mutual as exclusive.

Maybe one off the wrist was just what he needed now. At least it would help take his mind off the mini-bar. The thought of drinking before lunchtime did worry him a little, and would probably worry him a lot more once the effects of the alcohol wore off and the familiar feelings of remorse set in. Simon's relationship with alcohol was complicated, to say the least. Like many in his profession, he liked a drink or six to unwind after a long day's work or to get the juices flowing when a deadline loomed and the words weren't coming as thick and as fast as his schedule demanded. Like many of his persuasion, he also used alcohol to lower his inhibitions and boost his confidence on social occasions. It was a well-documented fact that rates of alcoholism within the gay community were significantly higher than they were among society in general. Indeed, Simon had even penned an article on the subject, explaining how most gay social interaction revolved around licensed premises and how many gay men nursed deep emotional scars and regularly used drink as a crutch. Of course, Simon didn't regard himself as one of the men described in the article. For one thing, he hardly ever ventured out to gay bars or clubs these days, the whole scene having gone completely mad in his opinion – all shirtless men with bulging muscles and eyes like saucers. And while most gay men seemed to drink bottled beer or alcopops, Simon had always prided himself on preferring a drop of the hard stuff. His favourite tipple was whisky and Coke, preferably Jack Daniel's, with plenty of ice.

As the call of the mini-bar rose to a level that made it increasingly difficult to ignore, Simon couldn't help but wonder if today was one of those days when, regardless of the time, he'd already earned himself a stiff drink. First thing this morning he'd been rudely awakened by the fire alarm. It rang through his skull like a power drill. When he realised it was only the phone he reached out from under the covers and knocked the receiver off the hook.

It was his editor in London, stirring him from his jet-lagged sleep to ask if the time of the Matt Walsh interview had been firmed up yet. Susie Butler was second in command on the *Sunday Globe* magazine, and had been openly vying for the top position for as long as anyone could remember. A short, flat-chested woman with a lantern jaw and a power bob, she was neither particularly pretty nor particularly popular, but survived on a combination of raw talent and ruthless ambition. Unlike many of her colleagues in the media, Susie hadn't got where she was today by attending the right college or knowing the right people. There were certain kinds of media women for whom such a steep career trajectory was almost an inevitability, but Susie wasn't one of them. As she never tired of saying, she wasn't born with a silver spoon in her mouth, or adopted by a rich media baron, or married to a publisher, or in any way given an unfair advantage in her attempts to climb the greasy media pole. Every break she'd ever had, she'd worked hard for, and considering how journalism was still a hideously middle-class profession, she was proud to have made it from where she had.

Despite Simon's middle-class background and Susie's habit of flexing her working-class roots whenever possible, she appeared to have taken quite a shine to him, possibly because he drank almost as heavily as she did, and possibly because she regarded every gay man she came across as something of a challenge – even a sexually repressed, sartorially challenged gay man like Simon. The first time the two of them met, over an extremely long lunch at the Groucho Club, Susie got exceedingly drunk and proceeded to tell Simon all about the time her fiancé dumped her for another man and how she'd been desperately trying to even up the score ever since. In fact, she said, she was quite possibly the only woman in Britain who would admit to a strong case of 'gay penis envy'. All this with one hand reaching out across the table and clutching his arm in a vice-like grip. Simon smiled weakly and let out a laugh that was a cry for help if ever there was one.

It was Susie who'd secured the interview with Matt Walsh,

and having built her reputation on her ability to inject a bit of A-list Hollywood glamour into the magazine whenever such things were called for, she wasn't about to take her eye off the ball and risk some hack ruining her chances of impressing her publisher and quite possibly landing that promotion – even when the hack concerned happened to be a personal favourite of hers. So when Susie phoned, she didn't waste valuable time asking Simon how the flight went, or what the hotel was like. She didn't concern herself with small talk. Instead, she got straight to the point. There was a lot riding on this interview, and while she had every faith in Simon's abilities, clearly it was in everyone's best interests to ensure that things ran as smoothly as possible. No pressure, of course, but she expected to be kept informed of any developments. Arrangements for the photo shoot would all be handled from London, but she wanted to know as soon as possible when and where the interview was taking place, and when she could expect Simon to file his copy. The deadline could always be extended by a few days if necessary, but that would be cutting things pretty fine in terms of the production schedule and, well, he knew how complicated these things could get.

He did indeed. So far Simon had left a total of four messages for Lee Carson and not one of his calls had been returned. The last time he called, some underling rejoicing in the name of Chad had informed him that Ms Carson was rather tied up at present and that she would call him back just as soon as possible. That was almost three hours ago, and still there was no response from the elusive Ms Carson. What did that woman actually do all day? She only had one client on her books after all, and it seemed pretty unlikely that Matt Walsh would be so difficult as to demand her full undivided attention every minute of every working day.

Surely even A-list celebrities were capable of entertaining themselves every once in a while, if only to give their managers and agents enough free time to manage their affairs and return their phone calls. Or maybe the rumours were true, and Walsh really was incapable of wiping his own backside without Lee Carson there to hold his hand. Maybe that would explain why Chad sounded so stressed.

Simon dreaded to think what it must be like working for a woman like Lee Carson. Hell probably, with a large helping of purgatory thrown in for good measure. Chad was evidently new to the job, and judging by his deflated tones on the phone, his days were probably numbered. Doubtless the poor kid was already heavily conditioned into the Hollywood way of thinking, and regarded the everyday megalomania of people like Lee Carson as perfectly reasonable behaviour under the circumstances. When the day of reckoning came, he would see his dismissal as a measure of his own failure, and quite possibly the worst fate that could have befallen him. But really it would be a blessing in disguise. Far better for him to get out now while he was still young enough to make a new start in life, and while he still had a soul. The alternative was too awful to even contemplate. The best years of his life spent in total servitude to some heartless Hollywood monster, his spirit slowly crushed by the daily grind of the machine. It gave Simon the shivers just thinking about it.

No sooner had the shivers started than Simon knew the battle for his own soul was well and truly lost. There was only one way to rid himself of the temptation that lay before him, and that was to yield to it. It was time for a drink. Rising from the desk, he stood and turned to face the mini-bar. And that was when he spotted it. A plain white envelope, tucked under his door. He picked it up and tore it open. Inside was a brief note, written in the style of a ransom letter, with large red and black letters cut from the pages of a magazine and pasted together. It reminded Simon of Jamie Reid's infamous artwork for the Sex Pistols' record *Never Mind the Bollocks*, except that the wording was a little longer and, given the nature of the subject matter, a shade more daring. *Matt Walsh Is A Closet Case*, the note read. *He's Screwing A Hustler Named Billy West. Ask Him Yourself If You Don't Believe Me.*

Simon grabbed the door handle and poked his head out of the door. The hallway was empty. The only sound was of a distant vacuum cleaner sucking up the dust created by someone staying in a room further down the hall. There were no sounds of retreating footsteps, no far-off echoes of someone fleeing the scene. For all Simon knew, the note could have been left hours ago. Whoever was responsible for delivering it, the chances were they'd made like Elvis and left the building by now. And whoever was responsible for writing it, something told him they were either a Hollywood insider, or someone with a wicked sense of humour. Looking at the note again, Simon suddenly realised why the typeface looked so familiar. The letters had each been cut from a copy of *Variety*.

Lee took several deep breaths and told herself to remain calm. It wasn't the end of the world. In the worst-case scenario, what she was faced with right now was the imminent destruction of everything she'd ever worked for. But so what? Maybe tomorrow the long-awaited big earthquake would finally strike and all her problems would vanish under a pile of rubble. It would be like the end of *Short Cuts*, where the rock fall hides the evidence of Chris Penn's heinous crime and nobody realises that he actually killed that poor girl. If only real life could be more like the movies. Only it wasn't, and it would take more than a natural disaster to sort this mess out. Lee wasn't sure what the present situation rated on the Richter scale, but by any estimation, things certainly weren't looking good.

The empty package sat in the wastepaper basket, its contents spread out across her desk. There was no covering letter, no mention of blackmail, no demand for a small fortune in used hundred-dollar bills, bundled into a sports bag and left at a phone booth. Just the photos. Or to be more precise, a series of glossy ten-by-eight prints, twenty in all, each featuring the same two people in a variety of different poses and settings, none of which looked entirely innocent or could easily be explained away. It was every tabloid editor's wet dream, and Lee's worst nightmare, there in glorious colour for all to see – a series of incriminating photos of Matt Walsh and some blond boy, and clear evidence that the man grinning from the cover of this month's *Vanity Fair* wasn't quite the hot-blooded heterosexual he claimed to be. Any fool could see that the people pictured in those photographs were in a relationship that involved a certain degree of physical intimacy. It didn't matter which way you looked at it. Nobody would ever have mistaken these guys for a couple of frat brothers.

So Lee's instincts had been right all along. Matt had been seeing someone. And not just seeing someone, but seeing them frequently enough and indiscreetly enough to actually run the risk of being seen with them. The photographs said it all. The boy entering Matt's mansion in Beverly Hills. The same boy leaving the next morning. Matt and the boy happily flipping steaks by the pool, Matt dressed in a bathrobe, the boy wearing nothing but a Speedo and a grin. The pair of them frolicking like puppies in the pool and relaxing in the hot-tub. A shot of them driving together in what must have been the boy's car. Matt hopping out of the car to buy a bunch of magazines from the news-stand at Laurel Canyon. Then the two of them walking together in what looked suspiciously like a public park. A close-up of Matt with the boy's head in his lap, stroking his hair. Judging by the evidence of the photographs, this boy wasn't just some passing piece of trade. He was someone Matt had actually grown attached to. Why else would there be a shot of them eating ice-cream together? People didn't eat ice-cream with someone they had just casually fucked and didn't plan on ever seeing again. And since when did Matt develop a taste for ice-cream? Just wait till his nutritionist got to hear about this!

In fact, fuck his nutritionist! What the hell was she thinking? If these photos got out there would be no further need for a nutritionist. Just as there would be no need for a personal trainer, or a chef, or a bodyguard, or a driver, or any of the people normally called upon to attend to the needs of a man in Matt's position. They'd all be out of work the moment the story broke. And she could give up any hope of talking Matt round and getting his career back on track. If this got out there'd be no career left. And if you'd blown it once, that was it. Few actors got a second shot at Hollywood stardom. The best he could hope for would be a fitness video, or a daytime soap, or the ritual humiliation suffered by those forced to work the theatre circuit. Then, if he was really lucky, in a few years' time his movies would be rediscovered by a new generation, and he would find work as one of those kitsch icons consigned to brief cameos where they parodied themselves in the vain hope that someone somewhere would take pity on them and pay for their retirement. It would all be over. Matt's glittering career, her fabulous lifestyle – all down the pan because of some pretty blond boy and a bunch of sleazy photos.

It was ironic, really. In fact, if the situation weren't so deadly serious, Lee would probably have found it fairly amusing. Only a few hours ago she was considering hiring someone to spy on Matt, actually paying someone to keep close tabs on her golden boy and report back to her as soon as they witnessed anything untoward. And now all of a sudden it turned out that someone else had already gone ahead and done the job for her. And not only had they spied on him. They'd even gone to the trouble of providing her with proof of their findings. All without her having to run the risk of jeopardising her relationship with her client, pay a hefty sum upfront or lift so much as a finger. It was almost touching.

Except of course it wasn't. She may have been in a mild state of shock, but Lee hadn't completely lost her marbles. People in this town rarely did anything purely out of the goodness of their heart, and she wasn't so naive as to assume that any of this had been done as a personal favour to her. The person who took these photos clearly had an agenda of their own, and it didn't take a genius to work out what that agenda might be. There was no mention of payment – yet. But that didn't rule out the possibility of blackmail. If the person responsible for taking these photos was simply interested in selling them to the tabloids, why send copies to her? And if one of the papers had already gotten hold of these pictures, she could be certain she'd have heard about it by now. They'd have been straight on the phone, angling for an exclusive interview to accompany the photographs, the interview they'd all been after for years, the one where Matt Walsh finally opened up and told the world that he was gay. The one where he came clean about all those years in the closet and shared the sordid secrets of his love life – the pool parties, the bus-boys, the midnight romps in the hot-tub, the flings, slings and sexual kinks of Hollywood's former action hero. All presented in the most sympathetic light possible, of course.

No, there had to be more to it than this. Someone was toying with her, and if there was one thing Lee couldn't stand, it was being toyed with. She'd had enough of that with Matt, not knowing where exactly he was coming from or what was going on. Now the truth was staring her in the face, it was high time she took charge of the situation. Maybe it was too late to stop the photos getting out. Maybe the best she could hope for now would be a damage limitation exercise. But what choice did she have? What else was she expected to do? Sit back and wait for the blackmailer to make his next move? Curl herself up into a little ball, crawl under her desk and wait for her world to come crashing down around her? Pray for a miracle? Lee hadn't been down on her knees in years, and she was damned if she was about to start crawling now.

She stared at the photos again. The boy was cute, she'd give Matt that. He'd had some pretty boys in his time, many of whom she'd personally vetted from an eager line-up of obedient office juniors and compliant mailroom boys. But this one – this one was something special. For one thing, he was clearly a natural blond, not one of those bleached wannabes Matt sometimes went for. Bleached blonds were a dime a dozen in LA, and while Lee was hardly an advert for the triumph of natural beauty over more inventive measures, that didn't prevent her from appreciating such qualities in others. No, the kid was certainly a looker, there was no denying that. In fact, he wouldn't have looked at all out of place in the latest catalogue from Abercrombie & Fitch. It was just a pity he wasn't posed alone in some catalogue modelling underwear, rather than cavorting with her client in a bunch of photos that could soon wind up on the front pages of the tabloids.

Maybe she was over-reacting. Maybe the photos weren't so incriminating after all. All they really showed was two men enjoying each other's company. There was no kissing, no nudity, no actual sex. Just two good-looking men in various stages of undress, demonstrating their affection for one another with a bit of horseplay and the odd hug. There were more incriminating shots in an Abercrombie & Fitch catalogue, and if the company who dressed half the gay men in LA could argue that their photos of buffed young men tugging at one another's boxers or sharing a shower weren't intended to be homoerotic, why shouldn't the same rules apply to these pictures? Or she could always claim that the photos had been faked, or manipulated in some way. Photos were manipulated all the time these days. All it took was a computer and some basic software. Any geek could do it. It was even possible to download photos of your favourite celebrity stark bollock naked from the internet. Most people knew that wasn't really Brad's dick they were looking at, or Britney's tits they were jerking off over. So who was to say these photos weren't created in a similar fashion, that they weren't quite what they purported to be?

There was always the boy, of course. Would he talk? Could he be bought off, or persuaded to disappear? Was he so head over heels in love with Matt that he would do anything to protect him? Or was he just another gold-digging starfucker? Would he take the money and run, or would he refuse to go quietly? Would he wait around for the media circus and grab his fifteen minutes of fame while he had the chance? He looked sweet enough in the photos, but who knew what was going on behind those blue eyes and that white smile? For all she knew, he could be the one who sent the photographs. He could have set Matt up from the start, luring him into a torrid love affair, encouraging him to take risks he would never normally take, knowing all the while that each time they were together there was a camera pointed at them. Staring down at the photos, it suddenly struck Lee that, laid out like that, they looked like the storyboard for a movie. And if she didn't act fast, this was one movie that wouldn't have a Hollywood ending.

She buzzed Chad and summoned him to her office. He was there in an instant, his face flushed, his eyes immediately darting to the photos spread across her desk, then darting away again before finally settling on the patch of floor just in front of his feet.

'Chad, I take it you've seen these photographs?'

'Yes, Ms Carson.'

'And you know who the man in the photographs is?'

'The blond guy, no. I've never seen—'

'Not the blond guy, Chad. The other man. You know who that is?'

'Yes, Ms Carson.'

'Then I'm sure you'll appreciate just how damaging these photographs could be.'

'Yes, Ms Carson.'

'And I'm also sure you'll appreciate the enormous opportunity I've given you here, not to mention the fact that I am in a position to help you further in the future.'

'Yes, Ms Carson.'

'So I take it I can rely on you not to breathe a word about these photos to anyone?'

'No, Ms Carson. I mean, yes, Ms Carson. I swear I won't tell a soul.'

'Thank you, Chad. That will be all.'

Clearly relieved to have escaped this lightly, Chad was gone in a shot. As soon as the door closed behind him, Lee reached for the phone and speed-dialled the number for Matt's cell. He answered on the third ring, his tone annoyingly jovial. 'Hey, Lee. What's up?'

'What's up?' she repeated coldly. 'What's up, Matt, is that we have a situation on our hands. A very serious situation. So whatever you're doing, drop it. I'll meet you at your place in an hour.'

CHAPTER THIRTEEN

Simon was still staring at the note and clutching a large whisky and Coke when the phone rang. It was Chad, calling from Lee Carson's office to confirm that his interview with Matt Walsh would take place tomorrow, at the Fox studio lot.

'The precise time of the interview hasn't been firmed up yet,' Chad explained. 'But I can let you have the full details later this afternoon.'

Simon thanked him and hung up.

This was turning into quite a day. First the note, and now this. An hour ago he was no closer to knowing when, where or even if he was going to get his promised interview with Matt Walsh. Now here he was receiving anonymous tip-offs about the man's private life and suddenly the publicity machine was grinding into action. What next? A surprise visit from a mysterious blonde in a trenchcoat? A strange phone call warning him not to get mixed up in Walsh's affairs? A shadowy figure lurking in the hotel lobby? A speeding car? A smoking gun?

Simon took a sip of whisky and tried not to let his imagination run away with him. He might be in the right place, with the right drink in his hand, but this wasn't a scene from *LA Confidential* and he was hardly cut out for the role of hard-bitten detective in a James Ellroy novel. Like many people who made their living interviewing famous celebrities, Simon had played many parts in his time – sympathetic listener, amateur psychologist, best friend, provocateur and hangman. But never once had he been asked to take the role of detective. He left that to the boys in the newsroom, keen to make their mark by exposing some hideous crime or government cover-up. If there was a character in a movie he could identify with, it was probably John Travolta in *Perfect*, where he played a *Rolling Stone* reporter wrestling with his conscience as he falls in love with Jamie Lee Curtis. Simon wrestled with his conscience on a fairly regular basis. And as for Jamie Lee Curtis, if he was to fall in love with a woman, it would probably be a woman with her many masculine qualities.

But never mind all that. The important thing was that his interview with Matt Walsh had been confirmed. Prior to Chad's phone call, Simon was beginning to wonder if Lee Carson was having second thoughts about letting him near her precious Matt, or if this was going to be one of those occasions where he was given the runaround for days, or possibly even weeks, before the person who'd previously agreed to be interviewed finally consented to sit down and tell him how wonderful their new film was. That was the trouble with world-famous celebrities. They lived in such a cocoon of praise, surrounded by so many sycophants, they were often inclined to develop a vastly overinflated sense of their own importance. They behaved as though the whole world revolved around them, and everyone else was at their beck and call, whether they happened to be on the payroll or not. What was it Gore Vidal once said? 'Stars are small people with big heads.' He got that right. The sad part was that these days it didn't seem to matter how big their heads got. There was always someone willing to smooth their ego and pander to their every whim. A thirty-foot trailer with its own hot-tub?

Certainly. A helicopter to and from the set? Why of course. A bowl of jellybeans with all the green ones taken out? No trouble at all.

That said, Matt Walsh wasn't known for throwing his weight around or making unreasonable demands just to remind people how important he was. He didn't act like a diva. Some would argue that he didn't really act at all, but that was beside the point. The point was, Matt Walsh did not have a reputation for being a prima donna. On the contrary, he went out of his way to charm everyone he met, journalists included. The current batch of interviews said it all. Simon had been through each one with a highlighter pen and a note-book, and they all told a similar story. Matt Walsh was good company, fun to be with, a megastar with his feet firmly on the ground, an all-round nice guy. Not quite as clean cut as Tom Cruise, and without the cloying cuteness of Tom Hanks, he still managed to come across as decent, down-to-earth and immensely likeable.

That was his public image, the face he presented to the world, the persona he used to seduce audiences and charm journalists and generally float through life winning friends and influencing people. But what was Matt Walsh really like? What went on in private? Was he really as easy-going as he made out? If so, he'd be the first major star Simon had ever met who didn't have an ego to match the scale of his achievements. It took certain qualities to get where Matt Walsh was today, and humility wasn't one of them. The entertainment industry was a tough business, and only the strongest of the species survived. Many famous people came from disadvantaged backgrounds, and had to fight tooth and claw to ensure that opportunity didn't pass them by. Many came from broken homes, and were still desperately searching for the love they were denied as children. Some were naturally gifted individuals just waiting to be discovered. Some possessed very little in the way of raw talent, and were largely driven by resentment and the grim determination to succeed where others had failed. And if they weren't screwed up in some way before they were famous, they were usually screwed up pretty badly afterwards. Fame was a tough thing to handle, as generations of drug-addled pop stars and alcoholic actors demonstrated only too well. As George Michael once said in an interview, it wasn't something extra that made a star, it was something missing.

There was certainly something missing where Matt Walsh was concerned, and it wasn't just the familiar story about his parents' divorce and his difficult upbringing. What was missing was anything resembling a personal life. He'd been linked to various women over the years, but never for very long and never with enough romantic conviction to silence the rumours. And in this day and age, when stars were constantly inviting readers into their lovely homes and auctioning off their wedding photos to the highest bidder, that surely begged a few questions. Was Walsh secretly dating the kind of strong, independent woman who wanted no part of the fame game and refused to be put in the spotlight, however beneficial it might be to her boyfriend's career? Was he emotionally crippled by his own fame and unable to form lasting relationships with anyone but his adoring audience? Or was he leading a double life, saying one thing in public and doing another in private, possibly with a hustler he paid to keep his mouth shut?

Simon had always known that Walsh would be a tough nut to crack. And if he was to stand any hope of chipping through that Teflon-coated exterior and finding answers to these questions, he would have to tread extremely carefully. There was no point walking in there tomorrow, waving the note around and accusing Walsh of things he would flatly deny before terminating the interview as soon as it had begun. It was a job that required timing, tact and a certain amount of cunning, one that would test all his skills as an interviewer. Luckily Simon had a wide range of tricks up his sleeve, a vast arsenal of weapons he'd accumulated over the years and tested on some of the toughest nuts around. He would ease Walsh into the interview with some innocuous questions about his new movie and his role as Hollywood's hottest action hero. He would compliment him on his performance and flatter him into thinking that, somehow, he actually rated him as an actor. He would build a rapport and establish a ground level of honesty from which Walsh would find it increasingly difficult to deviate without somehow giving himself away. He would ask a clever question, quoting something from an interview Walsh gave years ago and asking him if he still felt the same way now. This was an old trick of Simon's, a tactic he employed to let an interviewee know he'd done his homework and wasn't going to be fobbed off with the same old quotes they trotted out time after time.

Then he would ask him about his childhood. In Simon's experience, most stars would talk quite freely about their childhood. However traumatic it might have been at the time, they tended to see it as a safe topic, something way back in the past, safely removed from the life they were living now. In reality, a person's childhood was usually a pretty clear indicator of who they would become as an adult. And once the subject of someone's childhood had been broached and picked over, it was often far easier to bring them back to the present with a greater inclination towards open and honest discussion of the things that really mattered to them.

Simon would ask all these questions, and listen intently to whatever answers Walsh gave, all in the hope that gradually he would lower his defences and lay himself open. Because the truth was that only two questions concerned Simon now. Was there any truth in the allegations made in the note he held in his hand? And who the hell was Billy West?

Lee couldn't believe her ears. 'A hustler? You are joking! What did you do – pick him up on Santa Monica Boulevard?'

Matt glowered. 'Of course not. I stumbled across his website and we arranged to meet at a hotel.'

Lee laughed. 'Oh well, that's okay then! Problem solved! You realise, of course, that he's probably on the payroll at one of the tabs.'

She watched as the colour drained from Matt's face. Soon he was as white as the room they were standing in. Matt's Spanish-style mansion had been designed in 1926 by Wallace Neff, purveyor of palaces to the original Hollywood aristocracy. Like many of his contemporaries, who were often said to lack the colourful qualities of those great names of old, Matt's idea of a movie-star lifestyle was bland bordering on the ascetic. White walls met white marble floors. White drapes framed the windows. And in the centre of the room, two enormous white couches seemed to offer little in the way of comfort, but provided a convenient backdrop for a scattering of cushions in daring shades of cream.

'But he can't be,' Matt spluttered. 'He's not like that.'

'Really?' Lee said, dripping with sarcasm. 'So tell me, what exactly is he like? Forgive me for questioning your taste in men, but I think it's best we establish a few facts now, before your personal life is splashed all over the papers.'

Matt turned an even whiter shade of pale. 'He's just a kid,' he said, gesticulating wildly. 'He's not some cheap hustler. He wouldn't do anything to hurt me. I'm sure of it.'

He walked over to an enormous white couch and rested one hand on it for support. Lee looked around the room, wondering why anyone would settle for so much white furniture when there were so many perfectly serviceable neutral shades available.

'No good will come of this,' she foamed prophetically. 'I wish I shared your confidence, but from where I'm standing, this doesn't look good. This doesn't look good at all.'

Matt didn't respond. He simply stood with his back to her, his hand gripping the couch, his head hung.

'So where is he?' Lee asked finally. 'Is he here?'

Matt turned to face her. 'What?'

'Is he here now? Upstairs maybe? Or hiding out in the pool house?'

'No. He's gone to run some errands.'

'How do you know he hasn't gone to the papers? How do you know he isn't busy plotting with whoever took these photos?'

'I just know,' Matt said, none too convincingly.

'So how long has this been going on?'

'I don't know. Not long. Maybe the best part of a week.'

Lee eyed him suspiciously. 'Well you've certainly packed an awful lot of loving into a very short time. Judging from these photos, I'd say you were a lot more involved than that. And when exactly were you planning on telling me?'

'Christ, Lee! Spare me the injured woman routine. You're not my wife.'

Lee glared at him. 'No, I'm not. I'm someone far more important. I'm your manager. And if you want me to do my job effectively and sort this mess out for you, I suggest you quit stalling and start talking.'

Matt looked at her despairingly. 'What else could you possibly need to know?'

'Everything. I need to know everything there is to know about him. Where he lives. How I get in touch with him. Who his friends are. Everything.'

'And what if I was to say I didn't want you interfering in my private affairs?'

Lee bristled slightly but remained cool. 'The bottom line here is that your private affairs aren't going to remain private for very long if we don't do something about this situation, and fast. I can't help you if you're not prepared to help me. You have to work with me on this one, Matt. Do you have any idea how serious this is? Do you know what would happen if this got out? We're talking total career meltdown. They'll pick you clean and then go to work on the bones. Never mind all that art-house crap you've been spouting lately. You'll be lucky if you ever make another movie again. You'll be all washed up, dead in the water, yesterday's news. No one will want to touch you. No one.'

Matt collapsed on to the couch and buried his head in his hands. Finally he looked up at her. 'Okay,' he said. 'You win. So tell me, what should I do?'

Lee smiled triumphantly. 'Don't do anything. Just tell me everything I need to know. Then carry on as normal. You have a couple of interviews lined up for tomorrow. I know it's the weekend, but I thought it best we bring them forward and get them out of the way, before word gets out about these photos. Do the interviews. Turn on the charm. And for God's sake, stay away from that boy. The rest you can leave to me. I'm your manager. It's up to me to manage the situation.'

Ted Chalmers liked to leave the office a little early on a Friday afternoon – partly to beat the traffic, and partly to ensure that he arrived home in time for his favourite reality TV shows.

The shows changed on a regular basis. One week it would be *Extreme Makeover*, the next it would be *Fear Factor*, *Survivor* or even *The Swan*. Like a lot of people whose real lives weren't nearly as rewarding as they might have liked them to be, Ted watched an awful lot of reality TV. He could name the winners of every show of the past five years. But what really interested him was the losers. Like a lot of reality TV fans, part of the pleasure he gained in watching was a sense of superiority to the emotional casualties whose paltry ambitions were laid bare by the cameras and whose weight problems, self-esteem issues and other insecurities were paraded across the screen for the benefit of the millions of couch potatoes watching at home. Each show boasted its own odious new category of female victimisation, from Women Who Don't Know They're About To Be Dumped to Women Who Just Aren't Pretty Enough. There was even a show for Women Who Need A Gay Man To Teach Them How To Dress. And like the good little misogynist he was, Ted lapped them all up with just the right balance of guilty pleasure and cynical detachment.

If he succeeded in beating the traffic, Ted found he could make it home in less than an hour. Nothing could equal the sense of freedom as he cruised through the San Fernando Valley in top gear, past the mountains, through Bel Air and all the way to Santa Monica, where he lived, alone, in an overpriced apartment he could barely afford to keep up the repayments on, never mind furnish in what would be considered an appropriate fashion for an area so rich in entertainment industry titans. With his limited finances, the best Ted could manage was a trip to the Ikea in Burbank, where he blew most of his budget on a king-sized bed strong enough to support his considerable weight and large enough to accommodate a second person, should the need ever arise.

To date, the only person to have made bodily contact with the bed was Ted. Although he regularly enjoyed the company of male hustlers, he was far too security conscious to ever risk inviting them over to his place, where for all he knew they might end up conveniently losing the keys to the handcuffs and making off with the one possession he prized above all others – his car.

Today, as he climbed into the leather-lined, air-conditioned interior of his Chrysler convertible, Ted had a feeling that the drive home wouldn't be nearly as much fun as usual. The inside of his car was where Ted did most of his thinking, and this particular Friday afternoon he had an awful lot to think about. He hadn't been able to get this morning's meeting with Michael Rosetti out of his mind. All day it had been nagging away at him, flaring up at regular intervals like a particularly irritating pimple, or one of those Park Avenue princesses who'd never done an honest day's work in their lives and who occasionally popped up on *American Wifeswap*, where they traded places with some drudge from New Jersey and bitched the whole time while, back home, the drudge was enjoying the rewards of being temporarily wedded to an investment banker and was out getting a facial.

Ted didn't know Michael all that well. They'd only been introduced a couple of months ago, at one of those black-tie, red-ribbon, hundred-dollars-a-plate AIDS charity dinners regularly held in downtown LA in a spirit of solemn self-congratulation. It was during one of the many after-dinner speeches, with its references to 'angels', 'heroes' and the need to 'recognise the best within our community', that Ted and Michael discovered they had something in common – namely a large helping of internalised homophobia which they sought to externalise by pouring scorn on the charitable efforts of others. By the end of the evening their bond was sealed, each recognising in the other a little of himself, and neither having the courage to face up to the fact that, truly, theirs was an unhappy meeting of minds.

Today, Ted was more inclined to question the wisdom of the choices he had made that night. Ted liked to think of himself as a pretty good judge of character. And after this morning's performance, it was clear that Michael's character gave plenty of cause for concern. First there was that martyr complex of his. If he wasn't banging on about Lee Carson and the various injustices inflicted on him during his short term of employment, he was bitching about his mother and how much better his life would be if she would only loan him the money for the cosmetic procedures he had his heart so set on. Michael seemed to think that the moment he got his face fixed, all his problems would disappear. Clearly he shared Ted's passion for *The Swan*, only unlike Ted, Michael had been successfully brainwashed into thinking that plastic surgery really was the key to eternal happiness. 'It's only a scalpel, Michael,' Ted had told him. 'It's not a magic wand.' If Michael was wounded by the suggestion, he didn't let it show. Instead he treated Ted to a detailed account of the various procedures he'd been busy researching, together with the names of the best surgeons and the celebrities they were rumoured to have worked on.

Then there was the matter of that script of his. Michael had shown Ted the script in the hope that he might be able to pull some strings and bring it to the attention of someone in the story department. But was there more to it than that? Any fool could see that the script in its present form was virtually unfilmable, and whatever else Ted thought about him, it was clear that Michael Rosetti was no fool. As for the script, it was hackneyed, derivative, full of plot holes and populated by an entire cast of badly drawn characters, none of whom was even remotely likeable. All of which would be fine in today's Hollywood, where fresh ideas didn't count for much, story-lines were often sacrificed in favour of special effects, and walking clichés were widely regarded as a convenient short-hand for proper characterisation. If bad writing was a problem, half the movies in Hollywood would never get made.

No, the problem with Michael's script wasn't so much the quality of the writing. The real problem was that it was one long lawsuit from start to finish. Entitled *Starfucker*, it told the story of a movie star not unlike Matt Walsh who gets involved with a male hustler. Beautiful, blond and clearly doomed from the word go, the hustler starts off all Julia Roberts in *Pretty Woman* until the movie star tries to end the affair, at which point he suddenly stops being so sweet and innocent and turns into Glenn Close in *Fatal Attraction*. Realising that he's at the mercy of a bunny-boiler who could easily blow the lid on his career, the movie star calls on his manager, a woman not a million miles away from Lee Carson, who hatches a plan to do away with the hustler and make it look like suicide. The movie ends with the hustler following in the footsteps of all those disappointed young starlets who leapt to their death from the top of the Hollywood sign. As his car comes crashing through the sign, we cut to the movie star and his manager posing for the paparazzi at the premiere of his latest movie. Fade out and end credits.

Ted had read some cheesy scripts in his time, but never one quite like this. Clearly, it was the work of someone with a pretty big axe to grind, and very little interest in the finer points of script writing or the small details that made a story ring true. For one thing, it would be extremely difficult for a car to come crashing through the Hollywood sign, for the simple reason that the original wooden letters had rotted away many years ago and had been replaced with a reproduction sign made of toughened steel and weather-resistant concrete. As anyone with even a passing interest in local history could easily confirm, the sign originally read 'Hollywoodland' and was used to advertise the Hollywoodland Realty Company, until a mud slide washed away the 'land' part and the remaining letters were left to rot for the next forty years. By then, the sign had become such a part of the Hollywood landscape, as iconic in its way as the Bates motel or the *Hello, Dolly* set, it seemed only fitting that when the authorities threatened to pull it down, a 'Save Our Sign' committee was formed and the good people of Hollywood dug deep into their pockets and paid for a reproduction sign to be erected on the exact same spot. Result – a new sign built to last, but without the potential for dramatic scenes involving smashing cars and splintering wood, however poetic they might appear on paper.

What was more, it seemed highly unlikely that a man in Matt Walsh's position would be so stupid as to get emotionally involved with a hustler. Sure, Walsh had probably fucked a few hustlers in his time. What closeted gay movie star hadn't? Ted had met enough hustlers to know that men with their particular talents were extremely popular in Hollywood. In fact, no party was complete without a couple of hookers thrown in for good measure, if only to ensure that the appropriate egos were smoothed and nobody was reduced to sleeping with the pool boy or flashing their credentials at the Will Rogers Park. Hustlers were easy to get hold of, and just as easy to dispose of afterwards. That was the whole point of using them. But to actually get involved with someone who sold his ass for a living, and risk people finding out about it? That didn't sound like the Matt Walsh Ted knew. Not that they had ever been formally introduced. But Hollywood was a small town, and if there was one thing everyone was agreed on, it was that Matt Walsh hadn't got where he was today by taking unnecessary risks. Walsh wasn't just a movie star. He was a brand. His life was like a tightly programmed machine. There was no room for error, or for the kind of extracurricular activities that could quite easily damage the brand or short-circuit the entire system. Passionate affairs with male hustlers were not part of the programme. They did not compute.

Michael had tried to persuade Ted that the hustler in his script was more than just a ghost in the machine or a figment of his fevered imagination, that he was every bit as real as Matt Walsh, and a thousand times more real than Lee Carson. But if all that was true, and the entire script was based on the lives and actions of real people, what was the point of writing it? Michael knew, surely, that it would never get made, not when Walsh and Carson were so easily identifiable and certain to sue. So why go to the trouble of writing a script no studio would be willing to touch? It didn't make any sense. Was it some elaborate game of double bluff Michael was playing, daring Ted to take the script seriously, only to turn around at some later date and reveal that it was just a joke? Or was there some other method in his madness? Was he trying to tell Ted something? And if so, why not just come out and say it? He wasn't suggesting, surely, that Matt Walsh was really being blackmailed by a hustler, or that Lee Carson was capable of murder?

Ted turned the air-con all the way up to eleven, and drove home in a cold sweat. Thankfully, he'd had the foresight to take a copy of Michael's script. As soon as he got home he'd have another look and see if there wasn't something he'd missed.

CHAPTER FOURTEEN

Saturday morning found Casey back at the gym. Still wired from his night of heavy sex and serious substance abuse with Snakeman, and against the strict instructions of his surgeon, he'd decided to test his mettle by slipping into something slutty and attempting some gentle exercise. He arrived at Crunch shortly after eleven, dressed in low-rider jeans and a torn, sleeveless Christina Aguilera tour T-shirt several sizes too small. His search for a meaningful relationship would have to wait. Today Casey was feeling 'dirrrty'.

Of course he wasn't completely stupid. As a concession to his doctor, he'd decided to throw his usual routine out of the window and avoid attempting anything even remotely resembling a stomach crunch. At this rate the washboard abs he'd worked so hard to achieve would soon disappear under a layer of fat, but that was just a risk he was going to have to take. Imagine how much worse it would be if he'd followed his doctor's advice to the letter, stayed at home and spent last night pigging out on pizza. At least by driving over to see Snakeman he'd managed to burn off a few calories. Snakeman's sexual demands were so intense, Casey was certain to have dropped a few pounds through all that fucking. He'd also skipped dinner and breakfast, which were either the best or the worst meals to miss, depending on which revolutionary new eating plan you happened to be following. And with so much crystal still in his system, there was the distinct possibility that he wouldn't develop much of an appetite until tomorrow. So, it wasn't all bad news.

He was halfway through his workout, poised to do some bicep curls, when who should appear but the gym's resident gossip queens Bruce and Donald. Donald hadn't changed much. He was still as boss-eyed as ever, one eye zooming in on Casey's crotch while the other worked the room. Bruce, on the other hand, appeared to have splashed out on some laser resurfacing and was boasting a far smoother complexion than usual. Casey had no idea what a treatment like that actually cost, but whatever it was he reckoned it was worth every cent. From this distance, there was barely a pockmark to be seen.

As soon as he spotted Casey, Bruce whispered something to Donald and they began to make their way over, pausing briefly to get the low-down on a party held the previous night at a house in the Hills, and already rumoured to be the biggest gathering of A-grade gay beefcake anyone had ever seen. Their thirst for gossip temporarily quenched, they approached Casey with a spring in their step and sly smiles plastered across their faces.

'Hey, Casey,' said Donald. 'How are you doing?'

Casey nodded. 'Fine. I'm doing fine.'

'Only we heard you were stabbed,' Bruce piped up. 'Shouldn't you be in the hospital?'

Casey flinched. 'Good news sure travels fast around here. Honestly, guys, I'm fine. Really. It was nothing.'

His confidence clearly boosted by his recent skin treatment, Bruce refused to back off. 'It didn't sound like nothing,' he said, blatantly ignoring Casey's attempts to draw a line under the subject. 'From what I heard you were left bleeding to death on the sidewalk. If it hadn't been for some queen rushing you to the emergency room, you wouldn't be here now, having this conversation.'

Casey rolled his eyes. 'Yeah, and wouldn't that be a tragedy?' He stood up from the bench press and walked over to the water cooler. Bruce and Donald followed in hot pursuit.

'We haven't seen Billy in a while,' Bruce said meaningfully.

'Really,' Casey replied.

'It must be five days at least,' Donald chipped in. 'His routine will be really off.'

'I guess it will be,' said Casey, and suddenly realised he'd lost all track of time. Was it really five days? How the time flew by when you were busy getting stabbed and snorting crystal.

'Still, from what I hear he's getting plenty of exercise,' Donald went on. 'If you catch my drift.'

'I'm not sure that I do, Donald.'

'With Action Man,' Donald said. 'I can just picture them now – up to all kinds of manoeuvres.'

'So, is it true?' Bruce asked.

Casey frowned. 'Is what true?'

'Is it true that Billy's screwing Matt Walsh? Only I never had Billy down as a starfucker.' Bruce's lips formed a nasty little smile. Close up, Casey was pleased to see that his skin wasn't quite as smooth as it had first appeared. There were still some pockmarks below the cheekbones and some scarring around the eyes.

'I don't know what you're talking about,' Casey said casually. 'You shouldn't believe every piece of gossip you hear. Besides, everyone knows Matt Walsh is straight.'

Bruce laughed. 'Yeah, right. And I'm Pamela Anderson.'

Casey stared at him. 'No you're not,' he said sweetly. 'I'm sorry to be the one to break this to you, Bruce, but your

183

breasts aren't quite that perky. But never mind, there's a bench press free over there. Go and see if you can't pump them up a little more.'

And with that, Casey decided to call it a day. It was better that way, before he popped his stitches and things got really unpleasant. Before Bruce had time to come back with even a half-witty reply, he'd turned and headed for the changing rooms.

'Don't forget to say hi to Billy for us when you see him,' Bruce shouted after him. 'Or should I say, if you see him.'

There was a vicious tone to his voice that struck a nerve. Casey tried to ignore it, but as he entered the changing rooms and began to undress he found the words were still echoing inside his head. *If you see him.* The truth was, he hadn't seen Billy since Tuesday morning, which was the day he'd turned up to announce that he'd spent the night with Matt Walsh. And now that Casey actually thought about it, they hadn't even spoken on the phone. Casey had left several messages, and aside from that one message left on his answering machine at home, Billy had made no attempt to call him back. That wasn't like him. That wasn't like him at all. Even if he was busy, Billy knew better than to let Casey worry unnecessarily. And surely he'd be equally concerned himself by now? They were supposed to be friends after all. And that was what friends did – they looked out for one another.

As a rule, Casey and Billy checked in on a daily basis. And if either one of them left the other a message, their call was returned within a matter of hours, not left unanswered for days. That was just the way they did things. That was the deal between them, and although it wasn't often talked about, it had always been understood. That was how you operated when you were gay, and a hustler, and you lived in a world where gay rights weren't high on many people's list of priorities and plenty of people would be only too happy to see you dead. There were enough dangers associated with their lifestyle and line of work. There were all kinds of freaks and weirdos out there. A queer-basher with a crowbar could be waiting for you in a parking lot. A client could turn on you unexpectedly. You could be attacked while walking home with a bag full of porn. Anything could happen. Anything.

Casey examined his stitches and began to imagine all the things that might have happened to Billy. He could have been mugged. He could have been the victim of a car-jacking. He could have been held under house arrest by an overzealous client with a military fetish and forced to perform menial tasks like polishing the floor or cleaning the toilet bowl — with his tongue. He could have been dragged into the back of a delivery truck and sold into white slavery. He could have been abducted by aliens. Or he could simply be enjoying a whirlwind romance with one of the biggest stars on the planet and was too swept away by it all to spare a thought for his best buddy. But hadn't Casey mentioned in his message that he'd been stabbed and taken to the emergency room? Surely that would have prompted a response? Unless of course Billy's cell was switched off, or the battery was dead, or he just didn't give a fuck any more.

Casey took his towel from his locker and marched over to the showers. Standing naked as the water bounced off his impressive chest and ran in rivulets down the curves of his ass, it didn't take him long to attract attention. A few feet away, a guy with an enormous penis lathered himself into a state of arousal with a slow, one-handed motion eerily reminiscent of someone screwing in a light bulb. Sexual contact of any kind was strictly forbidden by the management, but this being West Hollywood there was always the odd club member who got carried away by some locker room fantasy he'd been harbouring since high school. At least this particular member had something to shout about. Usually with a dick that size, a guy was lucky if he could raise it to half-mast. Not this one. Within moments it was fully erect, its glistening head pointing straight up at the ceiling. It was an impressive performance by anyone's standards. Any other time, Casey would have been tempted to show his appreciation by following the enormous erection and its proud owner into the steam room. But not today. As the guy sidled over to him, busily tweaking his own nipples, Casey suddenly snapped. 'Please! Can't you see I'm busy here!'

His erection dwindling, the guy retreated huffily and went back to soaping himself. Luckily he'd followed his dermatologist's advice and chosen a shower gel that was one part moisturiser and wouldn't dry out his skin the way soap could. It looked like he might be in for quite a wait.

Grabbing his towel, Casey dried himself off, hurried over to his locker and got dressed. All the while he could feel the panic tightening in his chest. Something wasn't right. Something wasn't right at all.

Simon had met some monsters in his time. Only last year he'd taken a dive into the murky waters off the coast of South Africa, and come face to face with one of the fiercest predators known to man – a great white shark, three metres in length, lured up from the depths by the smell of fish guts and the promise of a free lunch. The dive was part of a press trip hosted by the local tourist board in an effort to persuade British tourists that Cape Town really was a safe place to visit, and Simon had gone along for the sightseeing and the great choice of seafood, oblivious to the fact that it wasn't just the little fish he'd be getting up close and personal with. How on earth it was decided that diving with great white sharks would help promote Cape Town as a safe haven for holiday-makers, Simon couldn't quite work out. But when the time came for him to slip on his wetsuit, climb into the metal cage and be lowered into the water, his heart was beating so fast he almost bottled it. The water was far colder than he'd been led to expect, and by the time the erstwhile star of *Jaws* finally put in an appearance, swimming up to the cage and moving in for his close-up, Simon was in serious danger of losing control of his bowels.

A similar feeling gripped him now. There was no metal cage designed for his protection, just a golf cart, winding its way across the Fox studio lot towards the building where the interview with Matt Walsh would take place. Stage 16 contained a 500,000-gallon water tank, which had been used extensively in the filming of *Surface Tension*, and it was here that Simon would finally meet the star of the movie. Luckily for him, there was no evidence yet of any great white sharks, just a small white woman exuding coldness from every pore. In the aftermath of his shark dive and much heated debate with experienced divers from three continents, Simon was willing to concede that the great white probably got an unfair rap, and that it wasn't quite the vicious man-eater of Hollywood folklore. It was a pity the same couldn't be said for Lee Carson. In the flesh, she was every bit as gruesome as her reputation suggested. Dressed in a silver-grey zebra-print jacket with matching trousers, she was as pale as a corpse, as if all the blood had been sucked up into her flaming red hair or run down into her crimson fingernails. Hard-faced didn't even begin to describe her. Her face was a testament to the mortician's art, a living death mask. Catching her eye, Simon thought he detected a slight stiffening of the sinews beneath the basilisk stare. He wondered if she ever blushed. Somehow he doubted it. She probably couldn't spare the blood.

It was a little after eleven a.m. as the golf cart and its two passengers trundled past the New York City street set and along the Avenue of the Palms. A large part of the Fox lot had been sold off when Century City was first developed, and some of the studio's facilities had been relocated elsewhere to make way for a glitzy array of hotels and shopping malls. Still a good part of the old Fox studios survived, and remained busy producing movies and TV dramas. It said something about Walsh's celebrity standing that he should choose a working studio as the setting for an interview. Not for him the usual low-key introduction in a hotel suite or a friendly lunch at the Ivy. This was a major Hollywood production number, and if the aim of the game was to remind Simon of how big a star Walsh really was, and how small and inconsequential he was in comparison, he would have to admit that it was working.

Of course it didn't help that his escort radiated all the affability of an industrial cooler. The conversation had been stilted, to say the least. Often in these situations, a star's agent or manager would attempt to ingratiate themselves to a journalist, to butter them up a bit before the interview began. Even the toughest of publicists would use this time to turn on the charm, to build a rapport, maybe even to share a joke. Not Lee Carson. The woman didn't do small talk.

Instead she had spent the best part of fifteen minutes lecturing Simon about the sanctity of his 'time with Matt'. He had been granted forty-five minutes of Matt's undivided attention, and to hear the way she described it, this was a miracle on a par with eradicating world hunger.

'Some people have to make do with fifteen, or thirty,' she said as they made their final approach to the building. 'You should consider yourself lucky. For you, Matt is willing to stretch it to the full forty-five.'

Simon could see how this might be interpreted as an act of great generosity on the part of Hollywood's busiest action hero. After all, these were forty-five minutes where Matt wouldn't be fighting fires or flexing his biceps aboard a nuclear submarine. Forty-five minutes where he wouldn't be getting his ass whipped or appearing bruised and bloodied in a baseball shirt. Forty-five minutes where he wouldn't be wowing audiences with his karate skills, and his only focus would be Simon and the list of questions he'd prepared in anticipation of the interview. It was up to Simon to make each of these forty-five minutes count, and right now the responsibility was weighing heavily on him.

He looked across at Walsh's manager and tried to engage her with a smile. She stared back at him, expressionless.

Casey left the gym with his hair still wet and his clothes somewhat dishevelled. It wasn't everyone who could wear low-rider jeans with a cropped T-shirt and impunity. Even in West Hollywood, such lethal combinations tended to attract attention. But for once, Casey wasn't aware of the looks he generated as he left the Crescent Heights mall and headed west towards San Vicente Boulevard. He was a man on a mission, and for once the mission wasn't to stop traffic or be spotted by a passing talent scout from a leading gay porn studio.

The West Hollywood Sheriff's Station on San Vicente boasted a Community Oriented Policing & Problem Solving Team, together with specialists in both hate crime investigations and gay, lesbian, bisexual and transgender community relations. It was a pity nobody had bothered to inform the grunt on the desk, who took one look at Casey's wild eyes and daring denims and decided that a little condescension was called for.

'People go missing all the time,' he said, nodding reassuringly. 'Your friend will probably show up in a day or two. They usually do.'

When Casey insisted that Billy wasn't the sort of person to go wandering off without telling anyone, he shrugged. 'They never are.'

By this point, Casey could feel his blood rising. It was bad enough that it had taken him this long to report Billy as missing, without some meathead in a uniform delaying things further by acting as though he couldn't care less. In a desperate attempt to spark some interest, Casey decided to play his trump card by explaining that the last time he heard from Billy, he was calling from Matt Walsh's house.

'Well, why didn't you say?' The cop smiled. 'They've probably flown down to Aspen for a couple of days. Either that, or they're busy picking outfits for the Oscars.'

Of course Casey didn't expect to get the most sympathetic hearing. He had already established that, when it came to crimes affecting the gay residents of West Hollywood, the Los Angeles Police Department weren't exactly beating a path to the door of the local gay and lesbian center. For all their talk of community policing, it was clear that the LAPD still existed to protect and serve some members of the community more than others. Maybe if they'd had a few gay riots on their hands, they might be inclined to take things a little more seriously. But of course Casey knew that would never happen. The gay men of West Hollywood would happily flock to the latest movie premiere or club opening, but they would never take to the streets in protest at anything. A riot was far too big a commitment.

Finally, when it became clear that Casey wasn't leaving until someone took him seriously, he was referred to the Missing Persons Unit. Someone there would file a report, and he would be notified as soon as they heard anything. Sorry if that wasn't enough to satisfy him, but investigations regarding missing persons presented a genuine challenge to law enforcement professionals, and while every effort was made to investigate all persons reported missing until the person was either found or determined to be a voluntarily missing adult, the Los Angeles Police Department had neither the authority nor the resources to find uprooted friends or relatives who had lost contact with one another. Concerned individuals interested in such matters were requested to employ other public and private resources, including the services of a private investigation firm.

And no, they hadn't recovered Casey's porn.

Simon was waiting in the hospitality suite at the Fox studio lot, where Lee Carson had deposited him before racing off to tie Matt's shoelaces or wipe his nose or whatever it was she actually did in these situations. This much Simon knew – the interview would begin at 11.30 a.m. precisely and end no later than 12.15 p.m. It was now 11.20 a.m. and Simon could feel his stomach tightening. He took a few deep breaths and reminded himself that he often felt this way before a big interview. It was just the adrenalin, nothing more. All this waiting around, all this cloak-and-dagger stuff – it was part of the process, just a few amateur theatrics thrown in for effect. The important thing was that he'd done his homework. He'd researched his subject. He'd prepared his questions. He'd planned his line of attack. He'd psyched himself up as best he could. What happened next was largely a question of fate. Either Walsh would give him a command performance, full of charm and poise and generic answers barely fit to print. Or Simon would provoke him into revealing a little more of himself than he intended.

At 11.25 a.m., a blushing blond boy appeared, introduced himself as Chad and proceeded to escort Simon down a series of corridors to a door marked 'Stage 16 Tank'. From behind the door, Simon could hear the echo of voices, like the sound produced by a small number of people in a very large sports hall.

Chad gently prised the door open, and there in the gloom of the darkened studio Simon saw the shadowy figure of a woman sat in what appeared to be a director's chair. In one hand she held a large stopwatch. On a small table next to her there was a bottle of water and a laptop computer. Occasionally she would take her eyes off the stopwatch and turn to the computer, tapping at the keys with one hand. Simon didn't recognise the woman at first, but as he approached she turned to face him and he saw that it was Lee Carson. She raised a finger to her lips and gestured for him to stop. He stopped dead in his tracks, his heart thumping.

As if on cue, the room fell silent and a female journalist emerged from the gloom, eyes shining. Lee waited for Chad to escort the journalist outside. She checked her stopwatch, looked at Simon and nodded. Simon stepped forward.

PART THREE

Matt

CHAPTER FIFTEEN

The first thing he noticed was the hair. Even in the half-light, it was the kind of hair that commanded attention. Perfect movie-star hair. Black and glossy and impossibly thick for someone fast approaching forty, it gave a whole new meaning to the phrase 'crowning glory', each filament an exercise in sleek perfection, glowing with the benefits of good genes, regular conditioning and a diet rich in oily fish and other essential superfoods. Not for him the dull, lifeless scalp-covering sported by so many of his contemporaries. His hair didn't just sit there keeping his head warm. It worked for him. It moved. It shone. It said that this was a man who was living in a L'Oréal world and loving it. This was a man who knew he was worth it. Then he turned his head, and Simon saw those big brown eyes and that megawatt grin and suddenly Matt Walsh was bounding over and welcoming him to LA.

He wasn't particularly tall. The official biog claimed six feet. Simon reckoned five ten was probably closer to the truth. Taller than many stars, but still no towering titan. But what he lacked in stature he more than made up for in personality. His presence filled the room. He was dressed in a brown cashmere sweater and tapered black pants. His eyes looked a little tired, and he hadn't shaved for two, possibly three days. But he wasn't cranky or difficult. Some stars could be coiled and defensive, only springing into life when they'd been around you for a little while and were satisfied that you weren't out to get them. Not Walsh. Right from the start he exuded a cool confidence. 'Fancy a dip in my pool?' he joked, gesturing to the 500,000-gallon water tank behind him, and he and Simon shared a laugh at the absurdity of the situation. The handshake, when it came, was firm but friendly, the perfect politician's handshake. It gave the impression that there was nowhere he would rather be than here, and nothing he would rather do than debate the merits of his latest movie and surrender himself to another friendly game of hide and seek with the media. Considering that stars of Walsh's calibre generally regarded journalists with deep suspicion bordering on outright hostility, this was no mean achievement.

But what really impressed Simon was how like Matt Walsh he was. Often people who projected well on screen were flat, two-dimensional, disappointing figures in real life. It took a camera to add that extra dimension, that special something people called charisma. In the flesh, most stars were like themselves on a dimmer switch. Only the occasional mannerism gave them away. Marilyn Monroe used to say that she could walk down the street as Norma Jean and not be recognised. It was only when she made a conscious effort to be Marilyn Monroe that anyone paid her any attention. Simon could see the sense in that. In order to live with long-term celebrity on the scale movie stars tended to generate, at some point a person had to compartmentalise their life into the reality versus the image. The image was the person they projected on screen; the reality was the person they were in private. Somewhere between the two was the person they presented in interviews. The secret was knowing how to slip between these various guises, and make each appear as natural and as effortless as breathing. Get the balance right and everyone was happy. Get the balance wrong and you'd wind up like the Whitneys and Courtneys of this world, constantly sparring with journalists, fighting with photographers and wondering what you'd ever done to deserve such a bad press.

Clearly, Matt Walsh had got the balance right. The person he'd chosen to be today was perfect for the occasion. Every bit as charismatic as the persona he projected on screen, he somehow gave the impression that what Simon was seeing was the man behind the image. His smile was bright, but not radioactive. He was self-assured without appearing too arrogant, charming without seeming too oily. He was expensively dressed, well groomed, but not too slick. The stubble on his chin was a clear indicator that here was one superstar who wanted to be seen as just one of the guys. His body language announced that he was friendly, accessible and not so bothered by the rumours that he was afraid of making male bonding gestures of body contact. When he gestured for Simon to sit down, he did so with one hand reaching for his shoulder and the other steering him towards a vast couch, positioned somewhat surreally at the edge of the water tank. Moments later he was slapping Simon on the back, asking him how the weather was in London and how he was finding it here in LA.

But of course Simon wasn't completely taken in. In many ways, Walsh was a lot like the studio they were sitting in. Just as the massive water tank was used to create the illusion that a drama was unfolding undersea, so Walsh was in the business of persuading people that he was whatever they wanted him to be. And lest Simon forget, somewhere in the gloom there was a woman with a stop-watch, quietly counting down the minutes until the allotted time was over and this whole performance would be brought to a close.

Simon took his tape recorder and placed it on the table in front of him. He opened his notebook. 'Okay,' he said. 'Let's start by talking about your new film. What made you decide to make another action movie?'

A few miles away in Santa Monica, Ted Chalmers was having lunch with his ex-therapist. Known as Dr Sheldon to his clients and Dr Zack to his friends, Zack Sheldon had been Ted's friend for a lot longer than he'd been his therapist. A tall, wiry man who spoke in carefully measured tones and wore a lot of beige, he gave the impression of being an extremely good listener with a genuine concern for the welfare of others. The truth was he was simply touting for new business.

In a previous life, Dr Zack had attempted to help Ted address his weight problem and heal his inner child. The fact that he had failed miserably on both counts ought to have signalled the end of their relationship, but by then Ted had successfully entered the transference stage and stubbornly refused to let go. Five years on, they were like a pair of ex-lovers trying to prove that they could be friends while constantly tiptoeing around the shared intimacies of the past.

Anyone watching them today would have thought them a very odd couple indeed. Although several years older than Ted, Dr Zack was a far better catch. Prematurely grey and chiselled, he had that slightly weathered rich daddy look that inspired rescue fantasies among his sexually frustrated female clients and went down equally well at certain bars in Silver Lake. Although by no means wealthy, he lived a fairly comfortable lifestyle, surrounding himself with designer furniture and an impressive circle of friends, few of whom weighed in at more than a hundred pounds or cleared less than two hundred thousand a year. And since Dr Zack had never even considered the possibility of becoming a chubby chaser, it was hard to see what he and Ted could possibly have in common. To the untrained eye, they were worlds apart.

But what Ted lacked in looks and disposable income he made up for in other ways. Like everyone else within a thirty-mile radius, Dr Zack was in thrall to the movie industry. His days off were usually spent running between movie theatres. On a good day, he could pack in two films before lunch and a further three before dinner, thereby ensuring that he was never in the embarrassing position of being lost for words at dinner parties. And since a number of his clients paid for their weekly therapy sessions from fortunes their husbands had amassed through their roles as production managers and executive producers up in Hollywood, Dr Zack felt it only fitting that he keep abreast of developments in the field of motion picture arts and sciences. In a small way, he was already part of the Hollywood food chain. Going to the movies was his way of paying something back to an industry that provided a steady supply of damaged souls with deep pockets, the likes of whom kept shrinks like him in flash suits and designer furniture.

Sadly, the sexual indiscretions of Hollywood powerbrokers, while good for business, were hardly the stuff that great dinner party conversations were made of. Aside from their wives, nobody really cared what studio execs got up to in their spare time. And even if they had, Dr Zack was duty-bound not to reveal the intimate personal secrets of those who came to him for professional help. Ted, on the other hand, was not only in a position to provide Dr Zack with tales involving names normally associated with the red carpet, but had very few qualms about breaking people's confidences, particularly to a man he considered to be safely outside the loop and the absolute embodiment of discretion.

'So how's work?' Dr Zack asked as they perused the menu

at Schatzi on Main, the self-styled 'world's most famous restaurant'. Ted had already complained that the food wasn't all that great, but the restaurant was owned by Arnold Schwarzenegger, and since Dr Zack was footing the bill he figured he was entitled to put his needs first. Only last week a friend was tucking into one of Arnold's home specialities when he spotted the man himself, pressing hands with the head waiter. For Dr Zack, opportunities like that were too good to pass up.

Ted looked up from his menu. 'I don't quite get the concept of Austrian cuisine,' he said mournfully. 'What's this? The Governor's Wiener Schnitzel. Is that supposed to sound appetising? And what's Arnold doing running a restaurant anyway? Doesn't he have enough on his plate?'

'He doesn't run it,' Dr Zack corrected him. 'He owns it. He leases it to some Austrian ice-cream mogul. So you can't tell me you won't be tempted by the dessert menu.'

'If I make it that far,' Ted said. 'The last time I ate here I lost my appetite by the time I'd finished my appetiser. Blue crab cakes. What the hell is that about?'

Dr Zack frowned. 'Well I have to say you're a real barrel of laughs today, Ted. Remind me never to dangle Arnold's Wiener in front of you ever again.'

Ted laughed. 'Sorry,' he said. 'I'm just tired, I guess. I didn't sleep too well last night.'

Dr Zack slipped into professional mode. 'What's up? Pressures of work? All those Hollywood egos getting you down?'

Ted gave a glimmer of a smile. 'Something like that,' he said. 'The thing is, I think someone's trying to fuck with me.'

Dr Zack stared at him. 'Sounds interesting. Tell me more.'

'I will,' Ted said. 'But first I need a drink. A large one.

Then maybe what I'm about to say won't sound quite so crazy.'

'It's not about being in control,' Matt Walsh said. 'It's about wanting to do my best. Everything I do, my name is on it. It's my name on that billboard. It's my name outside that movie theatre. It's my face people are paying their ten bucks to see. So naturally I want it to be the best work I'm capable of. I don't like going to see bad movies. And I sure as hell don't like making them.'

Simon smiled. 'Do you think you've made any bad movies?'

Walsh laughed. 'Good question. Do you?'

'I wouldn't say that exactly,' Simon said, playing for time. 'Maybe a couple of the earlier ones weren't so good.' This was somewhat disingenuous. The truth was, Simon hadn't seen a single Matt Walsh movie he didn't think was bad on some level. Even his better films were marred by the fact that you were never allowed to forget that this was Matt Walsh you were watching. As an actor, Walsh was rarely more than adequate. It wasn't his ability to fake emotions and recite his lines that made him interesting. It was something else entirely. Call it charisma. Call it star quality. Walsh had it in spades. He had the gift of being eminently watchable, even when he wasn't entirely believable.

'I know what you mean,' Walsh said. 'But those movies were kind of important, for me at least. They helped make me the person I am today. I remember when we were filming *Third Base*, I was so excited I could hardly sleep at night. I kept thinking to myself, "So this is what it means to be a movie star." I just felt incredibly fortunate to be given that opportunity at such a young age, and I was determined to learn everything I could about the art of acting. I was barely out of my teens and already I had my whole life mapped out. I knew this was what I wanted to do with my life. I wanted to make movies.' He paused for a moment, looking slightly embarrassed. Then he grinned. 'I just wasn't sure if I was cut out for the job.'

Simon frowned. 'Really? Why not?'

'I didn't know if I had what it takes, not just to be a movie star, but to be the kind of movie star everyone expected me to be. Y'know, the kind who always plays the hero and gets the girl, the romantic leading man. Right from the start, I was very conscious of the fact that there was a certain career path laid out in front of me. I just wasn't sure if that was the path I wanted to follow.'

'But it can't have been that tough,' Simon said. 'With your looks, I mean.'

Matt grinned. 'You shouldn't take things at face value. In some ways the path I took is the toughest one of all. It's a path many men have tried to go down, and have failed miserably. Because it's actually the most exposed. You're not hiding behind a false nose or a wig or something. You're really putting yourself out there. Plus there's always been this side of me that wants to push myself a little more, to dig a little deeper, to explore some of the darker sides to my character.'

Simon tried not to smile. 'Really?' he felt like saying. 'Because so far we haven't seen much evidence of that.' Instead he nodded. 'So is this darker Matt Walsh someone we can expect to see more of in the future?'

Walsh grinned. 'Possibly. It depends what comes my way. Believe it or not, there aren't that many interesting scripts out there. It's not as if I'm turning down great parts all the time. Having said that, I think the choices I've made have been the right ones, professionally speaking. I feel I've grown as an actor. And I've made some very successful movies. It's easy to knock success. It's not so easy to achieve it.'

Simon nodded. 'But when people knock movies like *Surface Tension*, or any big studio blockbuster for that matter, they're not simply knocking them because they're successful. They're knocking them because they regard them as being bloated and formulaic, lacking in imagination, always playing it safe.'

Walsh laughed. 'Hey, don't spare my feelings here!'

Simon blushed. 'Sorry. But you know what I mean. You must have heard it all before.'

'Maybe. But don't forget this is Hollywood we're talking about. Playing it safe is second nature here. And the stakes are high. A movie like *Surface Tension* costs millions of dollars to produce, and millions more to market. If that was your money, you'd play it safe too.'

Simon nodded. 'But it must be hard sometimes. Always playing it safe, I mean.'

Suddenly something in Walsh's manner changed. Gone was the easy charm and flirtatious body language of a few moments ago. All at once the energy level dropped and the megawatt grin faded. He was still smiling, but now the smile seemed rather brittle.

'Listen, I'm fully aware of my limitations as a person,' he said, defensively. 'I mean, you don't get where I am today without making certain compromises.'

Simon didn't miss a beat. 'Compromises? What sort of compromises?'

Walsh smiled weakly. 'Oh, you know. The usual Hollywood bullshit. People think you see it coming, but that isn't always the case. It happens so slowly, y'know? And when the pressures come, they come with silk gloves. Suddenly you find yourself being advised to do this or to do that, and you're never entirely sure where the advice is coming from. Then slowly things start to change. The people around you change. They watch, and they whisper. They pretend to be your friends, when really all they're after is a free ride. And you change too. You start to make choices, choices you never thought you'd make. And then one day you wake up and you're a different person. You're in a different place. And by then it's too late to find your way back.' He paused for a moment, staring off into the distance. 'It's easy to lose sight of yourself in this business,' he said finally. 'Be careful what you wish for.'

Simon's pulse was racing. This wasn't what he'd been led to expect at all. All that cloak-and-dagger nonsense beforehand, and now here was Matt Walsh, famously guarded movie star, opening up about the pressures of fame, talking about the kind of compromises a man would be required to make if, say, he was gay and wanted a career in Hollywood. Or was he? All he'd really said so far was that fame changes people. No big revelation there. Sitting here now, it was easy to put two and two together and make five. But take away the delivery, and the body language, and the words themselves didn't add up to all that much. If Simon wanted more, he'd have to push a little harder.

'I'm still not sure I understand,' he said. 'When you talk about losing sight of yourself, what do you mean exactly?'

Walsh looked him straight in the eye. 'Look at me now. What do you see?'

Simon hesitated before answering. 'I see Matt Walsh, star of *Surface Tension* and one of the biggest names in Hollywood.'

Walsh laughed. 'And is that all?'

'All?'

'Is that all you see when you look at me – a famous movie star?'

'Isn't that enough?'

'Most of the time, maybe. But there's more to life than making movies. And there's more to me than just being famous.'

Simon nodded. 'So what you're saying is that fame gets in the way of your personal life.'

At the mention of those two words, 'personal life', Walsh flinched slightly. There was a pause. 'I guess,' he said finally. 'Obviously you sacrifice a certain amount of your personal life in order to pursue your dream of becoming a famous actor. And once you've achieved your goal, it doesn't stop there. If anything, it gets worse. I don't mean to sound ungrateful. Nobody forced me to become famous. And I know it's hard for people to appreciate what it's like when you wake up in the morning and there's maybe a dozen photographers parked outside your house. But let me tell you, after a few years it can really grind you down.'

'Are you ever lonely?' Simon asked.

Walsh looked surprised. 'Am I ever lonely?' he repeated, pondering the question. 'I guess so. Sometimes. Don't get me wrong. I'm not the loneliest guy in the world. I have people I can call on. But there are times when I think it would be nice to lead a normal life, to do what normal people do, to enjoy that freedom.'

Simon smiled. 'Do you think it would be easier if you were married?'

Walsh held his gaze. 'I don't see why. I know a lot of married people, and some of them are among the loneliest people I know.'

'In a relationship, then?'

'How do you know I'm not in a relationship?'

'Are you?'

Before Walsh could answer, Lee Carson emerged from the

darkness, eyes blazing. 'Sorry to interrupt,' she said, her manner immediately betraying the fact that she wasn't sorry at all. 'But we're out of time.'

Walsh turned to her. 'You know what?' he said. 'I'm really enjoying this interview. Could we have another fifteen minutes?'

Simon smiled to himself. He must have seen this routine a hundred times. It was a familiar tactic, regularly employed by stars and their PRs the world over. First the PR announced that they were out of time. Then the star replied that they were enjoying this interview far too much to end it now and insisted on another ten or fifteen minutes. Then the PR shrugged and looked at the journalist as if to say, 'My, you are lucky', before quietly disappearing. It was a brilliant routine, designed to flatter journalists' egos and make them go away feeling incredibly grateful and more inclined to write a sympathetic piece. The truth, of course, was that the timing of the interruption had been agreed beforehand, and the total running time of the interview decided weeks ago.

At least that was usually how it went. On this particular occasional, the dynamics seemed rather different.

'But the schedule's already very tight,' Carson said, so forcibly that there was no doubt she meant every word.

Walsh didn't appear to be acting either. 'Screw the schedule,' he said, dismissing her with a wave of the hand. 'Another fifteen minutes isn't going to hurt.'

By now it was abundantly clear that this wasn't just a routine. If looks could kill, the look on Carson's face would have annihilated Walsh on the spot. The atmosphere became distinctly chilly as she stood staring at him and he sat studiously avoiding her gaze. Finally she left.

'That's better,' Walsh said. 'Now, where were we?'

Sensing that time was rapidly running out, and that he

should probably strike now while the iron was still hot, Simon took a deep breath. 'Actually, I was about to ask you about someone,' he said evenly. 'Someone I believe you might know. His name is Billy West.'

CHAPTER SIXTEEN

The moment his editor called the following morning, Simon could tell she wasn't happy.

'I'm not happy, Simon,' she said, lest he was in any doubt. 'If it's not too much trouble, would you mind telling me just what the hell you think you're playing at?'

Simon was still half asleep, only recently emerging from a dream in which Matt Walsh was showing him around his Beverly Hills mansion and the two of them were hanging out together like old friends. Somehow the fact that he'd blown his chances of ever being allowed within a mile radius of Walsh's home hadn't come back to haunt him. Until now.

'Susie,' he said, rubbing his eyes and reaching for the alarm clock. 'What time is it?'

'It's seven o'clock in the morning,' she snapped. 'I thought I'd wait a bit before waking you, though why I should spare a thought for your feelings right now I really have no idea. I had to drag myself out of bed this morning, just so I could come into the office and get a head start on some work for next week. Instead I arrived to find a dozen messages from Lee Carson, chewing my ear off about what happened yesterday. I'll spare you the gory details. I'm sure you'll get the general picture. Calling for your blood. Threatening to cancel the photo shoot. Referring me to her lawyers. That sort of thing.'

Simon gulped. 'Oh.'

Susie sounded as if she were about to explode. 'Oh? Oh! Is that the best you can do? The biggest interview we've had all year, about to go up in flames, and all you can say is "Oh"? For fuck's sake, Simon. You'll have to do better than that. A lot better.'

So Simon started to explain about the interview. How Matt Walsh was a lot more open than he'd been expecting. How the conversation developed into a discussion about the pressures of fame and the loneliness Walsh sometimes felt. How Walsh seemed only too happy to discuss certain aspects of his personal life. How Lee Carson tried to intervene and Walsh insisted on continuing, despite her obvious disapproval. How, given all this, it seemed only appropriate to pursue the conversation to its logical conclusion and bring up the name of the hustler referred to in the note. After all, Walsh might have taken this as his cue to open up completely and given Simon the scoop of his career. And just think how happy everyone would have been then.

'Hang on a minute,' Susie snapped. 'What's this about a note? Note from who?'

'That's the thing,' Simon said. 'I don't know who sent it. It was left under my door. All it said was that Walsh was definitely gay and that he was involved with some hustler called Billy West. That was it. It wasn't signed or anything. I'm guessing it was from someone connected to the industry in some way, but really that's all I have to go on.'

Susie didn't sound overly impressed. 'Let me get this straight,' she said, her tone distinctly chilly. 'You're telling me that some person or persons unknown left an anonymous note under your door, and that on the basis of that you went ahead and jeopardised an interview with one of the most powerful men in Hollywood. An interview, I might add, which I spent months setting up and would be very unhappy to lose at such a late stage in the game. An interview, I might also add, which would have done your career a power of good, but which is now unlikely to see the light of day. Right now the best you can hope for is that we cut it down to a thousand words and run it in the Style section. And I'm sure nobody wants to see that.'

'But I was so sure he was ready to open up to me,' Simon protested feebly. 'It was all going so well. And you know what these situations are like. Sometimes you just have to play a little dangerously.'

'Suggesting that a major movie star gets his kicks fucking male prostitutes isn't playing a little dangerously, Simon. Not when you haven't a shred of evidence. What the hell were you thinking? This isn't some sleazy tabloid we're running here. Our readers aren't interested in idle gossip and unsubstantiated rumours about people's sex lives. And the last thing we need right now is a lawsuit from Matt Walsh. I'm assuming you didn't show him the note?'

'Of course not. I haven't completely taken leave of my senses.'

'Well that's debatable for a start. I don't think you appreciate just how serious this is, Simon. This isn't some soap star you've offended here. This isn't some runner-up on *Pop Idol*. This is Hollywood. They do things differently there. You upset a man like Matt Walsh and pretty soon we'll be lucky if anyone on the West Coast is willing to talk to us. Word gets around. Stars close ranks. PRs become even bigger bitches to deal with. This isn't just your reputation you're risking here. It's mine too. So here's what you're going to do. You're going to get on the phone to Lee Carson. You're going to apologise profusely for any offence you might have caused yesterday, and put it down to a moment of madness or something.

You're going to assure her that no mention of this Billy person is going to appear in your interview. You're going to tell her exactly what she wants to hear, and see if you can't clean up this mess and rescue this interview. Do I make myself clear?'

Simon considered putting up a fight. Then his survival instincts kicked in and he thought better of it. 'Yes,' he said. 'Crystal clear.'

'Good,' said Susie. 'And Simon?'

'Yes?'

'Don't fuck up.'

Matt closed his eyes and waited for the makeup girl to conceal the evidence of another sleepless night. If only the rest of his problems could be erased so easily. Unfortunately, life wasn't like a photo shoot. It was more like a paparazzi shot. Life was usually what happened to you when you were busy doing something else. It caught you unawares, without your makeup on, when you weren't always looking your best.

It was like he told that journalist yesterday – things had a nasty habit of creeping up on you. Of course what he hadn't told that journalist was that it wasn't just the familiar pressures of fame he was alluding to. Matt had a secret. An open secret, admittedly. A secret known to at least half the people in Hollywood, and widely suspected by many more. But a secret nonetheless. And like all secrets, it seemed to grow larger and weigh heavier the longer he lived with it.

Of course it didn't help that celebrity had taken a very different shape over the past decade. As many stars had discovered to their cost, it was hard to have secrets now. The Garbo option was no longer available. These days you were never alone – not really, not when there were telephoto lenses and bugging devices and people paid to root around in your garbage. The media had the means necessary to intrude almost anywhere, and no methods were deemed too low. In gentler times, photographers generally waited for you to put in a public appearance before pointing their lenses at you. Now they came snooping around your home. And when some former associate betrayed your confidence and sold their story to the papers, no one batted an eyelid. Once there had been a name for people who kissed and told all to the media. Today they were invited on to talk shows and encouraged to talk some more. Celebrity gossip had never been more popular, and the right to privacy less respected. It was no wonder so many stars developed a reputation for being difficult, or lived in a constant state of paranoia. Just because you were paranoid, it didn't mean that someone somewhere wasn't out to get you. Matt knew full well there was a price on his head. The only question was when it would be paid.

It was all so much easier in the beginning. Matt knew he had a lot to be thankful for. There weren't many jobs where you were paid vast fortunes to do the one thing you'd excelled at since you were a kid. And he wouldn't have given up the trappings of fame for anything. After all these years it was hard to imagine a life without Lear jets and limousines. But he missed the freedom of the old days, before anyone knew who he was and he could go wherever he chose and do whatever he wanted, without this constant fear of exposure. He missed the simple pleasures. Driving over Coldwater Canyon in a 1965 Ford Fairlane convertible with the top down, music blazing, a bullet of cocaine in his pocket, on his way to Studio City to share a few lines with a casting agent he'd met one night at Mickey's. Screwing his brains out with some personal instructor called Troy at the gym in West Hollywood where Troy worked and men came to pump iron before pumping each other's asses in the steam room. Whole summers spent hanging out at the Will Rogers beach, flirting with the life-guards.

And the parties! He could still remember the thrill he felt arriving at some producer's mansion in the Hollywood Hills. It was the night of the Oscars. The guest of honour was a hot-shot director who had just won an award for his quirky look at child prostitution, and spirits were high. The host, whose parties were already the stuff of legend, truly excelled himself that night. His attention to detail exceeded the expectations of every man present. Lines of cocaine were laid out on silver trays. The champagne flowed. Cocktail waiters strutted like cocks before stripping down and getting jiggy with the guests. In the garden, drunken fumblings took place beneath twisted willows strewn with fairy lights and scenes of debauchery were softened by the warm glow of Chinese lanterns. The hot-tub bubbled away well into the early hours. And as dawn broke over the city, the remaining guests were served scram-bled eggs and croissants by muscle-studs in skimpy shorts and gold spraypaint – real life Oscars with pliant flesh and winning ways in the bedroom department. Matt may not have known what it was like to actually win an Oscar, but he held a few in his hand that night.

And then one day he found he couldn't walk into a grocery store without causing a shopping cart pile-up and suddenly everything changed. There were no more afternoons spent snorting cocaine, no more Troys and no more summers at the beach, flirting with lifeguards. There were still Oscar parties, but the hosts were generally far less imaginative and the wait-ers far less accommodating. As Matt quickly discovered, a career in Hollywood left its beneficiary profoundly compro-mised in many ways, and no one more so than him. Being a famous person with a precious public image to protect was hard enough. It was one of the unspoken truths about celebrity that you spent half your life in private planes and limos, and the other half sneaking around in back alleys and hiding out in fire escapes, waiting for your car to arrive. But for him it was stranger still. Being a famous person with a secret sexuality was like joining a cult. Suddenly he was required to cut ties with old aquaintances, to find new friends, fabricate elements of his past life and erase those bits that didn't sit too comfortably with the wholesome new image he was busy promoting. Soon there was hardly anyone in his life he could genuinely call on as a friend, or who knew him for the person he was. He was surrounded by people he'd known for barely five minutes, and whose only interest was in the person they wanted him to be.

It was at this point that Lee entered the picture and a few ground rules were established. Rule number one was that it was okay to be gay, just never during working hours. Matt reckoned he could live with that. He wasn't one of those people who made a big issue about his sexuality. He'd always been put off by those professional homosexual types who went around with a chip on their shoulder and a placard above their head, demanding to be seen as gay first and a human being second. As far as Matt was concerned, it was nobody's business who he slept with, so he figured the separation of work and private life shouldn't present too much of a problem. But then the working hours grew longer and longer, until pretty soon it was hard to say where work ended and his private life began. The premieres, the awards ceremonies, the public appearances – were they simply part of the job, or were they an extension of his private life? Turning up at premieres with a string of gorgeous women on his arm, inviting people to speculate about when he was going to settle down and get married, he felt the gulf between his private self and his public image grow wider with every photo opportunity.

He justified it to himself fairly easily at first. He told himself that his personal life wasn't there to sell papers, and that the public preferred their stars to retain an air of mystery. At a time when many of his contemporaries were lining up to spill their guts on *Oprah*, it was refreshing to see someone who conducted their affairs in the manner of an old-school celebrity, quietly and with dignity. And of course he always had Lee there to guide him, to remind him of how much was at stake, and to assure him that the choices he was making were the right ones. But the truth was he wasn't being mysterious. He was being duplicitous. And he wasn't conducting his affairs quietly or with dignity, at least not all of them. He was parading himself in public with a variety of starlets, some of whom knew the score, some of whom didn't, all of whom stood to benefit from the arrangement and were grateful for the kind of attention a date with Matt Walsh could generate.

There were boys too, of course. There were always boys. Even with the eyes of the world upon him, the opportunities for satisfying his basic instincts were never more than a phone call away. One celebrated gay porn producer ran what amounted to a stud farm, providing a steady supply of top porn stars to the best known of Hollywood's closeted gay elite. And he wasn't the only one. There were plenty of other networkers available. Some were mutual friends, and were happy to help out as a personal favour. Some were chauffeurs, and expected additional payment for providing a service other than driving. Some were people low down in the Hollywood pecking order, who preferred payment in kind to the cold, hard exchange of cash – an audition here, a personal reference there. But they all provided the same service – a regular flow of eager young men ready and willing to have discreet sexual liaisons with those who had something to hide. In Hollywood, there had always been people who arranged such things. Whether you referred to them as networkers or as pimps was simply a question of taste.

Matt had lost count of the number of boys he'd been introduced to by mutual aquaintances or arranged to meet in hotel rooms. Boys who knew the score and weren't too in awe of his celebrity. Boys who worked in mailrooms but had their sights on better things. Boys who called themselves actors but behaved more like prostitutes. Boys who were happy to perform acts he would never dare ask of mere civilians. Boys who could be trusted to keep their mouths shut. Boys who didn't need to be told when it was time to leave. Matt had met them all. For years his sex life had been an endless merry-go-round of carefully orchestrated casual affairs, each as physically gratifying and as emotionally unfulfilling as the last.

And then there was Billy. Matt had known Billy was special from the moment they met in that hotel room in Bel Air. He was beautiful, of course. That much Matt had been expecting. The photos on his website advertised the fact, although in truth they didn't really do him justice. He was far prettier in the flesh, when he wasn't frowning at the camera or striking a pose straight out of a Calvin Klein ad. The photos made him appear hard and knowing, when in person he was sweet and surprisingly naive. Matt wasn't prepared for that. Hustlers weren't exactly known for their naivety, certainly none that Matt had ever met. Some would play the innocent if they thought that was what turned you on, but any innocence was lost as soon as they hit the sack and threw themselves into one of their routines, begging to be fucked from behind or promising to give you the ride of your life. It was different with Billy. That night in the hotel room, barely a week ago, something happened that Matt wasn't expecting, and it had very little to do with sex. Something passed between them, something Matt had been missing for a long time, and it sent him spinning.

Matt was reluctant to call it love. It was far too early for that. And he certainly wasn't looking to get involved. His life was complicated enough, without the added burden of any emotional entanglements. A love affair was out of the question. There simply wasn't the space for it, not now when he had a movie to promote and problems with his manager to iron out. All he was hoping for was a little fun, something to take him away from himself. Well, he'd certainly found that. This past week had been nothing short of intoxicating. Matt had rediscovered feelings he hadn't felt in years. Passions extinguished long ago by the pressures of his career were suddenly rekindled. Emotions previously put on hold burst back to life. After a few days with Billy, it didn't seem to matter how famous he was. For the first time in years he felt reckless, abandoned and totally free.

And now it looked at though he was about to pay a high price for that brief taste of freedom. First those photos arrived, indicating that someone, somewhere had been monitoring his every move and wanted him to know it. How could he have been so careless? There was enough evidence in those photographs to blow the lid off his so-called secret life and give the media just the story they'd been waiting for. And to make matters worse, some journalist all the way from London had already got wind of the fact that he and Billy were an item. What the hell was going on? Had Billy been shooting his mouth off to the press? Was he involved in some kind of blackmail plot? Was the whole affair an elaborate sting operation, a set-up from start to finish? It pained Matt to think that someone he trusted could sell him out so easily, but what other explanation was there? Suddenly he didn't feel so reckless and free any more. He felt angry and betrayed and more desperate by the minute.

What made it worse was that Lee had warned him that this would happen. She could barely contain herself yesterday. When the journalist had uttered Billy's name and she came hurtling out of the darkness, he could see it written all over her face. The satisfaction. The look that said 'I told you so'. The triumphant look of a woman scorned and suddenly free to milk her fury for all it was worth. Oh, she had tried to disguise it, tried to make out that she was every bit as shocked and appalled by the situation as he was. But he could tell. He knew her too well. As angry as she was, there was a part of her that felt vindicated by what had happened, that was only too happy to be proved right. He could see it in her eyes.

The journalist didn't know what had hit him. And neither did Matt. Until yesterday, he'd been willing to do exactly as Lee said, to stay away from Billy and leave her to clear up his mess. She was his manager after all. It was her job to manage the situation. But by the time he returned to his mansion in Beverly Hills he wasn't so sure. Maybe it was time he took control of the situation. He'd lain awake thinking about it all night.

And now, as the makeup girl gave him one final dusting and he checked himself in the mirror, it all became perfectly clear. Matt knew what he had to do. He had to find Billy. Before someone else did.

CHAPTER SEVENTEEN

Casey woke on Monday morning with a bad feeling deep in the pit of his stomach. Whether this was a sign of something serious or was simply brought on by the exertions of the weekend he couldn't really tell, but a quick inspection of his stitches confirmed that the wound was healing nicely and the level of fat in his abdomen was visibly reduced. If he squinted, he could just about make out the contours of his abs. He thought about maybe planning a tattoo to celebrate, before remembering that tattoos were considered passé by everyone except Tommy Lee and a few actor types who still mistook them for something daring and cutting edge to flaunt whenever they were photographed leaving the Viper Room. Besides, nobody looked good with a tattoo floating above their pubes – not even Cher.

Hauling himself out of bed, he padded into the kitchen and made some coffee. Normally he only ever drank herb tea first thing in the morning, but he figured he could use the caffeine. It had been an arduous weekend. After leaving the police station on Saturday afternoon, Casey had wandered over to Billy's apartment building in the hope that his friend might be there, crashed out in front of the TV or catching up on his beauty sleep. But there was no answer when he rang the bell, and none of the neighbours had seen anyone leave or enter the apartment in days. This, of course, didn't really mean anything. The residents of West Hollywood were generally far too self-absorbed to keep track of anyone's movements but their own. Even the ones who stayed home all day had better things to do than keep a watchful eye on their neighbours – watch Mexican soaps for example, or spend an hour on their Abdominizer. Any attempts to get a Neighbourhood Watch scheme up and running were doomed to failure. There simply wasn't the commitment.

Casey had thought of breaking into Billy's apartment, but the lock proved extremely resistant and he didn't have the strength to kick the door down. Not for the first time, Casey was struck by how little real life resembled the movies. If this had been a movie he would have slipped into Billy's apartment no problem, quickly uncovering enough evidence to pinpoint exactly when and where his friend went missing before handing his findings over to the police and being applauded for his initiative. If this had been a porn movie, the police would have shown their appreciation in other ways, possibly involving handcuffs and an inventive use of their night sticks. But since no cameras were involved in the unfolding of this scene, Casey was left standing outside Billy's door feeling pretty powerless and wondering what exactly he was supposed to do next.

He had planned to spend Saturday night recovering from the excesses of Friday, but by the time he got home he was in serious danger of becoming depressed and was immediately sidetracked by the assortment of drugs he'd purchased from Snakeman. He did a few lines of coke first, before popping a pill and heading off to Mother Lode, where the lack of attitude was strangely disconcerting. From there it was on to Mickey's, where he watched the crowd go wild for some listless go-go boy and had the worrying feeling that nights like these weren't nearly as much fun as they used to be. He and

Billy had spent some great nights at Mickey's, dancing with their shirts off, stealing attention from the go-go boys and generally reassuring themselves that they were the hottest guys in the room. Here on his own, it wasn't half as much fun or nearly as reassuring. Was it just his imagination, or were people intent on acting as though he wasn't there? Even when he took his shirt off, he barely registered a second look. He knew it was time to leave when some old guy finally wandered up and attempted to tuck a five-dollar bill into the waistband of his jeans. Any other time, he might have found this funny. On this occasion he simply felt short-changed.

His mood hadn't improved much by the time he arrived at Rage, high on Ecstasy but feeling more anxious by the minute. He snorted a little crystal and was soon spinning around the dance floor with some Latin guy dressed in a Fred Segal top and sporting an elaborate growth of facial hair. Casey had recently taken a vow of chastity when it came to Latin guys, and normally he would have run a mile from anyone whose goatee suggested more than ten minutes in front of the mirror each morning. But such was the power of the crystal that soon his balls were aching and he wound up back at the guy's apartment, where his estimation of his new friend's character soon grew as he produced a sports bag bulging with sex toys and proceeded to demonstrate the unique attraction of each one in turn. One fuck led to another, and soon the air was heavy with the smell of poppers and the bed sheets sticky with lube. Condom wrappers were thrown around the room in wild abandon and half a dozen scented candles burned down until the flames finally flickered and powdered and died. In that strange timewarp brought on by a heady combination of uninhibited sex and copious amounts of drugs, Saturday soon turned into Sunday, and by the time Casey finally emerged blinking into the light, there wasn't an inch of his flesh that wasn't sore from friction or bruised black and blue. In short, he felt fabulous.

Sadly, his euphoria was short-lived. The fears over Billy's whereabouts came flooding back when he returned home to find his answering machine flashing and no word from either the police or his missing friend. It was Snakeman, inviting him to an orgy some friends of his were throwing together at a house in Echo Park. It was rumoured that one of the guests due to attend used to be a regular in *Beverly Hills 90210*, but even the prospect of some serious starfucking wasn't enough to lift Casey's spirits. He ordered a pizza, rolled a joint and scanned the TV guide for something to take his mind off his troubles. He started to watch a TV movie starring one of the original Charlie's Angels as a woman in peril, but lost interest when it was revealed that her dead husband wasn't really dead at all but was busy having an affair with her younger sister, played by the same actress in soft focus and an unconvincing wig. Around eleven p.m., he put on an old Jean-Claude Van Damme movie and began to masturbate, but his heart wasn't really in it and even the sight of Jean-Claude's naked butt failed to get his juices flowing. He switched on his computer, checked his emails and bagged a few pairs of briefs ready for mailing the following day. At midnight he popped a couple of Xanax and slipped into a troubled sleep. He dreamed of dildos and Van Damme. He dreamed of police officers and nipple clamps. He dreamed of Billy lying dead somewhere.

Now, as the caffeine coursed through his veins, Casey tried to clear his mind of such morbid thoughts. He thought of all the ways he could spend the day. He could get his hair done. His roots needed retouching and, at its current length, his faux-hawk was in serious danger of growing into a mohawk, which was a complete no-no, obviously. He could go to the Beverly Center and try on new clothes. His wardrobe was in desperate need of an overhaul, and although he was strapped for cash it was hard to argue when Macy's were having their half-yearly sale. He could go to the farmers' market and stock up on fresh vegetables. Money spent on food wasn't really money spent at all, and you could never have enough fresh vegetables. He could even make a day of it, unpack his juicer and spend the afternoon preparing fresh juices for the week ahead. That way, he would be guaranteed to meet his daily requirement of vitamins and introduce enough antioxidants into his system to combat the effects of all those free radicals the TV commercials were always warning him about.

Eventually he decided on the gym. It wouldn't cost him anything, and the exercise would help banish any thoughts of impending tragedy or destructive patterns of behaviour. The gym was where people paid for the excesses of the lifestyle they were living, and what could be more comforting than that?

Simon wasn't the least bit surprised to discover that Lee Carson was unavailable to take his calls. The woman had been difficult to pin down from the outset, and that was before he accused her client of being on intimate terms with a male prostitute. Nor was he surprised that Chad, who had once sounded so eager to please, now adopted a far chillier tone when answering the phone. Chad was probably feeling the brunt of Carson's wrath right now, and it wasn't hard to imagine that he might blame Simon for putting his boss in the mother of all bad moods.

What surprised Simon was just how unsupportive Susie was being. Editors were supposed to stand by their journalists in times of trouble. And it wasn't all that long ago that Susie was holding hands with him across the table at Joe Allen's, plying him with drink and telling him what a wonderful writer he was, and how thrilled she was to be working with him. So much for drunken flattery. A dozen dazzling cover features and one slight error of judgement later and now here she was practically accusing him of deliberately sabotaging the Matt Walsh interview and ruining her chances of promotion.

'But I've tried calling her,' Simon said. 'I've been calling her all morning. She won't speak to me. It's that simple.'

'Nothing about this situation is simple, Simon,' Susie snapped. 'Thanks to your little episode on Saturday, I have a photographer stranded in some hotel in Santa Monica, unable to book a studio because the shoot we were promised two months ago may not be happening. I have hair and makeup teams waiting to hear whether their services are still required or not, and a stylist who's threatening to sue me for breach of contract. And to top it all, I have a movie star who's probably in discussion with his lawyers as we speak, and a manager who won't rest until every remotely famous person in Hollywood is alerted to the fact that I'm in the habit of employing journalists who go out of their way to cause offence wherever possible. All of this is costing us money, and contrary to what you may think, we don't have a limitless budget we can fall back on every time someone chooses to cock things up so spectacularly.'

'But I didn't do any of this on purpose,' Simon protested. 'Maybe I made a mistake, but I'm doing everything I can to put it right. I've tried calling Carson. I've spoken to her assistant and asked him to convey to her how deeply sorry I am for what happened on Saturday. Short of turning up on Walsh's doorstep with a bunch of flowers and some sackcloth and ashes, I don't know what else I can do.'

'Well you'd better think of something,' Susie said. 'Without the photos or a second stab at Walsh this isn't looking like a cover feature. In fact, it may not make it into the magazine. I'll expect copy by Friday. Give me whatever you've got, and we'll see what happens with the photo shoot. In the meantime, if you hear anything from Carson, call me at once. And don't even joke about turning up at Walsh's house. The last thing I want to hear right now is that you've been arrested on a stalking charge.'

Simon tried to lighten the mood with a laugh, but it was too late. Susie had already hung up.

To: susie.butler@thesundayglobe.co.uk
From: lee.carson@leecarsonassociates.com
Subject: Matt Walsh

Susie,
Following Saturday's extraordinary turn of events, I'm sure you'll understand that I have decided to call off tomorrow's photo shoot. There will be no further dealings between my client and your publication, and any article you decide to run should avoid any reference to what was said on Saturday. For the record, my client has never even heard of the boy your reporter mentioned, and any attempt to suggest otherwise will result in legal action.
I trust that we understand one another.
Lee Carson

When Matt arrived at her office at lunchtime, the first thing Lee noticed was how tired he looked.

'You look worn out,' she said. 'Luckily the photographer is a total genius. I did push for Mario Testino, but apparently he's too busy photographing slum kids in Rio. But don't worry. I'm told this guy can perform miracles.'

'He'll need to,' Matt sighed. 'I feel like shit. I hardly slept a wink last night. No prizes for guessing why.'

'Well, I hate to say I told you so,' Lee said.

'Then don't,' Matt snapped. 'Don't say anything. I'm really not in the mood for one of your lectures.'

The car was already waiting. The driver, whose name was Dale, sensed immediately that something was up but said nothing. He'd worked for Lee long enough to know that the wrong words could easily land a man in trouble. They drove to the studio in silence.

'Remind me who these shots are for,' Matt said as they headed towards makeup.

Lee frowned. 'They're for *In Style*. The woman you met on Saturday. I thought you knew.'

'I thought I did those yesterday.'

'No, that was *Entertainment Weekly*. I did try to spread them out a bit more, but it was too late to reschedule. They go to press in two days.'

'Right. Well, feel free to leave whenever you want,' Matt said. 'You can send Dale back to pick me up later. I really don't need you to hang around.'

And with that he turned and walked away from her.

As she watched him go, Lee had the strangest feeling that this really was the beginning of the end.

By Monday afternoon, the news of Billy's whirlwind affair with Matt Walsh and subsequent disappearance was the talk of West Hollywood. Shop assistants gossiped as they persuaded customers to part with large sums of cash in exchange for artfully distressed jeans and T-shirts two sizes too small. Waiters whispered as they wandered from table to table, gathering information as they went. Hairdressers chatted over straightening irons and thinning heads of hair instantly thickened by the application of honey-blond highlights. Dermatologists dug for information as they applied powerful chemical peels and healing serums to complexions ravaged by years of steroid abuse. Mailroom boys neglected their duties as they debated the ethics of outing, and how the news of a movie star's homosexuality might affect the gay marriage debate. Office juniors hung around water coolers, exchanging tales of personal trysts in the Hollywood foothills and dreaming of the day when they too would climb all the way to the top of the totem pole and become some A-list action hero's boy toy. And in the glittery restaurants where discreet industry types studiously avoided flaming queens from all walks of life, long lunches were spent discussing the implications for Walsh's career and the potential impact on current stock options.

Arriving at the gym, Casey was immediately accosted by Bruce and Donald, who wasted no time in bringing him up to speed with the latest developments. Apparently, there were as many stories relating to Billy's sudden disappearance as there were vicious tongues willing to spread them. One story was that he was living it up in Miami, staying at the Delano under an assumed name and discussing a possible modelling contract with Donatella Versace while his movie-star boyfriend considered putting in an offer on Madonna's old house. In another version of events, he and Matt had been whisked away to Europe courtesy of Elton John, who'd offered them the run of his palazzo in Venice for a few months while he and David took a well-earned cruise with their dear friends David and Victoria Beckham. A less romantic, less star-studded theory suggested that Matt had already tired of Billy and replaced him with a younger model, and that Billy had gone home to Wisconsin to lick his wounds and indulge his appetite for all things dairy. Another insisted that he hadn't left town at all, but was last seen hanging around the Chateau Marmont, desperately searching for another star to hook his claws into. Finally there were those who said he was lying dead in a morgue somewhere, the victim of some Hollywood hitman hired by Lee Carson to prevent his affair with Matt Walsh from becoming public knowledge.

'The way I heard it, they beat his brains out with a gold-plated trophy,' Bruce said, relishing the drama of it all.

'What?' Casey said.

'He was beaten over the head with an Oscar,' Donald said gleefully. 'I guess that rules out Matt Walsh as a suspect.'

Casey wasn't in the mood for this kind of talk.

'There's nothing to suggest that Billy is dead,' he snapped. 'For all we know, he could have just taken off somewhere.'

'Sure,' Bruce said nastily. 'He could have. But don't you think it just a little bit strange that he hasn't bothered to call? My guess is he proved too much of a risk and they had to get rid of him. Either that, or he's blackmailing Walsh and he's had to go to ground for a while. Either way, he's dead meat. You know they do say that LA is the murder capital of the world. If you really want to kill someone, do it here. And if you want to dump a body, this is the place to dump it. The chances are you'll never get caught. The LAPD already have their work cut out keeping track of all the gangland killings you hear about every night on the news. One more stiff isn't going to make much difference.'

'Thanks for that, Bruce,' Casey said. 'Most illuminating. If I ever feel the urge to kill someone, I'll be sure to keep it in mind. Now unless you have any other pearls of wisdom you'd like to share, I actually came here to pump some iron.'

'Hey, no need to shoot the messenger,' Bruce said huffily. 'I'm just telling you what I heard. I don't want any harm to come to Billy. But you can bet your life someone does.'

Casey clenched his fists and watched as Bruce retreated to a safe distance with Donald. Suddenly a bench press became free and he hurried over to it, desperate to channel all this nervous energy into something productive. But it was no use. Even as the weights rose and fell, he could feel their eyes boring into the back of his head and hear their laughter as they found new audiences for their theories.

He left the gym shortly before four p.m., Bruce's taunts still ringing in his ears. At 4.42 p.m., a red Volvo convertible was found abandoned near the Hollywood sign and all bets were off. The search for Billy West was over.

CHAPTER EIGHTEEN

It was one of the many ironies associated with life in LA that while youth and beauty were widely recognised as qualities to be preserved at all cost, beautiful youths went missing all the time without so much as a thought for their sudden disappearance or untimely demise. The only thing that guaranteed them a place in the hearts and minds of their neighbours was a certain degree of fame, and it didn't really matter how that fame was achieved. Fame was the great leveller, the one thing understood by everyone as an indication that someone was worth caring about, whether they happened to have met them or not. It gave people permission to show an interest, and in a town where emotional detachment was more the order of the day, this was no mean achievement.

The death of Billy West would have warranted very little attention, would probably even have been dismissed as just another Hollywood 'homo-cide', had it not been for his known association with Matt Walsh. That the association was known had nothing to do with Simon Fowler's article, which appeared the following Sunday and, despite containing a few choice quotes, actually said very little about the world-famous movie star that most readers didn't already know. Lee Carson never did return Simon's calls, and with Susie breathing down his neck and the threat of legal action hanging in the air, he swallowed what little pride remained and delivered a glowing puff piece that was a testament to his talents as a stylist but a bitter disappointment to anyone hoping for some juicy revelation or startling new insight.

'It isn't easy being Matt Walsh,' the article began. 'Not that you'd know it from his latest screen outing. In *Surface Tension*, Walsh does exactly what we've come to expect. He smoulders. He bares his chest. He flexes his muscles. He performs feats of superhuman strength. He beats the bad guys and, naturally, he gets the girl. But behind the familiar screen persona is an intensely private man, and one for whom the pressures of fame have certainly taken their toll.

'Even when he's off-camera, Walsh spends much of his time at the centre of a storm of frantic agents, doting assistants, unctuous publicists and fretting hair and makeup people. Fiercely protected by his manager, the infamous Lee Carson, he has gained a reputation for being a little cold, a little distant, something of a control freak.

'The Matt Walsh I met was none of those things. Sure, I had to jump through a few hoops beforehand. Securing a meeting with Matt Walsh is no easy task. Like many Hollywood stars, his life is a tightly programmed machine. But any suggestion that he's unapproachable is dispelled the moment we meet. "I've told you things I haven't even told my therapist," he jokes at one point in our conversation. And while this may be stretching it a bit, it's certainly true that he's a far friendlier and more open figure than his reputation suggests . . .'

And so it went on, paragraph upon paragraph of pure hagiography, complete with well-worn observations about modern movie stardom and an extended plug for Walsh's latest movie. True to her word, Susie decided that the interview wasn't worthy of a place in the magazine and offered it to the editor of the Style section, where it was printed over two pages, sandwiched between a think piece debunking the myth of the metrosexual male and a straight man's guide to impressing women in the kitchen with six ways to breathe new life into the humble sausage.

To add insult to injury, on the day the article appeared, several tabloids led with a story concerning Matt Walsh and his 'close friendship' with a male prostitute. The editors in question had been secretly gunning for Walsh for years, only holding their fire because of the enormous power wielded by the Hollywood publicity machine and the threat of litigation. What gave them the confidence to run with the story now was a set of photographs identical to those delivered to the offices of Lee Carson a week earlier, FedExed to their news desks by an anonymous well-wisher and duly authenticated the day before publication. With these photographs as evidence, suddenly it was safe to suggest that Walsh was a shirt-lifter, although of course nobody used those actual words. There were far subtler ways to fan the flames of homophobia, and the British tabloids were well versed in them all. Time and again, Walsh was described in terms that cast doubts about his masculinity and left his personal morality open to question. Readers were alerted to the fact that many gay men indulged in anal intercourse, and invited to speculate about what Walsh got up to with boys 'practically half his age'. The spectre of Rock Hudson was raised, and readers reminded of all the stars who'd died of AIDS. One photo showed Walsh enjoying an 'unguarded moment' with his 'boy toy'.

A similar feeding frenzy ensued on the other side of the Atlantic, where further spice was added by the discovery that the prostitute in question was now dead and the subject of a police murder inquiry. According to reports, the body of a young man identified as Billy West was discovered in a car abandoned close to the Hollywood sign. The victim had been beaten over the head with a blunt instrument, and there were signs of recent sexual activity. No other details were confirmed, which only served to whet the public's appetite for ever more intense media speculation masquerading as reportage. Several supermarket tabloids competed for the most sensational coverage, quoting unnamed sources and describing the dead boy in terms that ranged from 'street hustler' to 'known drug addict', conveniently forgetting the fact that this was also somebody's son. A hefty price tag was put on the first photo of the body, and within days readers were treated to a shot of Billy laid out on the mortician's slab with half his skull caved in. The caption read: *Dead boy at centre of Matt Walsh scandal.*

Casey watched the whole drama unfold through a haze of cigarette smoke and eyes that grew redder by the day. Billy's death had affected him pretty badly. Night after night he lay awake, haunted by that picture in the papers. Eventually he bought himself a map of the stars' homes and drove over to Beverly Hills, wired on coke and determined to confront Matt Walsh over his part in Billy's downfall. It didn't take him long to find the house. The hordes of photographers gathered outside were a dead giveaway. But security was tight, and it wasn't long before the police were called to the scene and Casey was dragged kicking and screaming into the nearest squad car and warned to stay well clear if he knew what was good for him.

The sad truth was, Casey had never really known what was good for him. And in the present circumstances, the best that could be expected was that he would somehow learn to manage his own pain. Soon he was dedicating himself to the task of deadening his emotions the only way he knew how, ingesting vast quantities of coke and crystal and throwing himself back into his work with a level of enthusiasm some clients found a little disturbing. One night, in a motel room in Brentwood, his appetites got the better of him and he passed out. He came to the following morning propped up in the front seat of his car, covered in his own vomit. He couldn't remember how he got there, but he knew he was lucky to be alive. Some clients would have panicked and left him to choke to death on the bedroom floor.

The police interviewed Casey several times, first to eliminate him from their inquiries and then to establish a few facts about Billy's movements in the week leading up to his death. Casey told them everything they needed to know, plus a few things they didn't want to hear, like why didn't they act faster when he reported Billy missing? Maybe if they had, his friend would still be alive.

Finally they came and removed the answering machine with the recording of Billy's voice announcing that he was in Matt Walsh's bed.

America loved a good Hollywood show trial, and there was much excitement when it was announced that Matt Walsh was being charged with the murder of a male prostitute. The case had it all – profligate celebrity, lurid headlines, alleged sexual misconduct and a religious majority demanding an immediate clean-up of Sin City. Media commentators lined up to offer their two cents' worth, and fellow celebrities clamoured for their place in the spotlight. An actress who once starred opposite Walsh back in the early '90s and hadn't been seen since came out of retirement to condemn what she described as a ruthless cabal of closeted homosexuals, ruling Hollywood with an iron fist. No sooner were her views aired than Elizabeth Taylor stepped forward as a character witness, praising Walsh for his generous donations to her AIDS charities and refuting any suggestion that he was capable of an unkind word against anyone, let alone murder. The fact that she and Walsh had only met once in passing didn't seem to matter, either to the lady herself or to the dozens of TV news channels who broadcast her opinions up to twenty times in one day. When it came to actors of a certain persuasion, Ms Taylor was considered something of a local expert, and that alone lent her words a degree of gravitas.

In true Hollywood fashion, Matt Walsh immediately hired himself the best defence attorney money could buy and in due course was found not guilty of the murder of Billy West but saw his reputation dragged through the mud and his career fall apart. On the advice of his attorney, Matt had decided to throw himself at the mercy of the jury and confess that yes, he really was a homosexual, but no, he hadn't killed anyone. The subsequent revelations about his secret life drew gasps of astonishment from people who really ought to have known better, and in some cases actually knew far more than they were letting on. But as horrified as many of the jurors were, it soon became clear that there was very little solid evidence linking Walsh to the murder of Billy West, and in the absence of an eye-witness or any forensics placing him at the scene of the crime, they were left with no option but to deliver a verdict of not guilty.

Throughout the trial, Lee Carson kept an unusually low profile, only appearing once as a witness for the defence and insisting that, contrary to popular opinion, she had very little involvement in her client's personal affairs. For her court appearance, she opted for a tiger-print trouser suit with kitten heels. *USA Today* described it as 'a bold choice, cunningly evoking the image of a tigress called upon to defend her cub'.

In actual fact, Lee's testimony did very little to swing the jury in Matt's favour. Feigning surprise at the whole torrid affair, she refused to rule out the possibility that her client might have committed a crime of passion, stating only that he appeared to be under a lot of stress at the time and may have been pushed to the brink by the threat of blackmail. When it was suggested that she too had a motive for the murder of Billy West, and that she may indeed have been acting on her client's behalf, she immediately produced a cast-iron alibi. At the time of the murder, she was at a clinic in Beverly Hills, having her face injected with a combination of Botox and revolutionary new fillers.

As soon as the trial was over, she let it be known that she no longer had any interest in representing Matt Walsh. As she told a waiting reporter, the very fact that he had been involved with a male prostitute made her seriously question his integrity, and without integrity, what else was there?

The day he left court a free man, Matt called the woman he had once trusted with his life but would no longer trust to piss on him if he was on fire. She answered on the third ring. 'What the hell is going on, Lee?' he asked.

'Nothing,' she replied, as cool as a cucumber. 'I thought you might call, though I feel it only fair to warn you that you're wasting your time. Anything I have to say about this whole business I have already sworn under oath. And according to every news report I've seen this week, your career is officially over. So unless I'm very much mistaken, you and I have absolutely nothing left to say to one another.'

'That's where you're wrong,' Matt said. 'Our working relationship may well be over, but we still have some unfinished business. You may have fooled everyone else, but you haven't fooled me. I know you, Lee. I know what you're capable of. And more to the point, I know exactly how you felt about Billy. You made it perfectly clear. You told me you'd sort everything out. You told me you were going to manage the situation. If that isn't a statement of intent, I don't know what is.'

Lee laughed. 'Intent to do what?' she said. 'Crack his head open? It sounds to me as if this court case has really gotten to you, Matt. You're not thinking straight. Yes, I wanted the kid out of the picture. And yes, I'd have done everything in my power to stop you from making a total fool of yourself. But I didn't have him killed. And I certainly didn't kill him myself. I may be a ruthless bitch at times, but I still have standards.'

Much as he wanted someone to blame for Billy's death, something told Matt that Lee was telling the truth. Which only left one question. If she wasn't responsible for Billy's murder, who was?

If anyone was to determine the answer to that question, it certainly wasn't the LAPD. With their prime suspect cleared of any wrongdoing, and no other suspects in the frame, the chances of finding Billy West's killer were looking slimmer than Terri Hatcher at last year's Emmys. As each day passed, the trail grew colder. And with Matt Walsh no longer in the spotlight, the media soon lost interest and the pressure to solve the case was off. Who the hell was Billy West anyway? Just another hustler who had lived on the wrong side of the law and who died a violent death as many had before him. Officially, the inquiry was left open for several months. Unofficially, the case was closed the day Matt Walsh left court a free man.

With the trial over and Billy's death rapidly fading from public consciousness, Matt finally got the edgy role he'd been looking for, though not quite in the way he'd hoped. As soon as it was revealed that Matt Walsh was in fact a homosexual and had indeed been involved with a male hustler, Michael Rosetti sent out his script. Hollywood was a close-knit community, famously vindictive towards those who betrayed its confidences – unless of course the betrayal came in the form of a movie and could earn people a lot of money. Billy Wilder proved it with *Sunset Boulevard*. Tim Robbins proved it with *The Player*. And now Michael Rosetti was about to prove it with *Starfucker*.

No sooner was the script sent out than it was snapped up by Miramax. Within a matter of weeks, *Variety* announced that Michael's script had been bought by the studio for an undisclosed sum and was scheduled to go into production before the end of the year. Fearing that *Starfucker* was too controversial a title, the movie was given the far more palatable working title of *Star People*. Gregg Araki was lined up to direct. Several actors were being considered for the role of Matt Walsh, among them Dean Cain. In a touching display of gross self-aggrandisement, Lee Carson agreed to play herself in exchange for a hefty fee and a share of the profits. Lee wouldn't have been Michael's first choice for the role. He would have sooner seen it go to someone like Glenn Close – an actress with a hard edge and a proven track record of reaching deep into her soul and dredging up the least sympathetic qualities she could muster. But Michael was only the writer, and as he soon discovered, writers generally didn't call the shots when it came to casting.

So it was with mixed feelings that Michael tuned in to watch Lee's appearance on Larry King. It was great promotion for the movie, of course. But to see his nemesis happily gloating over the role he'd written in an effort to discredit her was too much irony for him to swallow.

At one point during the interview, the host attempted to put Lee on the spot, asking her if it wasn't a little weird playing herself in a movie based on real events.

'On the contrary, Larry,' Lee replied. 'It's the role I've been preparing for all my life.'

And in that moment, her rehabilitation was complete.

The morning after Lee's TV appearance, Ted Chalmers called Michael to congratulate him on the movie deal. 'There's just one thing', he added. 'I know it was you who murdered that hustler. And I can prove it too. I took the liberty of making a copy of your script. It's secured in a safety deposit box at the bank. The bank can verify when the box was last opened, which was two days before the police discovered the body. So as you can see, it does look rather bad from your point of view.'

For someone who'd just been threatened with blackmail, Michael's reaction was surprisingly cool. 'Not bad, Ted. Not bad at all. There's just one problem. If I was planning on committing such a heinous crime, why on earth would I provide you with enough evidence to convict me? It doesn't make any sense.'

Ted didn't flinch for a second. 'That's what I thought at first. Then I was having a conversation with this therapist friend of mine and suddenly it struck me. You wanted someone to know exactly what you'd done, to prove how smart you were. You're like one of those queens who boasts about his sexual conquests all the time. It isn't the doing it that gets you off. It's knowing you have an audience.'

Michael laughed. 'I can see I underestimated you, Ted.'

'There's just one thing I don't understand,' Ted said. 'Considering how much you hate Lee Carson, why work with her on the movie?'

'I won't be working with her,' Michael corrected him. 'She'll be working with me. There's a big difference. And you know what they say – success is the best form of revenge. Carson can think what she likes. It's still my movie. I made it happen. Carson was just a pawn. To be honest, I was hoping she'd kill the kid herself and save me the bother. God knows, I gave her enough motive. The photographs alone should have been enough to drive her into a murderous frenzy. I guess she isn't quite as tough as she makes out.'

'It does seem a little harsh, though,' Ted said. 'The kid dying like that.'

'You can't make an omelette without breaking eggs, Ted. You of all people should appreciate that. Besides, this is no time for cheap sentiment. You need to keep your tough negotiating head on. I assume that's why you're calling. I mean, if you had any intention of turning me in to the police, we wouldn't be having this conversation. So how much are you after? A few thousand, or are you going to get greedy?'

Now it was Ted's turn to laugh. 'I don't want paying off, Michael,' he said. 'What I want is worth a lot more than that. I want a share of the script, a writer's credit. I don't care how you go about it. Tell them we worked on the script together and you forgot to credit me. Whatever. Just think of it like this. If you pay me off now, there's nothing to stop me turning around in six months and demanding more. But if my name is on that script, that makes me an accessory. The deal ends here.'

'You'd do that?' Michael said, impressed. 'You'd incriminate yourself in a murder case, just for a writer's credit?'

'I'd do that and a lot more,' Ted replied. 'So do we have a deal?'

'And what about the therapist?' Michael asked. 'Is he in on the deal too?'

'He doesn't know the whole story,' Ted said. 'Only what I told him. It's just you and me. So, what do you say?'

While Ted negotiated the price of his silence with Michael, someone else was busy weighing up the cost of his own silence. The following week's issue of *Variety* would carry a double-page ad, the same ad that would appear in editions of *The Hollywood Reporter* and *Vanity Fair*. The ad would read simply: *In loving memory of Billy West.*

The total bill for this mark of respect ran into tens of thousands of dollars. Even with his career in tatters, Matt Walsh figured he could afford it.

ACKNOWLEDGEMENTS

First and foremost, a huge thank you to Antonia Hodgson, my editor, for her patience and understanding, not to mention her uncanny talent for always knowing exactly what I'm trying to say. Darling, you're a star and no mistake. Also worthy of a starring role is my agent Sophie Hicks at Ed Victor, who was enthusiastic from the start and who bears no resemblance to the vicious, bullying creature portrayed in these pages. Just so we're all clear on that.

And to all the other people who helped to make this happen. Thanks to Robin Morgan for first sending me to LA, Frank for the introduction to the Hollywood Hills, Fenton Bailey and Randy Barbato for the frozen margaritas and the West Hollywood boys for making Christmas in California so very memorable.

Thanks also to Jenny Fry, Raquel Leis-Rivera and Sarah Rustin at my publisher for all their hard work. A big thank you to Roland Mouret for Lee, Marc Almond for his support and Carl Miller for the loan of his books. For being there when I really needed a friend, I owe a huge debt of thanks to Elaine Finkletaub, one of the kindest, most thoughtful people I've ever known.

Thanks also to Mum and Windsor, Jac and Niv, Séan Cummings and Lee Garrett, William Gibbon, Shaun Given, Gordon John, Geoff Llewelyn and Michael Perkins,

Andrew Loxton and Paul Adams, Caroline McCartan, Mark Peddigrew, Caroline Reid, Frances Williams and especially Paulo.

Finally, I'd like to thank all the actors I've ever had the job of interviewing, all the hustlers I've ever had the pleasure of meeting and all the PRs who help make a journalist's life more interesting. Without them, etc., etc.